# ENERGY CRISIS

In the 21st Century, the United States has all but used up its oil supply. A new source must be found. Our atomic subtugs begin stealing oil from underwater deposits in enemy territory. But none of the last twenty tugs sent to bring back the desperately needed mineral have returned. Ensign John Ramsey of BuPsych is planted aboard the *Fenian Ram S1881* as an electronics officer. His assignment— find the saboteur in the four-man crew and bring back the oil.

"This is a fictional story of the future that we should pray will never become a news story of the present."
—*The Springfield Daily News*

# UNDER PRESSURE

## Frank Herbert

Formerly titled
*The Dragon in the Sea*

BALLANTINE BOOKS • NEW YORK

To the "special" men
of the United States Submarine Service
—chosen as crewmen on the first atomic submarines—
this story is respectfully dedicated.

SBN 345-23835-4-125

First Printing: March, 1974

Formerly titled *The Dragon in the Sea*

Cover painting by John Berkey

Printed in the United States of America.

BALLANTINE BOOKS, INC.
201 East 50th Street, New York, N.Y. 10022

The blonde WAVE secretary at the reception desk took the speaker cup of a sono-typer away from her mouth, bent over an intercom box.

"Ensign Ramsey is here, sir," she said.

She leaned back, stared up at the redheaded officer beside her desk. His collar bore the zigzag of electronics specialist over the initials BP—Bureau of Psychology. He was a tall man, round-faced, with the soft appearance of overweight. Freckles spotted his pinkish face, giving him the look of a grown-up Tom Sawyer.

"The admiral's usually a little slow answering," said the receptionist.

Ramsey nodded, looked at the door beyond her. Gold lettering on a heavy oak panel: *CONFERENCE ROOM—Sec. 1.* Security One. Above the clatter of office sounds, he could hear the tooth-tingling hum of a detection scrambler.

Through his mind passed the self-questionings he could never avoid, the doubts that had made him a psychologist: *If they have a rough job for me, can I do it? What would happen if I turned it down?*

"You can rest that here on the desk," said the receptionist. She pointed to a black wooden box, about a foot on a side, which Ramsey carried under his left arm.

"It's not heavy," he said. "Maybe the admiral didn't hear you the first time. Could you try again?"

"He heard me," she said. "He's busy with a haggle of braid." She nodded toward the box. "Is that what they're waiting for?"

Ramsey grinned. "Why couldn't they be waiting for me?"

She sniffed. "Enough braid in there to founder a subtug. *They* should be waiting for an *ensign*. There's a war on, mister. You're just the errand boy."

A wave of resentment swept over Ramsey. *You insolent bitch,* he thought. *I'll bet you don't date anything less than a full commander.* He wanted to say something biting, but the words wouldn't come.

The receptionist returned the sono-typer cup to her mouth, went back to her typing.

*I've been an ensign so long I'll even take lip from a WAVE yeoman,* he thought. He turned his back on her, fell to musing. *What do they want with me? Could it be that trick on the* Dolphin? *No. Obe would have said. This might be important, though. It could be my big chance.*

He heard the receptionist behind him take a sheet of paper from her machine, replace it.

*If I got a big assignment and came back a hero, she'd be the kind who'd try to beat Janet's time with me. The world's full of 'em.*

*Why do they want me in Sec. I?*

Obe had just said to bring the telemetering equipment for the remote-control vampire gauge and show up on the Sec. I doorstep at 1400. Nothing more. Ramsey glanced at his wrist watch. A minute to go.

"Ensign Ramsey?" A masculine voice sounded behind him. Ramsey whirled. The conference-room door stood open. A gray-haired line captain leaned out, hand on door. Beyond the captain, Ramsey glimpsed a long table strewn with papers, maps, pencils, overflowing ash trays. Around the table sat uniformed men in heavy chairs, almost like fixtures. A cloud of blue tobacco smoke hung over the scene.

"I'm Ensign Ramsey."

The captain glanced at the box under Ramsey's arm, stepped aside. "Will you come in, please?"

Ramsey skirted the reception desk, entered the

room. The captain closed the door, indicated a chair at the foot of the table. "Sit there, please."

*Where's the boss?* Ramsey wondered. His gaze darted over the room; then he saw Obe: a hollow-cheeked little civilian, straggly goatee, thin bird features, seated between two burly commodores like a prisoner under guard. The little civilian's radiation-blinded eyes stared straight ahead. The mound of a radar bat-eye box atop one shoulder gave him a curiously unbalanced appearance.

Ramsey sat down in the chair indicated, allowed himself an inward chuckle at the thought of the two commodores guarding Dr. Richmond Oberhausen, director of BuPsych. *Obe could reduce them to quivering jelly with ten words.*

The captain who had admitted Ramsey took a chair well down the table. Ramsey moved his black box to his lap, noted eyes following the movement.

*Obe has briefed them on my little invention,* he thought.

The hum of the detection scrambler was strong in the room. It made Ramsey's teeth ache. He closed his eyes momentarily, blanked off the pain, opened his eyes, stared back at the men examining him. He recognized several of the faces.

Very high braid.

Directly opposite at the other end of the table sat Admiral Belland, ComSec, the high mogul of Security, a steely-eyed giant with hook nose, thin slit of a mouth.

*He looks like a pirate,* thought Ramsey.

Admiral Belland cleared his throat in a hoarse rumble, said, "This is the ensign we've been discussing, gentlemen."

Ramsey's eyebrows went up a notch. He looked to Dr. Oberhausen's impassive face. The BuPsych chief appeared to be waiting.

"You know this ensign's Security rating," said Belland. "It's presumed we can talk freely in front of him. Would any of you care to ask him—"

"Excuse me, please," Dr. Oberhausen arose from between the two commodores with a slow, self-assured movement. "I have not acquainted Mr. Ramsey with any of the particulars of this meeting. In view of the assignment we have in mind, it would appear more humane if we did not treat him like a piece of dry goods." The sightless eyes turned toward Belland. "Eh, Admiral?"

Belland leaned forward. "Certainly, Doctor. I was just coming to that."

The admiral's voice carried a tone somewhere between fear and deference.

Ramsey thought: *Obe is running this meeting pretty much as he wants, and without these birds being certain they're outmaneuvered. Now, he probably wants me to pick up a cue and help him apply the clincher.*

Dr. Oberhausen sank back into his chair with a stiff, stick-like gesture. A punctuation.

Belland's chair rasped on the floor. He got to his feet, went to the side wall at his left, indicated a north-polar projection map. "Ensign Ramsey, we've lost twenty subtugs in these waters over the past twenty weeks," he said. He turned to Ramsey altogether like a schoolteacher about to propound a problem. "You're familiar with our pressing need for oil?"

*Familiar?* Ramsey restrained a wry smile. Through his mind sped the almost interminable list of regulations on oil conservation: inspections, issuance forms, special classes, awards for innovations. He nodded.

The admiral's bass rumble continued: "For almost two years now we've been getting extra oil from reservoirs under the marginal seas of the Eastern Powers' continental shelf." His left hand made a vague gesture over the map.

Ramsey's eyes widened. *Then the rumors were true: the sub services were pirating enemy oil!*

"We developed an underwater drilling technique working from converted subtugs," said Belland. "A high-speed, low-friction pump and a new type of plastic barge complete the general picture."

The admiral's mouth spread into what he probably imagined as a disarming grin. It succeeded only in making him appear even more piratical. "The boys call the barge a *slug,* and the pump is a *mosquito.*"

Dutiful chuckles sounded through the room. Ramsey smiled at the forced response, noted that Dr. Oberhausen maintained his reputation as Old Stone Face.

Admiral Belland said, "A *slug* will carry almost one hundred million barrels of oil. The EPs know they're losing oil. They know how, but they can't always be sure of where or when. We're outfoxing them." The admiral's voice grew louder. "Our detection system is superior. Our silencer planes—"

Dr. Oberhausen's brittle voice interrupted him. "Everything we have is superior except our ability to keep them from sinking us."

The admiral scowled.

Ramsey picked up his cue, entered the breach. "What was the casualty percentage on those twenty subtugs we lost, sir?"

An owl-faced captain near Belland said dryly, "Of the last twenty missions, we lost all twenty."

"One hundred per cent," said Dr. Oberhausen. The sightless eyes seemed to look across the room at a beet-faced lieutenant commander. "Commander Turner, would you show Mr. Ramsey the gadget your boys found?"

The lieutenant commander pushed a black cylinder about the size of a lead pencil down the table. Hands carried the object along until it reached Ramsey. He studied it.

"Mr. Ramsey's work, of course, involves electronics," said Dr. Oberhausen. "He's a specialist with the instruments used for detecting traumatic memories."

Ramsey caught this cue, also. He was the omniscient BuPsych electronics expert. The Man Who Knows Your Innermost Thoughts. *Ergo:* You don't have Innermost Thoughts in this man's presence. With an ostentatious gesture, Ramsey put his black box onto the table. He placed the cylinder beside it, managing to convey the impression that he had plumbed the mysteries of the device and found them, somehow, inferior.

*What the devil is that thing?* he wondered.

"You've probably recognized that as a tight-beam broadcaster," said Belland.

Ramsey glanced at the featureless surface of the black cylinder. *What would these people do if I claimed X-ray vision?* he asked himself. *Obe must have hypnotized them.*

Belland transferred his tone of deference-fear to Ramsey. "The EP's have been getting those things aboard our subtugs. We think there's a delayed-action device which turns them on at sea. Unfortunately, we've been unable thus far to dismantle one without exploding the anti-tamper charge."

Ramsey looked at Dr. Oberhausen, back to Belland, implying without words: "Well, if they'd turn these problems over to BuPsych . . ."

The admiral rallied some of his Pride of Department, said, "Turner believes he has it solved, however."

Ramsey looked at the beet-faced lieutenant commander. *And you'll be a rear-rank swabby if you fail,* he thought. The lieutenant commander tried to make himself inconspicuous.

The commodore to Dr. Oberhausen's right said, "Enemy agents aboard the tugs could be turning them on."

Dr. Oberhausen said, "To make a long story short, these devices have been leading the enemy to our secret wells."

"The real trouble," said Belland, "is that we're shot through with sleepers—people the EPs planted years ago—long before the war—with orders to wait for the right moment. People in the damnedest places." He scowled. "Why, my driver—" He fell silent, turned the scowl on Ramsey. "We're reasonably certain you're not a sleeper."

"Reasonably certain?" asked Ramsey.

"I am reasonably certain no one in this roon is a

sleeper," growled Belland. "But that's all I am." He turned back to the wall map, pointed to a position in the Barents Sea. "This is the island of Novaya Zemlya. Off the west coast is a narrow shelf. The edge is in about two hundred fathoms. It's steep. We've a well into the flank of that shelf tapping one of the richest oil reservoirs we've ever encountered. The EPs don't even know it's there—yet."

Dr. Oberhausen put a bony hand on the table, tapped a finger once. "We must make certain Mr. Ramsey understands the morale factor." He turned toward Ramsey. "You understand that it has been impossible to keep our losses completely secret. As a result, morale in the subtugs has dropped off to almost nothing. We need *good* news."

Belland said, "Turner, take it from there." The admiral returned to his chair, lowered himself into it like a battlewagon settling into dry dock.

Turner focused watery blue eyes on Ramsey, said, "We've screened, screened and rescreened our subtug crews. We've found one that looks good. They're at Garden Glen Rest Camp now and will be coming out in five weeks. However, they do not have an electronics officer."

Ramsey thought: *Great Grieving Freud! Am I going to be palmed off as a submariner?*

As though he had read Ramsey's thought, Dr. Oberhausen said, "That's where you come in, Ramsey." He nodded to Turner. "Please forgive me, Commander, but we're taking too much time with this."

Turner shot a glance at Belland, sank back into his chair. "Of course, Doctor."

Dr. Oberhausen arose, again with that air of vast assurance. "This is my field, anyway. You see, Ramsey, the previous electronics officer suffered a psychotic blowup at the termination of their last mission. It's the same problem you were working on with the men of the *Dolphin*. Amplified. The subtugs are smaller, a complement of only four men. The focal symptoms point to a kind of induced paranoia."

"The captain?" asked Ramsey.

"Precisely," said Dr. Oberhausen.

*We are now impressing the natives with our mysterious knowledge,* thought Ramsey. He said, "I noticed similar conditions in the battle-fatigue syndrome when I was on the *Dolphin.*" He patted the box in front of him. "The captain's emotional variations were reflected in varying degrees all through the ship's personnel."

"Dr. Oberhausen outlined your work with the men of the *Dolphin,*" said Turner.

Ramsey nodded. "I'm troubled by one point here. You say this crew rates high. That doesn't check if the captain is a borderline psychotic."

"Again, that's where you come in," said Dr. Oberhausen. "We were about to beach this captain. But now Battle-Comp tells us he and his crew have far and away the highest chance of success in this mission to Novaya Zemlya. But only if certain other conditions are present." He paused, tugged at an ear lobe.

Ramsey caught the signal, thought: *Ah, there's the bite. Somebody important hasn't agreed to this arrangement and it's vital to Obe that I get on that subtug crew. Who are we playing to? The admiral? No, he'd go himself if Obe said the word.* Ramsey's eyes abruptly caught the scowling glare of the commodore on Dr. Oberhausen's left, and at the same moment he noted for the first time the tiny sunburst on the commodore's collar. *A presidential aide! That would be the one.*

"One of the other conditions would be that they have secret psychological monitoring," said Ramsey. "How had you planned to link in my remote-control vampire gauge to this pivotal captain without his knowing?"

"An ingenious solution has been proposed by Admiral Belland," said Dr. Oberhausen. "Security has a new type of detector to combat those spy-beam transmitters. A speaker pellet is surgically imbedded in the neck and tuned to wave scanners which are similarly imbedded beneath the armpits. Microinstrumentation would permit us to include with the speaker the recorders you need."

Ramsey nodded toward the admiral. "Clever. You'd rig this subtug skipper that way, send me along to keep him in balance."

"Yes," said Dr. Oberhausen. "However, there has been some objection raised." The sightless eyes seemed to peer down at the commodore on his left. "On the grounds that you have no extended deep-tug combat experience. It's a specialized service."

The commodore grunted, glared at Ramsey. "We've been at war sixteen years," he said. "How is it you've escaped combat?"

*Old school tie,* thought Ramsey. He turned his telemeter box until one flat surface faced the commodore, squinted at the officer over it. *When in doubt, fire a broadside.*

"Every man we preserve for combat brings victory that much nearer," said Ramsey.

The commodore's leathery face grew dark.

"Mr. Ramsey has a special combination of training —psychology and electronics—which have made him too valuable to risk," said Dr. Oberhausen. "He has made only the most essential cruises—such as that with the *Dolphin*—when that was absolutely required."

"If he's so valuable, why're we risking him now?" demanded the commodore. "This all seems highly irregular!"

Admiral Belland sighed, stared at the commodore. "The truth is, Lewis, this new emotional-telemetering equipment which Mr. Ramsey developed can be used by others. However, his inventive talents are the very things which make his services so essential at this time."

"You may think me rude," said the commodore,

"but I'd like to know also why this young man—if he's as good as all that—is still"—he flicked a glance at Ramsey's collar bars—"an ensign."

Dr. Oberhausen held up a hand, said, "Permit me, my dear Admiral." He turned to the commodore. "It is because there are people who resent the fact that I have been able to keep myself and my top department heads out of uniform. There are those who do not see the necessity for this essential separation. It is regrettable, therefore, that those of my people in the lower echelons, who are required to wear uniforms, sometimes find it difficult to gain advancement no matter how talented they may be."

The commodore looked as though he were about to explode.

"By rights," said Dr. Oberhausen, "Mr. Ramsey should be at least a commodore."

Several fits of coughing broke out simultaneously around the table.

Ramsey suddenly wished he were anywhere else but under the eyes of this commodore. The latter said, "Very well, my objection is withdrawn." The tone of his voice said: *I will pass sentence in my own court.*

"I have planned," said Dr. Oberhausen, "upon completion of this mission, to have Mr. Ramsey released from the service and installed as head of a new department devoted to problems of submariners."

A harsh smile pulled at the corners of the commodore's mouth. "If he lives through it," he said.

Ramsey swallowed.

As though he had not heard, Dr. Oberhausen said, "The training will be a problem, but we have five weeks plus the full facilities of BuPsych."

Belland heaved his bulk from the chair, stepped to one side. "If there are no more questions, gentlemen, I believe we are all satisfied with Mr. Ramsey." He glanced at his wrist watch. "The medics are waiting for him now, and he's going to need every minute of the next five weeks."

Ramsey got to his feet, took his telemeter box under his arm, a question in his eyes.

"You're also going to be rigged as a walking detection system," said Belland.

Dr. Oberhausen appeared to materialize beside Ramsey. "If you'll come with me, please, John." He took Ramsey's arm. "I've had the essential material about Commander Sparrow—he's the captain of this subtug—and the other two crewmen reduced to absolute minimum. We've set aside a special ward at the bureau for you. You're going to be our prize patient for . . ."

Ramsey heard Turner speaking behind him. "Dr. Oberhausen called that ensign John. Is he the *Long John* Ramsey who . . ."

The rest was blurred as Dr. Oberhausen raised his voice. "It's going to be rough on you, John." They stepped into the outer corridor. "Your wife has been notified." Dr. Oberhausen lowered his voice. "You handled yourself very well in there."

Ramsey suddenly realized that he was allowing himself to be guided by a blind man. He laughed, found that he had to explain the laughter. "It was the way you handled that brassy commodore," he said.

"You don't lie at all well," said Dr. Oberhausen. "But I'll let it pass. Now, about the commodore: he's a member of the board which passes upon promotions for BuPsych men."

*Ensign* Ramsey abruptly found that laughter had left him.

Ramsey often referred to his five weeks' training for the subtug mission as "The time I lost twenty pounds."

They gave him three rooms in the sound wing of Unadilla Naval Hospital; blank white enclosures furnished in rattan and cigarette-scarred mahogany, a functional TV set, equally functional hospital bed on high legs. One room was set up for training: hypnophone, wall diagrams, mock-ups, tapes, films.

His wife, Janet, a blond nurse, received a weekend

schedule for visits: Saturday nights and Sundays. Their children, John Junior, age two, and Peggy, age four, were not permitted in the hospital, had to be packed off to their grandmother's at Fort Linton, Mississippi.

Janet, wearing a one-piece red dress, came storming into the sitting room of Ramsey's suite on their first Saturday night. She kissed him, said, "I knew it!"

"Knew what?"

"That sooner or later the Navy and that awful Obe would be regulating our sex life."

Ramsey, aware that everything he said and did in the hospital was being monitored, tried to shush her.

"Oh, I know they're listening," she said. She threw herself onto the rattan couch, crossed her legs, lighted a cigarette, which she puffed furiously. "That Obe gives me the creeking creeps," she said.

"That's because you let him," said Ramsey.

"And because that's the effect he wants to give," she countered.

"Well . . . yes," admitted Ramsey.

Janet jumped to her feet, threw herself into his arms. "Oh, I'm being a fool. They said I wasn't to upset you."

He kissed her, rumpled her hair. "I'm not upset."

"I told them I couldn't upset you if I tried." She pushed away from him. "Darling, what is it this time? Something dangerous? It isn't another one of those horrible submarines?"

"I'm going to be working with some oilmen," he said.

She smiled. "Oh, that doesn't sound bad at all. Will you be drilling a well?"

"The well's already drilled," he said. "We're going to see about increasing production."

Janet kissed his chin. "Old efficiency expert."

"Let's go to dinner," he said. "How're the kids?"

They went out, arm in arm, chatting about the children.

Ramsey's weekday routine began to 0500 when the

nurse entered with his wake-up shot to rouse him from the hypnophone drugs. High-protein breakfast. More shots. Blood test.

"This is going to hurt a little."

"Owoooooooch! Whatta you mean a little? Next time warn me!"

"Don't be a big baby."

Diagrams. Floor plans of Hell Diver Class subtugs.

They turned him over to a large subtug expert from Security. Clinton Reed. Bald as an egg. Thin eyes, thin nose, thin mouth, thick skin. Sense of duty as solid as his neck. Absolutely no sense of humor.

"This is important, Ramsey. You have to be able to go anywhere on this vessel, man any control blindfolded. We'll have a mock-up for you in a couple of days. But first you have to get a picture of it in your mind. Try flashing these plans and then we'll test your memory."

"Okay. I've finished the general layout. Try me."

"Where's the pile room?"

"Ask me something hard."

"Answer the question."

"Oh, all right. Its forward in the bulb nose; first thirty-two feet."

"Why?"

"Because of the teardrop shape of this class, and for balance. The nose gives the most room for shielding."

"How thick is the radiation wall behind the pile room?"

"I missed that."

"Twelve feet. Remember it. Twelve feet."

"Well, I can tell you what it's made of: hafnium, lead, graphite, and poroucene."

"What's on the aft face of the radiation wall?"

"Direct-reading gauges for the reactor. Repeaters are in the control room, forward bulkhead to the right of the first-level catwalk. Then there are lockers for ABG suits, tool lockers, doors to the tunnels leading into the pile room."

"You're getting it. How many tunnels into the pile room?"

"Four. Two top; two bottom. Not to be entered for more than twelve minutes at a time unless wearing an ABG suit."

"Fine. What's the rated horsepower?"

"Two hundred and seventy-three thousand, reduced to about two hundred and sixty thousand by the silencer planes behind the screw."

"Excellent! How long is the engine room?"

"Uh . . . nope. That one's gone, too."

"Look, Ramsey, these are important. You have to remember these distances. You have to get a feeling for them. What if you don't have any lights?"

"Okay. Okay. How long is the damned thing?"

"Twenty-two feet. It fills the whole midship section. The four electric engines are set two to a level with the gearbox for the drive below center aft."

"Gotcha. Here, let me take a flash of the aft section. Okay. Now try me."

"How many catwalks in the engine room and where located?"

"Look, I just flashed the *aft* section."

"How many catwalks and—"

"Okaaaay. Let's see: one center of the control deck going forward. One off center into machine stores on the second level below. One called A level into top stores. Same for bottom level: called B level. Short bridging catwalks from A and B levels to the engines and oxy tanks. And one very short to the conning-tower-retracted which lifts into a section of steps when the tower is extended."

"Good. You see, you can do this if you set your mind to it. Now, tell me how the four staterooms are placed."

"Staterooms yet."

"Stop dodging the question."

"Wise guy! Let's see: captain is top level starboard behind the electronics shack. First officer portside behind the recreation room-sick bay. Engineering officer starboard below the captain's quarters and behind the machine shop. Electronics officer portside below the first officer and aft of galley stores. That's the place for me. Gonna cut me a private door into galley stores."

"Where's the galley?"

"That's one I can answer. It's far port, top level, entered through the wardroom. Selector controls for the prepackaged meals are against the bulkhead separating galley and wardroom. The galley-wardroom unit is between control deck and rec room."

"What's behind the staterooms?"

"Machinery of the Palmer induction drive."

"Why an induction drive?"

"Because at the dive limit for Hell Divers, there can be no weak points in the hull, therefore no shaft through the hull."

"You're getting the drive on the hypnophone tonight. Every man blindfolded. There'll be a model for you to work on day after tomorrow."

"Oh goody!"

"What's the pressure hull limit for Hell Divers?"

"Three thousand and ten pounds to the square inch or 7000 feet."

"Stick to your first answer. Pressure varies with different water conditions. You'd be okay at 7100 feet in one place, dead at 6900 another. Learn to depend on your static pressure gauge. Now let's go to the atmosphere composition. What's a vampire gauge?"

"A little device worn on your wrist during deep dives. Needle goes into your vein, tells you if your $CO_2$ diffusion is fast enough so you won't crock out. It also tattles on nitrogen."

"What's minimum diffusion?"

"When you get below .200 on $CO_2$ you get the jeebies. If your blood $CO_2$ count goes to four percent you're in trouble. With nitrogen it's different. The subtug atmosphere is supposed to be entirely cleared of it. A small quantity of helium is substituted."

"How do you get by with the high atmospheric pressure?"

"Aerobic carbonic anhydrase is fed into the atmosphere by the ventilator system. This speeds up the $CO_2$ loading and unloading of the blood, prevents gas bubbles forming."

"You're good at that. Did you know it before?"

"My emotional telemeter is just a glorified vampire gauge."

"Oh, sure. Now, why is the electronics officer so important?"

"Contact with the exterior control motors is by coded wave pulse. If the E-system breaks down when a subtug is submerged, it stays submerged."

"Right. Now, let's go through the plans again."

"Not again!"

"Start with the reactor room. In detail."

"Slave driver!"

The nightly hypnophone sessions flooded Ramsey's mind with the new knowledge: pressure hull, resonating hull, tank hull . . . pressure compensating system . . . header box . . . reactor controls . . . search and sounding . . . diving plane controls . . . valve controls . . . pile check-off . . . sonoran automatic-navigation board . . . atmosphere controls . . . automatic timelog, Mark IX . . . external and internal TV eyes, specifications for servicing of . . . gyro controls . . . two controls . . . plastic barge, oil, components of . . . needle torpedoes, external racking system . . . torpedo homing systems . . . scrambler systems . . . systems . . . systems . . . systems . . .

There were times when Ramsey's head felt filled to the bursting point.

Dr. Oberhausen appeared in Ramsey's quarters on the fourth day of training. The doctor's unpressed clothes gave him the appearance of a bedraggled robin. He came in quietly, sat down beside Ramsey, who was seated in a viewerscope-sequence training hookup.

Ramsey pulled the fitted faceplate away from his

eyes, turned to Dr. Oberhausen. "Ah, the chief of the inquisition."

"You are comfortable, Johnny?" The sightless eyes seemed to stare through him.

"No."

"Good. You are not supposed to be comfortable." The doctor's chair creaked as he shifted his weight. "I have come about the man Garcia who is engineering officer of this crew."

"What's wrong with him?"

"Wrong? Have I said anything was wrong?"

Ramsey completely disengaged the viewerscope, sat back. "Come to the point."

"Ah, the impatience of youth." Dr. Oberhausen sighed. "Do you have a file on Garcia?"

"You know I have."

"Get it please, and read me what you have."

Ramsey leaned to his right, took a file folder from the bottom ledge of his coffee table, opened it. Garcia's picture on the inside front cover showed a short man—about five feet seven inches—slim. Latin features—dark. Black curly hair. Sardonic half smile. The picture managed to impart a sense of devil-may-care. Under the photograph a note in Ramsey's handwriting: "Member Easton championship water-polo team. Likes handball."

"Read to me," said Dr. Oberhausen.

Ramsey turned the page, said, "Age thirty-nine. Came up from ranks. Ex-CPO machinist. Ham radio license. Born Puerto Madryn, Argentina. Father cattle rancher: José Pedro Garcia y Aguinaldo. Mother died at birth of daughter when Garcia age three. Religion: Catholic. Wears rosary around neck. Takes blessing of priest before each mission. Wife: Beatrice, age thirty-one."

"Do you have her picture?" asked Dr. Oberhausen.

"No."

"A pity. I am told she is quite beautiful. Continue, please."

Ramsey said, "Educated at New Oxford. That accounts for his British accent."

"I grieved when the British Isles were destroyed," said Dr. Oberhausen. "Such a lovely culture, really. So basically solid. Immovable. But that is weakness, also. Continue, if you please."

"Plays bagpipes," said Ramsey. He looked at the doctor. "Now there's something: a Latin American playing the bagpipes!"

"I see nothing wrong with that, Johnny. For certain moods, nothing is more soothing."

Ramsey raised his gaze to the ceiling. "Soothing!" He looked back at the BuPsych chief. "Why am I reading this?"

"I wanted to get the full flavor of Garcia in mind before imparting the latest morsel from Security."

"Which is?"

"That Garcia may be one of these *sleepers* who are giving Security so many *sleepless nights.*"

Ramsey snorted. "Garcia! That's insane! As well suspect me!"

"They are still investigating *you,*" said Dr. Oberhausen. "As to Garcia—perhaps; perhaps not. Counter-Intelligence has turned up the description of a sleeper supposed to be in the subtugs. The description fits Garcia. Security almost called off the mission. I convinced them to go ahead by suggesting that you be primed to watch Garcia."

Ramsey returned to the color photograph in his file folder, observed the sardonic smile. "I say we're chasing shadows. And that may be what the EPs really want. If it's carried to its illogical extreme, certain Security-thinking is first cousin to paranoia—dementia praecox type."

Dr. Oberhausen lifted himself from the rattan chair. It gave off a reedy creaking. "Do not say that to the Security gentlemen when they come to brief you on Garcia," he said. "Oh, and one other thing: the commodore is sharpening knives with which to carve you if there is some error on this mission."

"I have you to thank for that," said Ramsey.

"I take care of my own," said Dr. Oberhausen. "Fear not on that score." He waved toward the viewerscope. "Continue with your studies. I have other work."

Ramsey waited for the door to close, threw the file folder back onto the coffee table, took twenty deep breaths to calm his nerves. Presently, he leaned to the right, captured the folders on the other two crew members, scanned them.

*Commander Harvey Acton Sparrow.* Age forty-one. Picture of a tall, thin man with balding sandy hair, a face of sharp planes, stooped shoulders.

*He looks like a small-town college professor,* thought Ramsey. *How much of that is conditioned on his early desire to teach mathematics? Does he resent the fact that his hardcrust Navy family forced him to follow in the old man's footsteps?*

Father: Rear Admiral Acton Orwell Sparrow, lost with subcruiser *Plunger* in Battle of Irish Sea, 16 October 2018. Mother: Genene Cobe Sparrow. Invalid (heart), lives at Watters Point Government Rest Home. Wife: Rita. Age thirty-six. Blonde? Childless.

*Does Sparrow know that his wife is unfaithful?* Ramsey asked himself. *Most of their friends are aware of it.*

Qualifications: navigator—superior; gunnery officer—superior; medical officer (advanced first aid and pressure syndrome)—excellent; general submarine competence—superior.

Ramsey turned to the other folder.

*Lieutenant Commander Leslie (none) Bonnett.* Age thirty-eight. Picture of a heavy-bodied man (just under six feet) with brown wavy hair (artificial wave?), aquiline nose, overhanging eyebrows, the look of a brooding hawk.

Orphan foundling. Raised at Cape Neston Home for the Unwanted.

*For the Unwanted!* thought Ramsey.

Married four times. Two children—one by each of first two wives. Maintains marriage relationship with number four: Helene Davis Bonnett. Age twenty-nine. Miss Georgia of 2021.

*The Unwanted*, thought Ramsey. *He's carrying out an unconscious revenge pattern against women, getting even with the mother who deserted him.*

Qualifications: navigator—good; supply officer—excellent; gunnery officer—superior (top torpedo officer of subtugs four years running); general submarine competence—excellent plus.

Ramsey looked at the note in the psych record: "Held from advancement to his own command by imperfect adjustment to deep-seated insecurity feelings."

*The Unwanted*, he thought. *Bonnett probably doesn't want advancement. This way, his commander supplies the father authority lacking in his youth.*

Ramsey tossed the folders back onto the coffee table, leaned back to think.

*An association of twisted and tangled threads.*

*Sparrow and Bonnett were Protestants, Garcia a Catholic.*

*No evidence of religious friction.*

*These men have evolved a tight working arrangement. Witness the fact that their subtug has the highest efficiency rating in the service.*

*What has been the effect of losing Heppner, the other electronics officer? Will they resent his replacement?*

*Damn! Heppner was the wrong one to go! A case history with no apparent clues. Quiet childhood. Calm home life. Two sour notes: a broken love affair at age twenty-four; a psychotic blowup at age thirty-two. It should have been someone like Bonnett. The Unwanted. Or Captain Sparrow. The frustrated mathematician.*

"Sleeping?"

It was Reed, the constant tutor.

"It's three o'clock," he said. "I brought a layout

plan of the electronics shack on these Hell Divers."
He handed a blueprint to Ramsey, pointed as he
spoke. "Bench here. Vise there. Wrench kit. Micro-
lathe. Vacuum pumps. Testingboard plugs."

"Okay, I can read."

"You have to be able to plug into that test board
in total darkness," said Reed. He sat down squarely
in the rattan chair lately occupied by Dr. Oberhausen. "Tomorrow you're going to start training on a
mock-up."

"Tomorrow's Saturday, Clint!" Ramsey glared at
him.

"You don't get out of here before 1800," said Reed.
He bent forward over the plan. "Now, concentrate on
that plug layout. This here is emergency lighting. You'll
be expected to find it the first time."

"What if it takes me two tries?"

Reed leaned back, turned his flinty gaze on Ramsey.
"Mr. Ramsey, there's something you should understand so thoroughly that it's second nature to you."

"Yeah? What's that?"

"There is no such thing as a *minor* accident on
a submarine."

Commander Sparrow trotted down the ramp from
the tube landing, slowed as he stepped into the cav-
ernous, floodlighted gloom of the underground submarine moorage. A fine mist of condensation from the
rock ceiling far away in upper blackness beat against
his face. He picked his way through the pattern of
scurrying jitneys, darting, intent people. Ahead of
him, the bulbous whale mound of his subtug rose
above the pier; a 140-foot Wagnerian diva center
stage beneath banks of floodlights.

Instructions from the final Security session jangled
through his mind.

"Your crew has the top Security rating of the service, but you must remain alert for sleepers."

"In my crew? Hell, man, I've known them all
for years. Bonnett's been with me eight years. Joe

Garcia and I served together before the war. Heppner and—" His face had crimsoned. "What about the new E-officer?"

"You won't need to worry about him. Now, the inspectors assure us there are no enemy signal devices aboard your boat."

"Then why this gadget in my neck?"

"That's just an added precaution."

"What about this new man? What's his E-rating?"

"He's one of the best in the service. Here, look at his record."

"Limited combat experience in gulf patrol! He's practically a dryback!"

"But look at his E-rating."

"Limited combat!"

A jitney driver shouted at Sparrow, bringing him out of his reverie. He glanced at his wrist watch: 0738—twenty-two minutes until castoff. His stomach tightened. He quickened his steps.

*Damn Security's last-minute details!*

Across the ebony velvet of the mooring pool he could see the glow tubes outlining the marine tunnel. Down the 160-mile slant of that tunnel, out into the underwater deeps of De Soto Canyon and the Gulf of Mexico—and beyond—ranged the enemy. An enemy grown suddenly, terrifyingly, one hundred percent effective against vessels such as his.

It came to Sparrow that the marine tunnel formed a grotesque birth canal. This cavern carved under a Georgia mountain was nestled in the earth like a fantastic womb. When they took their vessel out to do battle they were born into a terrible world that they did not want.

He wondered what BuPsych would think of an idea like that. *They'd probably rate it as an indication of weakness,* he thought. *But why shouldn't I have a weakness? Something about fighting a war a mile and a half under the ocean—the unrelenting pressure of water all around—exposes every weakness in a man. It's the pressures. Constant pressures. Four men iso-*

lated in pressure, held in a plasteel prison as they are held in the prisons of their souls.

Another jitney scurried across Sparrow's path. He dodged, looking up at his boat. He was close enough now to make out the name plate on the retractable conning tower high above him: *Fenian Ram S1881*. The boarding ramp swooped down from the tower in a long graceful curve.

The dock captain, a moonfaced lieutenant commander in fatigues, hurried up to Sparrow, a check list in his hands.

"Captain Sparrow."

Sparrow turned without stopping. "Yes? Oh, hullo, Myers. Are all the ready crews off?"

Myers fell into step beside him. "Most of them. You've lost weight, Sparrow."

"Touch of dysentery," said Sparrow. "Got some bad fruit up at Garden Glenn. Has my new electronics officer showed up?"

"Haven't seen him. His gear came along earlier. Funny thing. There was a sealed box with his stuff. About so by so." He gestured with his hands. "Cleared by Admiral Belland."

"ComSec?"

"None other."

"Why was it sealed?"

"It's supposed to contain some highly delicate instruments to monitor your new long-range search equipment. It was sealed so no zealous searcher could foul the works."

"Oh. I take it the new long-range gear is installed?"

"Yes. You're battle-checking it."

Sparrow nodded.

A cluster of men at the foot of the boarding ramp snapped to attention as the two officers approached. Sparrow and Myers stopped. Sparrow said, "At ease."

Myers said, "Sixteen minutes, Captain." He held out his hand, shook with Sparrow. "Good luck. Give 'em hell."

"Right," said Sparrow.

Myers headed for the foot of the dock.

Sparrow turned toward a heavy-bodied, hawk-faced man beside the ramp, First Officer Bonnett. "Hi, Les."

"Good to see you, Skipper," said Bonnett. He tucked a clipboard under his left arm, dismissed three ratings who were with him, turned back to Sparrow. "Where'd you and Rita go after the party?"

"Home," said Sparrow.

"So'd we," said Bonnett. He hooked a thumb toward the submarine behind him. "Final safety inspection's completed. Spare gear checked out. But there's a bit of a delay. Heppner's replacement hasn't reported."

Sparrow cursed inwardly, felt a stomach-gripping surge of frustration-anger. "Where is he?"

Bonnett shrugged. "All I know is that Security called and said there might be some delay. I told them—"

"Security?"

"That's right."

"Suffering Jesus!" barked Sparrow. "Do they always have to wait until the last minute? They had me—" He broke off. That was classified.

"They said they'd do their best," said Bonnett.

Sparrow pictured the complicated arrangements which would pass the *Fenian Ram* through their own defense network outward bound.

"It could take another day to set up a new passage time."

Bonnett glanced at his wrist watch, took a deep breath. "I told them 0800 was the latest. They wouldn't answer a damned one of my—" He fell silent as the ramp beside them rattled to descending footsteps.

Both men looked up, saw three figures coming down: two ratings carrying heavy-duty electronics detection gear, followed by a short wiry man with dark Latin features. He wore stained service fatigues, carried a small electronic search box under his right arm.

"Don José Garcia," said Sparrow.

Garcia shifted the search box to his left arm, stepped

down to the dockside. "Skipper! Am I glad to see you!"

Sparrow moved back to permit the ratings to pass with their load, looked questioningly at the search box under Garcia's arm.

Garcia shook his head. "For God and Country," he said. "But sometimes I think I overdraw my account with God." He crossed himself. "The Security chaps have had us at this floating sewer pipe half the night. We've been over it from stem to stern four distinct times. Not a blip. Now, I say to you: they want me to make another search after we get underway down tunnel!" He raised his eyebrows. "I ask you!"

"We'll have to do it," said Sparrow. "I've allowed time before our first contact point for total deep-dive inspection."

"I say," said Garcia. He grinned. "You know, I've already gone and rigged for it."

Sparrow answered the grin, felt some of the tensions inside him begin to unknot.

Bonnett glanced significantly at his watch. "Twelve min—"

The whine of a command jitney's electric motor intruded upon him. All three men turned toward the sound. It came down the dark line of mooring slots. its single light casting an erratic Cyclops gleam upon the damp concrete. The jitney swerved up to the ramp, jerked to a stop. A redheaded man with a round, innocent face sat beside the driver, clutching his uniform cap in his hands.

Sparrow saw ensign's bars on the man's collar, thought: *That will be my new E-officer.* Sparrow grinned at the man's obvious relief upon a safe arrival. The recklessness of the base jitney drivers was a standard service joke.

The new man put his cap over his red hair, stepped out of the jitney. The machine rebounded from his weight. The driver whirled the jitney back the way they had come.

The ensign stepped up to Sparrow, saluted, said, "I'm Ramsey."

Sparrow returned the salute, said, "Glad to have you aboard."

Ramsey handed his service record to Sparrow, said, "No time to send these through channels."

Sparrow passed the papers to Bonnett, said, "This is Mr. Bonnett, first officer." He turned to Garcia. "Mr. Garcia, engineer."

"Good to meet you," said Ramsey.

"We'll soon dissuade you of that illusion," said Garcia.

Sparrow smiled, offered his hand to Ramsey, was surprised to feel strong muscle in the new man's grip. The fellow just *looked* soft. Bonnett and Garcia also shook hands.

Ramsey was busy cataloguing his first visual impressions of the three men in the flesh. It seemed strange to be meeting these people for the first time when he felt that he already knew them. And that, he knew, would have to be concealed. Odd bits of knowledge about the personal lives of these men—even the names of their wives—could not be in the memory of a new man.

"Security said you might be delayed," said Sparrow.

"What's got Security on its ear?" asked Ramsey. "I thought they were going to dissect me."

"We'll discuss that later," said Sparrow. He rubbed at the thin scar on his neck where the Security surgeons had imbedded the detection-system speaker. "Castoff is 0800. Mr. Garcia will take you aboard. Get into fatigues. You'll be assisting him in a final spy-beam inspection as we get underway."

"Yes, sir," said Ramsey.

"Your gear came along hours ago," said Garcia. He took Ramsey's arm, propelled him toward the ramp. "Let's get with it." They hurried up the ramp.

Ramsey wondered when he could break away to

examine his telemeter box. He felt an anxiety—a need to study the first reports on Sparrow.

*That mannerism of rubbing his neck,* thought Ramsey. *Extreme nervous tension well concealed. But it shows in the tight movements.*

On the pier, Sparrow turned to look across the mooring basin at a string of moving lights. "Here comes our tow, Les."

"Do you think we'll make it, Skipper?"

"We always have."

"Yes, but—"

"For now is our salvation nearer than when we believed,' " said Sparrow. " 'The night is far spent, the day is at hand: let us therefore cast off the works of darkness, and let us put on the armour of light.' " He looked at Bonnett. "Paul wrote that to the Romans two thousand years ago."

"A pretty wise fellow," said Bonnett.

A bos'n's whistle sounded at the head of the dock. A swifty crane came darting up to take away the boarding ramp. Ratings hurried to attach the hooks, looked inquiringly at the two officers.

Men hurried along the pier, a new purposefulness in their movements. Sparrow swept his gaze over the scene. "We're being asked to perform," he said. He gestured for Bonnett to precede him up the ramp. "Like the man said: Let's get with it."

They climbed to the conning tower. Bonnett ducked for the cable rack which mounted the float for their TV periscope. As a matter of routine, he glanced at the housing, saw that it was secured for dive. He grasped the ladder arms, slid down into the subtug.

Sparrow remained topside. Around him, the mooring basin appeared a vast lake. He looked at the rock ceiling's blackness.

*There should be stars,* he thought. *Men should get one last look at stars before they go under the sea.*

On the pier below, scurrying figures moved to cast

off the magnetic grapples. For a moment, Sparrow felt like a useless pawn being thrown into a sacrifice position. There had been a time, he knew, when captains conned their vessels away from the dock, shouting orders through a megaphone. Now, it was all automatic—done by machines and by men who were like machines.

A surface tug swung up to their bow, slapped its tow grapples onto them. White water boiled from beneath the tug's stern. The *Fenian Ram* resisted momentarily, as though reluctant to leave, then began a slow, ponderous movement out into the basin.

They cleared the slot, and another tug slid alongside their stern. The magna-shoe men leaped onto the *Ram*'s silencer planes, hitched the tow and guide cables of the long plastic tube which stretched out across the dark water of the basin. Their shouts came up to Sparrow in the tower like the clear noise of children. He tasted a sudden oil-tainted breeze and knew they had crossed the path of a ventilator duct.

*No special fanfare, no brass bands, no ceremony for the departure of a raider,* he thought. *We are as a reed shaken with the wind. And what go we out into the wilderness to see? No John the Baptist awaits us. But it's a kind of baptism all the same.*

Somewhere in the darkness a klaxon hooted. *Turn and identify the man next to you. Another Security scheme: Show your identification when the horn sounds. Damn Security! Out here I identify myself to my God and none other.*

Sparrow looked astern at the set of the tow. *Oil. War demanded the pure substance born in the sediment of rising continents. Vegetable oil wouldn't do. War was no vegetarian. War was a carnivore.*

The tow tug shifted to the side of the *Ram* and now the sub was being nosed into the traveler rack which would carry it down to the underwater canyon and the gulf.

Sparrow looked at the control console in the conning tower, and the green *clear-away* light. He flashed the standby signal to the tug below him and, with a practiced motion, touched the controls to retract the tower. It slid smoothly into the sub, its plasteel lid twisting into the groove seats.

A chest microphone hung beside the tower console. Sparrow slipped it on, spoke into it: "Rig for dive."

He focused his attention on the dive board in front of him.

Back came Bonnett's voice, robbed of life by the metallic mutes of the intercom: "Pressure in the hull."

One by one, the lights on Sparrow's dive board shifted from red to green. "Green board," he said. "Stand by." Now he could feel the hull pressure and another pressure in his stomach. He closed the signal circuit which told the outside crews that the subtug was ready to go down tunnel.

The *Ram* shifted, lurched. A dull clang resonated through the boat. Across the top of the dive board amber lights flashed: they were in the grip of the tunnel elevator. Twenty hours of free ride.

Sparrow grasped a handhold beside the dive board, swung down and out onto the engine-room catwalk. His feet made a slithering sound on the catwalk padding as he made his way aft, crawled through the control-room door, dogged it behind him. His gaze paused for a moment on the hand-etched brass plate Heppner had attached beside the door—a quotation from some nineteenth-century pundit:

"No one but a crazy man would waste his time inventing a submarine and no one but a lunatic would go down in it if it were invented."

Through the gulf shelf in the Florida elbow, De Soto Canyon slashes the soft peninsula limestone like a railroad cut: fourteen fathoms where it starts in Apalachee Bay, more than two hundred and sixty fathoms where it dives off into the ocean deeps south of Cape San Blas and east of Tampa.

The gulf exit of the marine tunnel opens into the

canyon wall at fifty fathoms: a twilight world of waving fan kelp, red fingers of gorgonian coral, flashing sparkles of reef-dwelling fish.

The *Fenian Ram* coasted out of the dark hole of the tunnel like a sea monster emerging from its lair, turned, scattering the fish, and slanted down to a resting place in the burnt-umber mud of the canyon bottom. A sonar pulse swept through the boat. Detectors in the triple hulls responded, registered on control gauges of the navigation deck.

Garcia's clipped accent—oddly squeaking in the oxygen-high atmosphere—repeated the check list as he watched the Christmas tree lights of the main board. ". . . no leaks, trim weights balanced, external salvage air clear and pressure holding, atmosphere free of nitrogen, TV eyes clear and seeing, TV periscope surfaced and seeing; periscope gyro checks with—" His laughter echoed through the intercom: "Seagull! It tried to land on the peri-box as I started to reel in. Lit on its fanny in the water."

Bonnett's crisp tones interrupted: "What's it like topside, Joe?"

"Clear. Just daybreak. Going to be a good day for fishing."

Sparrow's voice rasped over the speakers: "Enough of that! Was there anyone up there to spot the gull's flop? They could've seen our box."

"Negative, Skipper."

Sparrow said, "Les, give me the complete atmosphere check. Vampire gauges everyone. Follow the check. Report any deviations."

The patient inspection continued.

Ramsey interrupted. "I'm in the induction-drive chamber. A lot of static here as I entered."

Garcia said, "Did you go back by the lower shaft tunnel?"

"Lower."

"I noticed that myself earlier. We'll rig a ground for the scuff mat. I think that'll fix it."

"I grounded myself before entering."

Sparrow said, "Run that down, Joe. Les, where are you?"

"Second-level catwalk in the engine room."

"Relieve Joe on the main board. Ramsey, get into your shack. Contact with base in eleven minutes."

"Aye, Skipper."

Sparrow moved from his position on the control deck below Garcia to a point at the first-level door which was open to permit visual inspection of the big gauges forward on the radiation wall. *That room in the bow,* he thought. *That's what worries me. We can see into it with our TV eyes; gauges tell us what's happening. But we can't touch it with our bare hands. We don't have a real feeling for that place.*

He mopped his forehead with a large red handkerchief. *Something, somewhere is wrong.* He was a sub-tug skipper who had learned to depend on his feeling for the boat.

A string of Spanish curses in Garcia's voice, rendered metallic by the intercom, interrupted his reverie.

Sparrow barked: "Joe! What's wrong?" He turned toward the stern, as though to peer through the bulkheads.

"Wiper rag in the rotor system. It was rubbing the induction ring every revolution. That's Ramsey's static."

"Does it look deliberate?"

"Did you ever come across a *silk* wiping rag?" The sound of a grunt came over the intercom. "There, by heaven!"

Sparrow said, "Save that rag." Then: "Ramsey, where are you?"

"In the shack warming up the transmitter."

"Did you hear Joe?"

"Yes."

"Tell base about that rag. Tell them—"

"Skipper!" It was Garcia's voice. "There's oil in the atmosphere back here!"

Sparrow said, "A mist of oil plus static spark equals an explosion! Where's that oil coming from?"

"Just a minute." A clanking of metal against metal. "Open pet-cock in the lube system. Just a crack. Enough to squirt a fine spray under full drive."

Sparrow said, "Ramsey, include that in the report to base."

"Aye, Skipper."

"Joe, I'm coming back there," said Sparrow. "We're going over that drive room with a microscope."

"I've already started."

Bonnett aid, "Skipper, would you send Ramsey up here after he gets off the contact? I'll need help checking the main board."

"Hear that, Ramsey?" asked Sparrow.

"Aye."

"Comply."

"Will do."

Sparrow went aft, dropped down to the lower level, crawled through the shaft tunnel and into the drive room—a cone-shaped space dominated by the gleaming brass induction ring, the spaced coils. He could smell the oil, a heavy odor. Garcia was leaning into the coil space, examining the induction ring by magnifying glass.

"They're just little things," said Sparrow. "But taken together—boom!"

Garcia turned, his eyes glittering in the harsh work lights. "I don't like the feel of things, Skipper. This is a bad beginning. This is starting like a *dead-man* mission."

Sparrow took a deep breath, exhaled slowly. With an abrupt motion, he thumbed the button of his chest mike. "Ramsey, when you contact base, request permission to return."

"Aye, Skipper."

Ramsey's thoughts leaped. *What will that do to morale? The first raider in months turns back without getting out of the gulf. Bad.* He stared at the wavering fingers of the dial needles. His contact timer hit the red line, buzzed. He rapped out the first pulse with its modulated message: "Able John to Red Hat. Over."

The speaker above his head hissed with background noise like a distant surf. Presently, a voice came out of it, overriding the noise: "This is Red Hat. Over."

"Able John to Red Hat: We've discovered sabotage aboard. A silk rag was put in the motor system of our drive room. A static spark from the rag could've blown us out of the bay. Over."

"Red Hat to Able John. Stand by, please. We are routing your message to Bird George."

*"Security!"*

Again the speaker came to life. "Bird George to Able John. This is Teacher. What is the situation? Over."

*Clint Reed!* Ramsey could almost see the humorless face of his Security teacher. *Teacher Reed. Impromptu code.* Ramsey bent over his own mike: "Teacher, this is Student." He repeated the story of sabotage.

"Teacher to Student. What's your suggestion? Over."

"Student to Teacher. Permit us to go on with inspection out here. There's less chance for an unknown factor. Just the four of us aboard. If we check safe, allow us to continue the mission. Bad for morale if we came back. Over."

"Teacher to Student. That's the way we see it. But stand by." Pause. "Permission granted. How much time do you need? Over."

Ramsey turned on his intercom microphone. "Skipper, base suggests we continue the inspection here and not return if we check secure."

"Did you tell him what we'd found?"

"Yes, sir."

"What'd they say?"

"That's there less chance for a Security slip out here. Fewer personnel. They suggest we double-check each other, give every—"

"Suffering Jesus!"

"They want to know how much time we'll need."

Silence.

"Skipper, they—"

"I heard you. Tell them we'll need ten hours."

Ramsey turned back to his transmitter. "Student to Teacher. Skipper says give us ten hours. Over."

"Teacher to Student. Continue as ordered. We'll clear new checkpoints for you. Over and out."

Ramsey sat back, thought: *Now, I've really stuck my neck out. But Obe said this one has to go through.*

Bonnett's voice rasped over the intercom: "Ramsey! If that contact's over, get your ass up here and help me on this board!"

"Coming."

In the drive room, Sparrow hefted a socket wrench, looked at Garcia crouched under the secondary coils. "They want this one to go through, Joe. Very badly."

Garcia put a contact light on two leads. It glowed. "Yes, and they give us a green hand like that Ramsey. A near dryback."

"His service record says limited combat in gulf Security patrols."

"Get the priest and the parish!" He shifted to a new position. "Something odd about the chap!"

Sparrow opened the plate over a condenser. "How so?"

"He strikes me like a ringer, a chap who pretends to be one thing when he's actually something else."

"Where do you get that idea?"

"I really couldn't say, Skipper."

Sparrow shrugged, went on with his work. "I dunno, Joe. We'll go into it later. Hand me that eight-inch flex wrench, please."

Garcia reached up with the wrench, turned back to his own work. Silence came over the little room, broken only by the sound of metal on metal, buzzing of test circuits.

Sparrow ducked through the door into the control room, stood silently as Bonnett and Ramsey reinstalled the final cover plate of the main board.

Bonnett straightened, rubbed the back of his neck. His hand left a grease smear. He spoke to Ramsey:

"You're a boy, Junior. We may make a submariner out of you yet. You've just gotta remember that down here you never make the same mistake once."

Ramsey racked a screw driver in his tool kit, closed the kit, turned, saw Sparrow. "All secure, Skipper?"

Sparrow didn't answer at once. He looked around the control room, sniffed the air. Faint smell of ozone. A distant humming of stand-by machinery. The round eyes of the indicator dials like symbiotic extensions of himself. The plucking disquiet remained within him.

"As secure as mortals can make it—I hope," he said. "We'll repair to the wardroom." Sparrow turned, ducked out the way he had entered.

Ramsey put his tool kit into its wall rack. Metal grated against metal. He shivered, turned. Bonnett was going through the door. Ramsey stepped across the control room, ducked through the door, followed Bonnett into the wardroom. Sparrow and Garcia already were there, Garcia seated to the right, Sparrow standing at the opposite end of the table. Ramsey's eyes widened. An open Bible lay on the table before Sparrow.

"We invoke the help of the Almighty upon our mean endeavors," said Sparrow.

Bonnett slipped into a chair at the left.

Sparrow indicated the seat opposite himself. "Will you be seated, please, Mr. Ramsey?"

Ramsey lowered himself into the chair, rested one hand on the green felt of the table cover. Sparrow towered above them at the other end of the table. *The Giver of the Law with hand upon the Book.*

*Religious services,* thought Ramsey. *Here's one of the binding forces of this crew. Participation Mystique! The consecration of the warriors before the foray.*

"What is your religion, Mr. Ramsey?" asked Sparrow.

Ramsey cleared his throat. "Protestant Episcopal."

"It's not really important down here," said Sparrow. "I was merely curious. We have a saying in the subtugs that the Lord won't permit a *live* atheist to dive below a thousand feet."

Ramsey smiled.

Sparrow bent over the Bible. His voice rumbled as he read: " 'Woe unto them that call evil good, and good evil; that put darkness for light, and light for darkness; that put bitter for sweet, and sweet for bitter! Woe unto them that are wise in their own eyes, and prudent in their own sight!' "

He closed the Bible, lifted his head. It was a movement of power, of authority. Ramsey received an impression of deep strength.

"We do our job with what we have at hand," said Sparrow. "We do what we believe to be the *right* thing. Though it grieve us, we do it. We do it that the godless shall perish from the earth. Amen."

Sparrow turned away, placed the Bible in a case against the bulkhead. With his back still turned to them, he said, "Stations, everyone. Mr. Ramsey, contact base, tell them we are ready to go. Get the time for the first checkpoint."

Ramsey got to his feet. Foremost in his thoughts was the almost physical need to examine the first telemeter record on Sparrow. "Yes, sir," he said. He turned, ducked through the door to the companionway and across into his shack, contacted base.

First checkpoint in four hours.

Ramsey relayed the information to Sparrow.

"Zero the automatic timelog," said Sparrow. "Check in, everyone."

"Garcia here. Drive and tow secure."

"Bonnett here. Main secure."

Ramsey looked at his board in the electronics shack. A queer sensation of belonging here passed over him. A sense of familiarity, of association deeper and longer than the five weeks of training. "E-board secure," he said. "Two atmospheres in the hull." He looked to the vampire gauge on his wrist. "Diffusion normal-plus. No nitrogen."

Back came Sparrow's voice over the intercom: "Les, slide off."

Ramsey felt the subtug lurch, then a faint whispering pulse of power. The deck assumed a slight upward incline, leveled. Presently, it tipped down.

*We're headed into the deeps,* thought Ramsey. *Physically and mentally. From here on it's up to me.*

"Mr. Ramsey, come to the control deck," Sparrow ordered.

Ramsey closed down his board, went forward. Sparrow stood, hands behind his back, feet braced slightly apart almost precisely in the center of the control deck. He appeared framed in a background maze of pipes, wheels, levers, and dials. To his right, Garcia worked the tow controls; to his left, Bonnett held the high-speed pilot wheel. The big static pressure gauge high in the control bulkhead registered 1,310 pounds, increasing; they were below 3,000 feet.

Without turning, Sparrow asked, "What's in that little box that came aboard with your effects, Mr. Ramsey?"

"Monitoring equipment for the new search system, sir."

Sparrow's head moved to follow the flickering of a tow-control dial; he turned back. "Why was it locked?"

"It's extremely delicate and packed accordingly. They were afraid someone—"

"I'll want to see it at the first opportunity," said Sparrow. He stepped over behind Bonnett. "Les, is that a leak in compartment nine?"

"There's no moisture or pressure variant, Skipper. It has to be condensation."

"Keep an eye on it." Sparrow stepped back beside Ramsey.

*I'm going to find out quick if that disguise system in the box satisfies his curiosity,* thought Ramsey.

"What's your hobby?" he asked Ramsey.

Ramsey blinked. "Astronomy."

Bonnett spoke his shoulder: "That's a peculiar hobby for a submariner."

Before Ramsey could reply, Sparrow said, "There's nothing wrong with astronomy for a man who goes to sea."

"The basis of navigation," said Ramsey.

Sparrow glanced sidelong at Ramsey, returned his gaze to the board. "I was thinking as we moved out across the mooring basin back at base that we were entitled to a last look at the stars before going under the sea. They give one a sense of orientation. One night before we left Garden Glen I was struck by the clarity of the sky. The constellation of Hercules was—" He broke off as the *Ram*'s nose tipped upward.

A brown hand moved over his controls to correct for the deflection.

"Hercules," said Ramsey. "Do you mean the Kneeler?"

"Not many call him that any more," said Sparrow. "I like to think of him up there all these centuries, guiding mariners. The Phoenicians used to worship him, you know."

Ramsey felt a sudden wave of personal liking for Sparrow. He fought it down. *I must remain clear-headed and objective,* he told himself.

Sparrow moved to the left to get a clearer view of the pilot gauges. He studied them a moment, turned to Ramsey. "Has it ever occurred to you, Mr. Ramsey, that these Hell Diver subtugs are the only remaining spaceships that mankind has developed? We're completely self-contained." He turned back to the control board. "And what do we do with our spaceships? We use them to hide under the liquid curtain of our planet. We use them to kill one another."

Ramsey thought: *Here's a problem—a morbid imagination vocalized for the benefit of the crew.* He said, "We use them in self-defense."

"Mankind has no defense from himself," said Sparrow.

Ramsey started to speak, stopped, thought: *That's*

*a Jungian concept. No man is proof against himself.*
He looked at Sparrow with a new respect.

"Our underground base," said Sparrow. "It's like
a womb. And the marine tunnel. A birth canal if I
ever saw one."

Ramsey thrust his hands into his pockets, clenched
his fists. *What is going on here?* he asked himself.
*An idea like that should have originated with Bu-
Psych. This man Sparrow is either teetering on the
ragged edge or he's the sanest man I've ever met.
He's absolutely right about that base and the tunnel
and we've never spotted the analogy before. This
bears on our problem. But how?*

Sparrow said, "Joe, secure the tow board on automatic. I want you to go with Mr. Ramsey now and
test out the new detection gear. It should be ranged
on our first checkpoint." He looked to the big sonoran
auto-nav chart on the forward bulkhead and the red
dot showing their DR position. "Les, surface the peri-
box and get a position reading."

"Right, Skipper."

Garcia closed the final switch on his board, turned
to Ramsey, "Let's go, Junior."

Ramsey looked at Sparrow, a wish to be part of
this crew uppermost in his mind. He said, "My friends
call me Johnny."

Sparrow spoke to Garcia, "Joe, would you also
initiate Mr. Ramsey into the idiosyncrasies of our atmospheric system? The carbonic anhydrase phase regulator would be a good place to start."

Ramsey felt the rejection of his first name like a
slap, stiffened, ducked through the aft door and into
the companionway.

Garcia followed, dogged the door behind them,
turned, said, "You'd better know something about the
subtugs, Ramsey. A new hand is always known by his
last name or anything else the crew feels like calling
him until after the first combat. Some guys hope they
*never* get called by their first name."

Ramsey cursed inwardly. Security had missed that

point. It made him appear like a green hand. Then he thought: *But this is a natural thing. A unit compulsive action by the crew. A bit of magic. Don't use the secret name of the new man lest the gods destroy him . . . and his companions.*

In the control room, Bonnett turned to Sparrow, sniffed. He rubbed a hand across the back of his neck, turned back to the control board. "He's green," he said.

"He appears willing, though," said Sparrow. "We can hope for the best."

Bonnett asked, "Aren't you worried about that last minute Security check-up on the guy?"

"Somewhat," said Sparrow.

"I can't help it," said Bonnett. "The guy—something about him—I dunno. He strikes me as a wrongo." Bonnett's shaggy brows drew down in thought.

"It could've been routine," said Sparrow. "You know the going over they gave us."

"I'm still going to keep an eye on him," said Bonnett.

"I've some paper work," said Sparrow. "Steady as she goes. Call me before the first checkpoint."

"What's the watch schedule?" asked Bonnett.

"That's what I'm going to be working on," said Sparrow. "I want to set it up so I can spend some time with Ramsey while we're still in comparatively safe waters. I don't want him goofing when the chips are down."

Sparrow ducked for the aft door, went down the companionway and into the wardroom. The first thing that struck him as he entered was the color of the wardroom table cover—a cover and a color he had seen thousands of times.

*Why is it that Navy wardrooms always have green table covers?* he asked himself. *Is it a little of the color of the growing land? Is it to remind us of home?*

In the electronics shack, Garcia and Ramsey closed down the board after testing the detection gear.

"What now?" asked Ramsey.

"You'd better log a little sack time," said Garcia. "It's Les's watch. The skipper's probably setting up the schedule right now. You may be called next. Things are pretty loose the first day or so."

Ramsey nodded, said, "I am tired." He turned aft, said, "See you later."

Garcia's "Righto" floated after him.

Ramsey hurried to his room, dogged the door, dragged out the telemeter box, unlocked it, extracted the first record strips, sat back to examine them.

Pituitra and adrenaline high points showed early on the scrolls. Ramsey noted that one was before he arrived and the other coincided with the moment pressure was first bled into the hull.

*The first tense moments,* he thought. *But that's normal.*

He reeled the scrolls of telemeter tape forward to the moment the sabotage was discovered, doublechecked the timed setting, scanned backward and forward across the area.

*Nothing!*

*But that can't be!*

Ramsey stared at the pattern of rivets on the bulkhead opposite him. The faint whispering of the drive seemed to grow louder. His hand on the blanket beside him felt every tuft, every thread. His nostrils sorted out the odors of the room: paint, oil, soap, ozone, perspiration, plastic . . .

*Is it possible for a person to go through anxiety without glandular changes?* he asked himself. *Yes, under certain pathological circumstances, none of which fit Sparrow.*

Ramsey remembered the sound of the captain's voice over the intercom during the period of stress: higher pitched, tense, clipped.

Again, Ramsey examined the tape. *Could the telemeter be wrong?*

He checked it. Functioning perfectly. Could there

be disfunction in the mechanism within Sparrow's flesh? Then the other fluctuations would not have registered.

Ramsey leaned back, put a hand behind his head, thought through the problem. Two major possibilities suggested themselves: *If Sparrow knew about the wiper-rag-oil-spray thing then he wouldn't be anxious. What if he planted the rag and set that lube-system pet-cock himself? He could've done it to disable the ship and stop the mission because he's lost his nerve or because he's a spy.*

*But there would've been other psychomotor indications which the telemeter would have registered.*

This led to the other possibility: *In moments of great stress Sparrow's automatic glandular functions are taken over by the higher cortical centers. That could tie in with the known paranoiac tendencies. There could be a systematic breakdown of normal function under stress: such a turning away from fear that the whole being believes there could be no danger.*

Ramsey sat bolt upright. *That would fit the pattern of Sparrow's religious attitude. An utter and complete faith would explain it. There had been religious paranoiacs before. They'd even tried to hang the label on Christ.* Ramsey frowned. *But of course Schweitzer made the ones who tried look like fools. Tore their arguments to shreds.*

A sharp rap on Ramsey's door interrupted his thoughts. He slipped the tapes into the false bottom of the telemeter box, closed the lid, locked it.

Again the rap. "Ramsey?" Garcia's voice.

"Yes?"

"Ramsey, you'd better take a couple of anti-fatigue pills. You're scheduled for the next watch."

"Right. Thanks." Ramsey slipped the box under his desk, went to the door, opened it. The companionway was empty. He looked at Garcia's door across the companionway, stood there a moment, feeling the ship around him. A drop of moisture condensing from the overhead fell past his eyes. Abruptly, he had to fight off a sense of depression. He could almost feel the terrible pressure of water around him.

*Do I know what it is to be truly afraid?* he asked himself.

The *Ram* moved to the slow rhythm of the undersea currents, hiding under every cold layer her crew could find because the cold water damped the sound of her screw; creeping between the walls of underwater canyons like a great blimp with a tail because the canyon walls stopped the sound of her passage.

Watches changed, meals were eaten. A chess game started between Sparrow and Garcia. The automatic timelog's hands swept around, around, around, and around, clocking off the deadly dull routine of danger. The red dot marking their position on the sonoran chart crept around the tip of Florida, up the Atlantic coast, and out into the ocean—a mite creeping toward Iceland.

Five days, thirteen hours, twenty-one minutes from point of departure.

Sparrow entered the control room, stooping for the door, pausing inside to sweep his gaze over the dials— his *other* sense organs. Too much moisutre in the atmosphere. He made a mental note to have Garcia check that on his watch. Now, it was Bonnett's watch. The main board was set up for remote control. A repeater board was missing from its rack.

On the sonoran chart, their position marker stood almost due east of the northern tip of Newfoundland, and on a line south from the southernmost tip of Greenland: course sixty-one degrees, twenty minutes. The static pressure gauge registered 2360 pounds to the square inch: about 5500 feet below the surface.

Sparrow stepped across the control room, ducked through the door and out onto the engine-room catwalk. The catwalk padding felt soft under his feet.

Bonnett stood on the lower catwalk, back to Sparrow, staring down to the left. Sparrow followed the direction of his first officer's gaze: the door sealing one of the emergency tunnels into the reactor room.

*Something odd about Bonnett's movements,* thought Sparrow. *Looks like he's counting.*

Then Sparrow recognized the motion: Bonnett was sniffing the air. Sparrow took an experimental whiff himself, smelled the omnipresent stink of their recirculated air plus the ozone and oil normal to the engine room. He strode out onto the catwalk, bent over the railing. "Something wrong, Les?"

Bonnett turned, looked upward. "Hi, Skipper. Don't know. I keep smelling something rotten in here."

Sparrow's lips twisted into a half smile. "How can you tell in this stinkpot?"

"I mean actually rotten," said Bonnett. "Carrion. Rotting meat. I've been getting it for several days—every time I go past here."

"Has anybody else noticed it?"

"They haven't said."

"Its probably your imagination, Les. After five days in this floating sewer pipe everything stinks."

"I dunno, Skipper. I can sort out most of the smells. This one doesn't fit."

"Just a minute." Sparrow stepped to the connecting ladder, dropped down to Bonnett's level.

"Take a sniff, Skipper."

Sparrow drew in a deep breath through his nose. There *was* a faint carrion odor in the air, but then meat got high quickly in the heavy oxygen of a subtug's atmosphere. "Could it be a dead rat?" he asked.

"How would it get aboard? Besides, we went over the *Ram* with a fine-tooth comb. A mosquito couldn't—" He broke off, turned, stared at the radiation bulkhead.

"There's one place we didn't comb," said Sparrow.

"Still, we looked it over with the internal eyes," said Bonnett. "There—" He fell silent.

"Let's take another look," said Sparrow.

He led the way back to the control room, keyed

the master screen to the reactor-room scanners, one by one.

"Nothing," said Bonnett. He looked at Sparrow, shrugged.

Sparrow glanced at his wrist watch. "Joe went off stand-by about an hour ago." He looked at the now blank screen. "Get him up to that tunnel door anyway. Put Ramsey on stand-by here in the control room. I'm going forward." He stooped for the forward door, went out onto the catwalk, dropped down to the lower level.

In the control room, Bonnett went to the communications panel, buzzed Garcia. A sleepy voice came on the speaker. "Yeah?"

"Skipper wants you forward. Number-one reactor-room tunnel."

"What's up?"

"He'll tell you."

Bonnett closed the circuit, opened the call network. "Ramsey."

"Aye. In the rec room."

"Stand by on the control deck."

"Right away."

Bonnett clicked the call switch off, joined Sparrow at the tunnel door forward. Garcia was with them almost immediately, still buttoning his shirt, his black hair tumbled over his forehead. "Something wrong?"

Sparrow said, "You made the last pile check, Joe. Did you open the tunnel doors?"

"Sure. But I didn't go inside. The Secuirity crew gave us a clean—"

"That's okay. Did you smell something?"

Garcia frowned. "You mean like with my nose?"

"That's right."

"I don't believe so." Garcia scratched his head. "Why?"

"Take a sniff," said Bonnett.

Garcia wrinkled his nole, inhaled. Again. "Rotten."

"Les has been smelling it for a couple of days."

"Has anybody checked the ventilator duct?" asked Garcia.

"First thing," said Bonnett. "I couldn't be certain. Far enough in there it'd be a race between bacteria and sterilizing radiation."

"With the bacteria winning as soon as we hit high oxy," said Sparrow. He pointed to the screened outlet of the tunnel vent. "It's worst right there. Joe, get me a length of our spare high-pressure tubing."

"How long?"

"About twenty feet. Something that'll bend for the center dip of the tunnel and reach out into the open section."

"Righto." Garcia went aft and into machine stores.

Sparrow turned to a wall rack, broke out a portable TV eye and spotlight. "All of us have a blind spot on the reactor room. We don't like to think about it. We count on the stationary eyes being arranged for maximum inspection. This way we'll lose one portable eye and one spotlight when they get hot, but we'll see into the odd corners."

Garcia returned with the tubing. "What're you going to do?"

"Rig a portable eye and light on the end," said Sparrow.

Garcia blushed. "I didn't think of that."

"Like I was telling Les," said Sparrow. "Our minds don't function right on—"

Ramsey's voice came from the speaker on the bulkhead above them. "I have you on my screen here. What's doing?"

Bonnett thumbed his chest mike. "Something rotten in this .pile-room tunnel."

Sparrow looked up from where he was rigging the TV eye and light to the tubing. "Have him take it from the portable board you left up there on the catwalk railing. We may need his help."

Bonnett relayed the order.

Presently, Ramsey came out on the catwalk above them, checked the portable control board. He leaned over the railing, looked down at them. "I just smelled it," he said. "Do you think it's a rat?"

"Don't know," said Bennett.

"Here." Sparrow passed the tubing to Garcia, turned to the tunnel door, undogged it, paused. He looked up at Ramsey. "Take that board back a ways."

Ramsey complied, moving about ten feet back along the catwalk.

Sparrow nodded to Bonnett. "Les, move over a bit."

Bonnett stepped back out of line of the door. "What're you expecting?"

Sparrow nodded toward the fixed radiation counter above the tunnel door. "It may be a little warm. Keep an eye on that thing."

Garcia brought a portable radiation snooper from its wall rack, stood beside Sparrow.

"Okay," said Sparrow. "Here goes." He pulled the door open.

Garcia gagged.

"Wheee-ew!" gasped Sparrow.

"If you'll excuse the pun," said Bonnett, "I don't like the smell of that."

Ramsey leaned over the railing. "That's no rat," he said. "Too much of it."

Sparrow took the length of tubing, snapped on the light. It was turned so that its beam flashed full into Ramsey's eyes, blinding him momentarily. When Ramsey's vision returned, Sparrow had the tube pushed into the tunnel. Garcia was bent over the portable receiver beside the door, staring into the screen.

Ramsey tuned one of his own circuits to the portable unit, gasped as Garcia barked, "Skipper! Look at this!"

The screen showed part of the downward curve of the tunnel floor. Just within view were the soles of a man's shoes and part of his legs. The picture stopped just below the knees.

Bonnett looked at Ramsey, who caught a glimpse of staring eyes under the shaggy brows. Sweat glistened on the first officer's forehead. "You getting this on your screen?" he asked.

Ramsey nodded. Because of the angle of view, the men below him had a foreshortened, gnome-like appearance. A trick of acoustics brought their voices to Ramsey with a faint ringing quality. He felt like a man observing a marionette show.

Bonnett turned back to examine the fixed meter above the door. "Radiation's up slightly," he said.

"Nothing the filters can't take care of," said Garcia.

Sparrow was bending over to maneuver the TV eye and light farther into the tunnel. Garcia moved the portable receiver back where Bonnett could see it.

"Anything?" asked Sparrow.

"More leg," said Bonnett.

Ramsey became conscious of a low murmuring, realized that Garcia was whispering: "Holy Mary, Mother of God . . ." The engineering officer's hands were tolling the Rosary under his shirt.

Sparrow gave the tubing a gentle twist.

"Knife!" blurted Bonnett.

Ramsey saw it on his panel. The hilt of a knife projected from the chest of the man in the tunnel.

"Get a record camera on this," ordered Sparrow.

"I have it up here," called Ramsey. He pulled the camera from its rack beside the control board, hung it over the receiver screen.

Sparrow pushed the tubing farther into the tunnel until the scanner picked up the man's face. "Anybody recognize him?"

"I think I've seen him," said Garcia. "That's a rating uniform. Looks like atomic tech insignia." He shook his head. "But he's not one of the Techs I let aboard for the final embarkation check."

Sparrow turned, looked up at Ramsey. "How about you, Ramsey?"

"He's a special Security officer attached to Admiral Belland's office," said Ramsey. "His name's Foss or Foster. Something like that."

"How do you know?" asked Bonnett.

Ramsey suddenly realized he had committed a tactical error. "When I was with the gulf patrol," he said. "This bird was our Security liaison."

The lie came easily. He remembered the last time he had seen the man: Belland's outer office, Teacher Reed performing the introductions.

"Do you know what he was doing here?" asked Sparrow.

Ramsey shook his head. "I can guess. He was probably making a special check when somebody caught him."

"Caught him at what?" asked Garcia.

With an abrupt intake of breath, Ramsey realized that Garcia was the suspected sleeper.

"It was probably the other way around," said Bonnett. "This Security officer caught somebody doing something and—"

"Doing what?" barked Sparrow. He turned to a locker to the left of the tunnel. "Joe, help me into an ABG suit." He opened the locker, pulled out a suit.

Garcia moved to help him.

Presently, Sparrow's voice came to them over the suit communicator: "Les, get a contamination bag and lead box for this man's effects. Leave it at the hatch here. Joe, get into another suit to help me when I bring him out. Ramsey, monitor me and get a still record of the items I hold up for you. Get a repeater on my suit's radiation snooper. I may be too busy to watch it."

"Right," said Ramsey.

Garcia already was pulling on another suit. Bonnett was moving aft toward the door into machine stores.

Sparrow ducked for the door, clambered clumsily into the tunnel. Immediately, the radiation-snooper repeater on Ramsey's board picked up the count.

"It's hot in there," said Ramsey. "I read it 5000 milli-R here."

"I see it," said Sparrow. "Tune to my helmet scanner."

Ramsey tuned another screen on his board to the

scanner on Sparrow's helmet. The screen showed a gloved hand: Sparrow's. The hand moved out of range and revealed a portion of the dead man's uniform.

"Note," said Sparrow. "He left a note. Get a voice record of this as I read it and then photograph it. It's dated April 16, time 0845."

*Our embarkation day,* thought Ramsey. *At that time we were in the marine tunnel.*

Sparrow's voice continued: " 'To Captain H. A. Sparrow from Lieutenant Arthur H. Foss, SYO-2204829. Subject: Extra Security inspection subtug *Fenian Ram* this date.' "

The captain cleared his throat, continued: " 'Pursuant to new Security policy, I was making a special investigation of your atomic components following the regular check by the pile crew. This was to be a quick tunnel crawl for a look at the end plate and manuals. I did not wear an ABG suit because of the anticipated short time of the check and to maintain secrecy.' "

Garcia had moved up to the tunnel mouth, hovering over it in his ABG suit like some other-world monster. "You want me in there, Skipper?" he asked.

"Wait out there, Joe," said Sparrow. He went on reading: " 'My snooper's switch was accidentally turned off as I crawled through the tunnel and I received no warning that it was hot.' " (Sparrow's voice quickened.) " 'I found that one of your hafnium damper rods had been taken from the pile in the secondary bank and hidden in the tunnel. I was directly on top of it before I noticed it. There was no mistaking what it was. I turned on my snooper and immediately saw that I'd had a lethal overdose.' "

Sparrow paused. "May the Lord be merciful to him," he said. He continued with the note: " 'It was obvious that the damper rod had been selected for a timed overload, but the timing was not immediately apparent. It could have been set to blow at the base. Therefore, I made haste to slip the rod back onto the pile-room manuals and replaced it. I also repaired the alarm-system wiring where it had been cut to hide the sabotage.' "

Sparrow stopped and Ramsey saw the note (through the scanner) change position as the Skipper shifted. "Joe, did you notice any peculiar reaction from the alarm system?" asked Sparrow.

"Not a thing," said Garcia.

Sparrow grunted, continued with the note: " 'When the damper had been replaced, I looked for the communicator box at the pile end. It had been smashed. I then crawled back, thinking I'd get the medics to ease my dying. The tunnel hatch had been dogged from the outside and I was trapped. I tried to attract attention by calling through the vent, but there was no response. My own portable communicator would not work inside the shielding of the reactor wall.' "

Sparrow's voice stopped. "That explains it," he said.

Ramsey bent over his panel mike. "Explains what?"

"This tunnel vent opens from the inside. It should've been closed. But if it'd been closed we wouldn't have noticed—" He fell silent.

Ramsey's thoughts went to the actions of that Security officer: alone in the tunnel with the certain knowledge he was dying and nothing could save him. Spending his last minutes to guard the safety of others.

*Would I have been as brave?* he wondered.

Sparrow said, "He put the knife in himself rather than go out the slow way alone in here. He says he doesn't know who sabotaged the pile and tripped him."

"He could've attracted somebody," said Ramsey. "If he'd shorted one of—"

"And he'd have chanced shorting the wrong circuit and kicking every damper rod out onto the pile-room floor," said Garcia.

"But the gravity catches—"

"How could he know what'd been fouled up in

there?" demanded Garcia. His voice was choked with emotion. "But suicide!"

Sparrow said, "Joe, who were the last dock crewmen aboard?"

"Two snoopers I let aboard. I believe you saw them leave."

Ramsey thought: *Garcia again.* He leaned over the catwalk railing, called down to Garcia. "Joe, who were—" Then he remembered that Garcia's suit would damp out the sound and turned back to his mike: "Joe, who were those men?"

The blank faceplate of Garcia's suit tipped upward toward Ramsey. "Two new ones. Their names are on the gangway check list."

Sparrow said, "Record this from the note, Ramsey." He read: " 'Whoever sabotaged your pile was hoping it would blow while this subtug was in the marine tunnel. Such a blowup would eliminate the subtug base until a rerouted tunnel section could be built. Obviously, the enemy knows of the existence of this base. Security should be notified at once.' " The skipper's voice lowered. " 'Please tell my wife that my last thoughts were of her.' "

Garcia said, "Those dirty, evil—" He choked.

Sparrow held up the note for his suit scanner while Ramsey photographed it.

"Is there anything else?" asked Ramsey.

"A notebook filled with what looks like Security code. Yes, here's a notation from Lieutenant Foss: 'See that Security Section Twenty-Two gets this notebook.' "

Ramsey saw the book through Sparrow's suit scanner.

Sparrow said, "Record the pages as I hold them up, Ramsey." He flipped through the pages for the scanner, said, "I have the contents of his pockets. I'm coming out." He backed out to the tunnel entrance.

Bonnett returned from the rear storeroom dragging a bulky contamination bag and a small lead box. He looked up at Ramsey, said, "I listened in on the storeroom portable while I was getting this stuff. Lord, how I'd like to have my hands on the rats who scragged that poor guy!"

"You mean who almost scragged us," said Ramsey. He bent over his panel mike: "Joe, you'd better get that stuff from Les. He shouldn't go any closer to the tunnel without a suit."

Garcia's voice issued from the speaker: "Righto." He went back to the engine-room floor to Bonnett, returned to the tunnel with the contamination bag and lead box.

Sparrow emerged from the tunnel, turned, said, "Ramsey, record these items as I put them in the box. One Mark XXVII hand-snooper, one wrist-type communicator, one flashlight, one wallet with the following items: a picture of woman and child inscribed 'All our Love, Nan and Peggy,' one ID card issued to Lieutenant Senior Grade Arthur Harmon Foss, SYO-2204829, one base gate pass, one mess-hall pass, one driver's license, currency and coins to sixteen dollars and twenty-four cents."

He turned back to the tunnel, picked up another bundle tied in a handkerchief, untied the handkerchief clumsily with his heavily gloved hands. "Here's some more: one fountain pen, one key ring with four keys, one fingernail clipper, one minicamera. The telltale's turned red: film's been ruined by radiation. One pocket recorder with wire blank."

Sparrow dropped the bundle into the box. Garcia sealed it.

Ramsey glanced at his wrist watch, noted the time. *The telemeter record of Sparrow's reactions: what will it show for this period?* he asked himself.

Garcia straightened from the lead box. "What's the pile end like?" he asked.

Sparrow nodded his head toward the tunnel mouth, a grotesque gesture in the bulky suit. "Just as he described it. Everything back as it should be. All except the communicator box. Smashed. Why?"

"Maybe whoever did it anticipated the inspection," said Garcia.

"Maybe."

Ramsey's hands moved over his portable control panel, compensating for a minor course deflection caused by an upward current. When they were back on true, he looked over the railing. Garcia and Sparrow were just sealing the Security officer's body into the contamination bag.

Sparrow said, "Les, when we get him out of here, flush this area out with the detergent hoses. Let me know what the radiation count is."

Ramsey punched the switch on his panel mike: "Skipper, that note could've been faked to throw us off. Did you think of that? It strikes me the man would've used his recorder."

Garcia said, "And taken the chance of having his message accidentally erased? No sir." He dragged the sacked body under an engine-room hoist.

Sparrow said, "Les, when you get this place cleaned, get into a suit and make another inspection of the end plate and manuals of that tunnel. I'm eight minutes from my limit."

Bonnett acknowledged.

Garcia passed a snooper over the contamination bag. "Hot," he said. "We'll have to get him overboard within twelve hours. Otherwise, I wouldn't be responsible for the filters clearing our air." He racked the snooper, turned back, rigged a net under the bag.

Meanwhile, Bonnett had gone down the starboard side of the engine-room, donned an ABG suit from that side, and moved to the detergent hoses at the tunnel mouth.

Garcia took the slack out of the hoist line, turned toward Sparrow. "Skipper, why don't you get Les to help you here and let me crawl the tunnel? That's my department."

The faceplate on Sparrow's suit turned toward Bonnett, who hesitated beside the tunnel door. "Okay, Joe. Les, give me a hand here."

Bonnett stepped to Sparrow's side.

Garcia went to the tunnel door, turned back, and looked up at Ramsey. The quartz viewplate gave him the appearance of a one-eyed monster. He turned back to the tunnel, bending down as he snaked his way inside. Presently, his voice came over the speaker to Ramsey: "You with me, Junior?"

"I read you."

"My suit snooper says it's hotter than a two-dollar pistola where the shield curve ends here. I'm at the halfway mark. Here's the tunnel communicator box. It's a mess." (Pause) "I'm now at the manuals." (Long pause.) "The mirrors show no visible evidence of sabotage on this face of the pile. All secure. I'm coming out."

In Ramsey's mind a single thought: *If Garcia's really a sleeper, what's he actually doing in there? Why was he so anxious to make that inspection?*

Ramsey wondered if he could think up an excuse to make a personal inspection of that tunnel.

*Probably not,* he thought. *Sparrow wouldn't risk having three of his crewmen take a near-limit dosage. He'd have no reserve if something else made it necessary to crawl one of the tunnels.*

Ramsey resolved to make as thorough an inspection as possible using the internal scanners.

Sparrow and Bonnett were hoisting the contamination bag up to the discharge tubes below the retracted conning tower. Sparrow said, "Ramsey, take your board back against the aft bulkhead. That bag's leaking some."

Ramsey complied, racking his board on the catwalk rail.

Sparrow left the hoist to Bonnett, stepped into the decontamination chamber against the port pressure hull, emerged without his ABG suit. He looked up to Ramsey, his long face drawn into serious lines. "Is Joe on his way out?"

"He's on his way," said Ramsey.

"Foss's ID card shows he was Catholic," said Sparrow. "Ask Joe if he'll read the service for the dead."

Ramsey relayed the request.

Garcia, emerging from the tunnel, paused. "He couldn't have been Catholic," he said. "Either that, or he was murdered. A good Catholic doesn't commit suicide."

Sparrow heard Garcia's voice on the speaker, said, "Suffering Jesus! He's right." He looked thoughtful for a moment, found his chest mike, asked, "Will you read the service?"

Garcia said, "Under the circumstances, yes." He closed the tunnel door, dogged it, stepped into a decontamination chamber, and emerged without a suit.

Bonnett swung up to the central catwalk, anchored the hoist's load with a side line, returned to the lower deck, and reeled out the detergent hoses. He began to spray the area.

Sparrow and Garcia mounted to the catwalk beside Ramsey.

"We'll surface at midnight local time for burial," said Sparrow. He went aft through the number-one door without glancing up at the bundle swinging from the hoist.

Ramsey, watching Bonnett at work below him, again had the feeling of looking at a marionette show. *Last act, scene one.*

Garcia, beside him, said, "My watch coming up. I'll take it on the main control deck." He released Ramsey's portable board from the rail, carried it up to the central catwalk, ducked through the door in the aft bulkhead.

Ramsey followed, turned at the door for one last look at the long bundle swaying in the hoist net: a body in a sack. He turned, passed through the control room, went directly to his quarters and pulled out the telemeter tapes.

*No significant deviations!*

He coded the tapes for identification, placed them in the false bottom, lay back on his bunk. Around him he could feel the faint vibrations of the subtug: a feeling as of life. He seemed to fit into the pattern of the room, one with the crisscross of pipes overhead, the ventilator ducts, the repeaters for the electronics-shack instruments, wall mike and speaker.

Presently, he fell asleep, dreamed that he was a deep-dwelling fish trying to figure out a way to climb to the light of the surface far away above him.

The problem was that a terrible pressure held him trapped in the deeps.

At midnight they committed the body of Lieutenant Foss to the ocean. A cold, starless night, a high-running sea. Ramsey stood shivering on the deck while Garcia mumbled the service for the dead.

"Into Thy hands we commend this spirit."

For Lieutenant Arthur Harmon Foss; last act, last scene.

Afterward, they homed into the depths as though fleeing the scene of a crime. Ramsey was startled by the faraway look in Sparrow's eyes, heard the captain whispering the lines from the first chapter of Genesis:

" '. . . and darkness was upon the face of the deep. And the Spirit of God moved upon the face of the waters. . . .' "

From some recess in his memory, Ramsey recalled the next lines: " 'And God said, Let there be light: and there was light.' "

Ramsey thought: *If there is a God, let him make things right for that brave guy.* It was his nearest approach to a prayer since childhood. He was surprised at the stinging sensation in his eyes.

Then another thought mingled with the memory of Garcia's voice: *And what if Garcia is the sleeper?*

The thought spurred him to hurry into the electronics shack, examine the contaminated tunnel through the internal scanners. The scanners showed only the pile-room end. Nothing appeared amiss. Ramsey activated one of the control-room scanners to check on Garcia. The engineering officer was bent over the portside grab rail, knuckles white from the pressure of his grip upon the rail, his forehead pressed against the cold metal of the pressure hull.

*He looks ill,* thought Ramsey. *I wonder if I should go down and relieve him?*

As Ramsey watched, Garcia straightened, slammed a fist against the hull surface so hard his knuckles bled. The *Ram* took this moment to tip slightly from the thrust of an undersea current. Garcia whirled to the controls, corrected for the deflection. Ramsey could see tears streaming down his face.

Abruptly, Ramsey switched off his screen, feeling that he had eavesdropped upon the workings of a man's soul and that it was wrong to have done so. He stared at his hands, thought: *Now that's a strange reaction for a psychologist! What's come over me?* He reactivated the screen, but now Garcia was calmly going about the business of his watch.

Ramsey returned to his quarters with the strong sense that he had blinded himself to something vital. For almost an hour, he lay awake on his bunk, unable to resolve the problem. When he fell asleep it was to sink again into the dream of the fish.

He awoke to his next watch with the feeling of not having slept at all.

There had been a time when people thought it would solve most seafaring problems to take ocean shipping beneath the surface storms. But, as had happened so many times in the past, for every problem solved a new one was added.

Beneath the ocean surface flow great salt rivers, their currents not held to a horizontal plane by confining banks. The 600 feet of plastic barge trailing behind the *Ram* twisted, dragged, and skidded— caught by currents flowing through 60 degrees at right angles to their course. If the current set downward the *Ram* tipped upward and had to fight against the climb. If a current took the tow upward, the *Ram* headed down. Variations often gave the subtug's deck a stately rolling and tipping as though the vessel was beset by a slow-motion storm.

Automatics took care of most of the deflections, but many were sufficient to cause wide course error. Because of this, a portable gyro repeater always accompanied the man on duty.

Bonnett carried such a repeater on his remote-control panel as he prowled the engine room during his watch. The little timelog repeater beside the gyro dial showed seven days, eight hours, and eighteen minutes from departure. The *Ram* had moved forward deep into the ocean no man's land south of Iceland.

*Maybe it'll be a milk run,* he thought. *For all our detectors have shown, we could be alone in the whole damned ocean.* He fell to remembering the night before departure, wondered if Helene was really faithful to him. *So damned many Navy wives . . .*

An amber light glowed at the upper corner of his board, the signal that someone had entered the control room. He spoke into his chest mike: "I'm on the second-level catwalk in the engine room."

Sparrow's voice came out of the board speaker: "Continue as you are. I'm just restless. Thought I'd look around."

"Right, Skipper." Bonnett turned to examine the master control gauges on the reactor bulkhead. Ever since they'd found the dead Security officer, Bonnett had been nursing an uneasy feeling about the room in the subtug's nose.

A sudden needle deflection on his control board caught his attention. The outside water temperature had dropped ten degrees: a cold current.

Ramsey's voice came over the intercom: "This is Ramsey in the shack. My instruments show a sharp ten-degree temperature drop outside."

Bonnett thumbed his mike switch: "What're you doing up and about, Junior?"

"I'm always nervous when it's your duty," said

Ramsey. "I couldn't sleep, so I came in here to run an instrument check."

"Wise guy," said Bonnett.

Sparrow's voice joined them: "Find out how deep it is, Ramsey. If it doesn't extend below our limit, we can hide under it and pick up speed. Ten degrees will cloud a lot of noise."

"Right, Skipper." Pause. "Sixty-eight hundred feet, give or take a few."

"Les, take her down," said Sparrow.

Bonnett racked his control console onto the catwalk railing, took electronic hold of the diving planes. Abruptly, his static pressure-gauge repeater showed what his sense of balance already had told him: they were going down too fast; an upcurrent was following them, lifting the tow. Bonnett fought it until they were inclined at a safe three degrees.

The *Ram* leveled at 6780 feet.

In the shack, Ramsey looked at his own repeater for the master pressure gauge: 2922 pounds to the square inch. Instinctively, his gaze went to the pressure hull beside him—a small length of it seen through a maze of pipes and conduits. He tried to fight away from the thought of what would happen if the hull should implode: bits of protein pulp floating amidst shattered machinery.

*What was it Reed had said?* It came back to Ramsey clearly, even to the impersonal tones of his instructor's voice: "An implosion of external equipment at extreme depths may set up a shock wave which will split your hull wide open. Of course, it'd be all over for you before you'd hardly realized what happened."

Ramsey shivered.

*What is Sparrow's reaction to the increased danger?* he wondered. Then: *I don't really care as long as his ability keeps me safe.*

This thought shocked Ramsey. He suddenly looked around his electronics shack as though seeing it for the first time, as though he had just awakened.

*What kind of a psychologist am I? What have I been doing?*

As though answering a question from outside himself his mind said: *You've been hiding from your own fears. You've been striving to become an efficient cog in this crew because that way lies a measure of physical safety.*

Back came the answer: *You're afraid of your own personal extinction.*

"It'd be as though I'd died *en utero*," he said, speaking the thought softly to himself. "Never born at all."

He found that he was trembling, bathed in perspiration. The plug holes of the test board in front of him seemed to stare back—a hundred demanding eyes. He suddenly wanted to scream, found he couldn't move his throat muscles.

*If there was an emergency now, I'd be helpless,* he thought. *I couldn't move a finger.*

He tried to will the motion of the index finger of his right hand, failed.

*If I move I'll die!*

Something touched his shoulder and he almost blanked out in frozen panic. A voice spoke softly beside his ear and it was as though the voice had shouted loud enough to split his eardrums.

"Ramsey. Steady boy."

"You're a brave man, Ramsey. You took it longer than most."

Ramsey felt the trembling of his body had become so violent that his vision blurred.

"I've been waiting for this, Ramsey. Every man goes through it down here. Once you've been through it, you're all right."

Deep, fatherly voice. Tender. Compassionate.

With all his being, Ramsey wanted to turn, bury his head against that compassionate chest, sob out his fears in strangled emotion.

"Let it go," said Sparrow. "Let it come. Nobody here but me, and I've been through it."

Slowly at first, then in gasping sobs, the tears came. He bent over the bench, buried his face in his arms. All the time, Sparrow's hand upon his shoulder, a feeling of warmth from it, a sense of strength.

"I was afraid," whispered Ramsey.

"Show me the man who isn't afraid and I'll show you a blind man or a dolt," said Sparrow. "We're plagued with too much thinking. It's the price of intelligence."

The hand left Ramsey's shoulder. He heard the shack door open, close.

Ramsey lifted his head, stared at the test board in front of him, the open intercom switch.

Bonnett's voice came from the speaker: "Ramsey, can you give us a sound-distance test now?"

Ramsey cleared his throat. "Right." His hands moved over the board, slowly, then with rapid sureness. "There's enough cold stuff above us to blanket force speed," he said.

The speaker rumbled with Sparrow's voice. "Les, give us force speed. Ramsey, we are within ninety pounds of pressure limit. Remain on watch with Les until you are relieved."

The humming of the *Ram*'s electric motors keened up a notch, another.

"Right, Skipper," said Ramsey.

Garcia's voice came over the intercom. "What's up? I felt the motors."

"Cold layer," said Sparrow. "We're gaining a few knots while we can."

"Need me?"

"Come up here on stand-by."

Ramsey heard the voices over the intercom with a peculiar clarity, saw the board in front of him with a detail that amazed him: tiny scratches, a worn plug line.

Back came the memory of his blue funk and with it, a detail his mind had avoided: Sparrow calling to him over the intercom to make the sound-distance test.

*And when I didn't answer, he came immediately to help me.*

Another thought intruded: *He knows how green I am—has known it all along.*

"Ramsey."

Sparrow stood in the shack doorway.

Ramsey stared at him.

Sparrow entered, sat down on the bench stool beside the door. "What are you, Ramsey?"

He cleared his throat. "What do you mean?"

"Every man has to wrestle with his shadow down here. You held out a long time."

"I don't understand you."

"This life makes you face your fears sooner or later."

"How did you know I was afraid?"

"Every man's afraid down here. It was just a matter of waiting until you found out you were afraid. Now, answer my question: What are you?"

Ramsey stared past Sparrow. "Sir, I'm an electronics officer."

A faint smile touched Sparrow's eyes and mouth. "It's a sad world we live in, Ramsey. But at least Security picks its men for their courage." He straightened.

Ramsey accepted this silently.

"Now, let's have a look at that little box of yours," said Sparrow. "I'm curious." He stood up, went out into the companionway, turned aft.

Ramsey followed.

"Why not keep it in the shack?" asked Sparrow.

"I've been using my time off to check it."

"Don't wear yourself out." Sparrow dropped down to the lower level, Ramsey behind him. They entered Ramsey's room. The humming of the induction drive came through the bulkhead.

Ramsey sat down on his bunk, brought out the box, put it on his desk, and unlocked it. *Can't let him look too close,* thought Ramsey. He noted that the disguise system was working.

Sparrow peered into the box with a puzzled frown. *What's he expect to find?* Ramsey wondered.

"Give me a rundown," said Sparrow.

Ramsey pointed to a dial. "That monitors the sweep of the primary search impulse. The first models were plagued by feedback echo."

Sparrow nodded.

Ramsey indicated a group of signal lights. "These separate the pulse frequencies. They flicker red when we're out of phase. The particular light tells me which circuit is bouncing."

Sparrow straightened, shot a searching glance at Ramsey.

"Tapes inside make a permanent record," said Ramsey.

"We'll go into it at greater length some other time," said Sparrow. He turned away.

He expected some Security gadget, thought Ramsey.

"Why'd Security plant you on us?" asked Sparrow.

Ramsey remained silent.

Sparrow turned, stared at him with a weighing look. "I won't force this issue now," he said. "Time enough for that when we get home." His face took on a bitter expression. "Security! Half our troubles can be traced to them."

Ramsey maintained his silence.

"It's fortunate you're a good electronics officer," said Sparrow. "Doubtless you were chosen for that quality." A sudden look of indecision passed over his features. "You *are* a Security man, aren't you?"

Ramsey thought: *If he believes that, it'll mask my real position. But I can't just admit it. That'd be out of character.* He said, "I have my orders, sir."

"Of course," said Sparrow. "Stupid of me." Again the look of indecision. "Well, I'll be getting—" Abruptly, he stiffened.

Ramsey, too, fought to keep from showing surprise. The pellet imbedded in his neck had just emitted a sharp *ping!* He knew that the identical equipment in Sparrow had also reacted to a signal.

Sparrow whirled to the door, ran forward to the control deck, Ramsey on his heels. They stopped before the big master board. Garcia turned from his position at the monitor controls. "Something wrong, Skipper?"

Sparrow didn't answer. Through his mind was running a senseless rhyme born of the twenty kills the EPs had made in the previous months: *Twenty out of twenty is plenty . . . twenty out of twenty is plenty . . .*

Ramsey, standing behind Sparrow, was extremely conscious of the charged feeling in the control room, the stink of the atmosphere, the questioning look on Garcia's face, the clicking of automatic instruments, and the answering response of the deck beneath his feet.

The pellet in his neck had begun sending out a rhythmic buzzing.

Garcia stepped away from the board. "What's wrong, Skipper?"

Sparrow waved him to silence, turned right. Ramsey followed.

The buzzing deepened. Wrong direction.

"Get a signal snifter," said Sparrow, speaking over his shoulder to Ramsey.

Ramsey turned to the rear bulkhead, pulled a snifter from its rack, tuned it as he rejoined Sparrow. The instrument's speaker buzzed in rhythm to his neck pellet.

Sparrow turned left; Ramsey followed. The sound of the snifter went up an octave.

"Spy beam!" said Garcia.

Sparrow moved toward the dive board, Ramsey still following. The sound from the snifter grew louder. They passed the board and the sound deepened. They turned, faced the board. Now, the signal climbed another octave.

Ramsey thought: *Garcia was in here alone. Did he set up a signal device?*

"Where's Les?" asked Sparrow.

"Forward," said Garcia.

Sparrow seemed to be trying to look through the wall in front of him.

*He thinks it may be Bonnett sending that signal,* thought Ramsey. With a sudden despair, he wondered: *Could it be?*

Sparrow spoke into his chest microphone: "Les! To the control room! On the double!"

Bonnett acknowledged and they heard a clang of metal as he slipped on the catwalk; then he shut off his microphone.

Ramsey frowned at his snifter. The signal remained stationary although Bonnett was moving. But then a signal device could have been left hidden forward. He moved the snifter to the right, aiming it toward the center of the dive board. The signal remained constant.

Sparrow had followed the motion.

"It's in the board!" shouted Ramsey.

Sparrow whirled toward the board. "We may have only a couple of minutes to get that thing!"

For a mind-chilling instant, Ramsey visioned the enemy wolf packs converging for another kill—twenty-one.

Garcia slammed a tool kit onto the deck at their feet, flipped it open, came out with a screw driver. He began dismantling the cover plate.

Bonnett entered. "What's wrong, Skipper?"

"Spy-beam transmitter," said Sparrow. He had found another screw driver, was helping Garcia remove the cover plate.

"Should we take evasive action?" asked Ramsey.

Sparrow shook his head. "No, let them think we don't know about it. Steady as she goes."

"Here," said Garcia. "Pull on that end."

Ramsey reached forward, helped pull the cover

plate away from the board, revealing a maze of wiring, transistors, high-pressure tubes.

Bonnett picked up the snifter, passed it in front of the board, stiffened as the signal increased in front of the tube bank.

"Joe, stand by on the auxiliary dive board," said Sparrow. "I'm shutting down this whole section."

Garcia darted across to the auxiliary board on the opposite side of the control room. "Auxiliary operating," he called.

"Wait," said Bonnett. He held the search box steady before a tube, reached in with his free hand and pulled the tube from its socket. The signal continued, but now it emanated from Bonnett's hand as he waved the tube in front of the snifter.

"A self-contained power unit in that little thing!" gasped Ramsey.

"Suffering Jesus save us," muttered Sparrow. "Here, give it to me." He took the tube from Bonnett's hand, gritted his teeth at the heat of the thing.

Bonnett shook the hand which had held the tube. "Burned me," he said.

"It was in the ZO2R bank," Ramsey said.

"Smash it," said Garcia.

Sparrow shook his head. "No." He grinned mirthlessly. "We're going to gamble. Les, take us up to discharge depth."

"Six hundred feet?" asked Bonnett. "We'll be sitting ducks!"

"Do it!" barked Sparrow. He turned to Ramsey, extended the tube. "Anything special about this you could use to identify it?"

Ramsey took the tube, turned it over in his hand. He reached into his breast pocket, pulled out a tiny record camera, began photographing the tube from all angles.

Sparrow noted the ready availability of a record camera, but before he could comment on it, Ramsey said, "I'll have to look at the enlargements." He glanced up at Sparrow. "Do we have time to give this thing a more thorough going over in the shack?"

Sparrow looked to the static pressure gauge. "About ten minutes. Whatever you do, don't stop that signal."

Ramsey whirled, hurried to the shack, Sparrow behind him. He heard Sparrow speaking into a chest mike as they ran.

"Joe, get a garbage disposal container and ready a tube to discharge that spy beam. With any luck at all, we're going to send the EPs chasing after an ocean current."

Ramsey put a piece of soft felt on his workbench, placed the tube on it.

"If you've ever prayed, pray now," said Sparrow.

"Nothing this small could have an internal power source to give off that much signal," said Ramsey.

"But it does," said Sparrow.

Ramsey paused to wipe perspiration from his hands. A thought flitted through his mind: *What will the telemeter record show on Sparrow's endocrine balance this time?*

"Devilish thing!" muttered Sparrow.

"We're playing a big gamble," said Ramsey. He placed calipers over the tube, noted the measurements. "Standard size for the ZO2R." He put the tube in a balance scale with another of the same make. The spy tube sank, unbalancing the scale.

"It's heavier than the standard," said Sparrow.

Ramsey moved the balance weights. "Four ounces."

Bonnett's voice came over the bulkhead speaker above their heads: "Estimating discharge depth in four minutes. We've picked up a free ride on a current."

Sparrow said, "Do you think you can find out anything else about that thing?"

"Not without tearing it down," said Ramsey. "Of course, there's a possibility X-ray would show some internal detail we could figure out." He shook his head.

"There'll be more of those aboard," said Sparrow. "I know there will."

"How?"

Sparrow looked at him. "Call it a hunch. This mission has been marked." He glared at the tube on the bench. "But by all that's sacred, we're going to come through!"

"Two minutes," said Bonnett's voice over the speaker.

Ramsey said, "That's it. Let me examine what we already have."

Sparrow scooped up the tube, said, "Move out to full limit."

"They may detect our pulse," said Ramsey, then colored as he felt the metronomic response of the speaker in his neck.

Sparrow smiled without mirth, turned, stooped for the door, and disappeared down the companionway. Presently, his voice came over the intercom: "We're at the tube and ready to blow this thing, Les. Give me the static gauge readings."

Back came Bonnett's voice: "Four-ninety, four-seventy, four-forty . . . four hundred even!"

Ramsey heard the faint "chug!" of the discharge tube, the sound carried to him through the hull.

Sparrow's voice rang over the intercom: "Ride the vents!"

The *Ram*'s deck tipped sharply. The humming of the motors climbed through a teeth-grating vibration.

Ramsey looked to the dial showing their sound-transmission level. Too high. The silencer planes would never cover it.

Sparrow's voice boomed from the speaker: "Ramsey, take over the internal-pressure system on manual. Overcompensate for anticipated depth. We'll worry about Haldane charts and depth sickness later. Right now, I want that cold level and 7000 feet over us."

Ramsey acknowledged, his hands moving to the controls as he spoke. He glanced at the vampire gauge on his wrist. Diffusion rate low. He stepped up the release of carbonic anhydrase into the atmosphere.

Sparrow again: "Ramsey, we've fired a salvo of

homing torps on our back path. Delayed timing. Track the signal if any of them blow."

"Aye, Skipper." Ramsey plugged a monitor phone into one of the board circuits ahead of him, glanced to the telltale above it. As he did, he noted that the pellet in his neck had almost lost the sound of the tube behind them. His hands continued to move the internal pressure ahead of the depth requirement. The outside pressure repeater above his head showed 2600 pounds to the square inch, still climbing. Abruptly, the temperature recorder responded to their entrance into the cold current.

Ramsey spoke into his chest mike: "We're in the cold, Skipper."

Back came Sparrow's voice: "We have it here."

Ramsey's pressure repeater climbed through 2815 pounds, steadied. He felt the deck beneath him come up to level. Relays clicked, a bank of monitor lights flashed green. He sensed the ship around him—a buoyant, almost living thing of machines, plastics, gases, fluids . . . and humans. He could hear Sparrow's voice over the open intercom giving orders in the control room.

"Force speed. Change course to fifty-nine degrees, thirty minutes."

The secondary sonoran chart at Ramsey's left noted the course change. He looked at the red dot marking their position: almost due south of the western tip of Iceland, directly on the sixtieth parallel of latitude. Automatic timelog reading: seven days, fourteen hours, twenty-six minutes from start of mission.

"Ramsey, anything on those fish we sent back?"

"Negative, Skipper."

"Stick with the shack. We're going to start tearing down the board. We'll have to check every tube for deviation from standard weight."

"We'll have to go over the shack and the E-stores, too," said Ramsey.

"Later." Sparrow's voice conveyed a calm surety.

Ramsey glanced at his wrist watch, correlated it

with the timelog. *What will the telemeter show?* he asked himself. Again, he felt that his mind had made a failing grasp at an elusive piece of essential knowledge. Something about Sparrow. Ramsey's gaze ranged over the board in front of him. His ears felt tuned for the slightest sound over the monitor phones. He glanced at the oscilloscope in the right bank: only background noise. For a fleeting instant, Ramsey felt that he was one with the ship, that the instruments around him were but extensions of his senses. Then it was gone and he could not recapture the feeling.

In the control room, Sparrow fought down the twitching of a cheek muscle. He replaced a tube in the sonoran system, extracted another, read the code designation from the tube's side: "PY4X4."

Garcia, beside him, ran a finger down a check list: "Fifteen ounces plus."

Sparrow checked it on a balance scale. "Right on." He replaced the tube, said, "You know, when I was in high school they were saying that someday they'd run systems like this with transistors and printed circuits."

"They did for a while," said Garcia.

"Then we got into sweep circuits," said Sparrow. He pulled out an octode cumulator tube, read off the code, checked the weight.

"We could still get by with lighter stuff if it weren't for high atmospheric pressures." He went on to another tube. "What we need is a dielectric as tough as plasteel."

"Or an armistice," said Garcia. "Then deep-tug equipment would be specialty stuff."

Sparrow nodded, pulled another tube from its socket.

"Skipper, what is that Ramsey?" asked Garcia.

Sparrow paused in the process of weighing a tube, looked at Garcia. "I *think* he's a Security man planted on us."

"That occurred to me," said Garcia. "But have you asked yourself yet who planted the spy beam on us? He could be a sleeper. He could be, Skipper."

Sparrow's hand trembled as he reached for another tube to weigh. He brought back his hand empty, wiped the palm on his shirt, looked down at Garcia. "Joe—" He broke off.

"Yes?"

"Has it ever occurred to you that humanity's basic problem is all wrapped up in the idea of Security?"

"That's a big mouthful, Skipper."

"I mean it, Joe. Look, I know what I am. I can even tell you what my conception of myself is. How you have nothing to fear from me. Les can do the same thing. And you. And Ramsey." He wet the corners of his mouth with his tongue, stared wide-eyed at Garcia. "And any one of us or all of us could be lying."

"That's not a Security problem, Skipper. That's a problem in communications. Ramsey's department."

Sparrow turned back to the board without answering, went on with his patient inspection.

"I'd like to know what that last-minute Security inspection of Ramsey was all about," said Garcia.

"Shut up!" barked Sparrow. "Until there's proof positive to the contrary, he's one of us. So are you and Les. And so am I." His mouth twisted in faint amusement. "We're all in the same boat." The lips thinned. "And we've a bigger and more immediate problem." He balanced a tube on the scales, replaced it. "How can we break radio silence to notify home base of what we've discovered?"

A distant dull thump pounded through the hull. A second one.

Ramsey's voice over the intercom: "Skipper! Two hits! Blast pattern identical to our fish!" His voice rose in pitch: "Breaking up noises! Two sources. Skipper! We got two!"

"God forgive us," said Sparrow. "God forgive us."

More thudding sounds resonating through the hull, a strange double beat.

"Anti-torp seekers," said Ramsey. "They've knocked out the rest of our fish."

"Those men didn't stand a chance," said Sparrow.

His voice lowered, became almost inaudible. " 'He that smiteth a man, so that he die, shall be surely put to death. And if a man lie not in wait, but God deliver him into his hand; then I will appoint thee a place wither he shall flee. But if a man come presumptuously upon his neighbour, to slay with guile; thou shalt take him from mine altar, that he may die.' "

Across from him, Bonnett held up a tube. "Joe, what's standard on a GR5?"

Garcia glanced at Sparrow, who turned abruptly back to his examination of the board. "Eight ounces," said Garcia.

"That's what I make it," said Bonnett. "But this one tops thirteen." A tone of suppressed excitement vibrated in his voice.

Sparrow looked aft, lips trembling.

"I think I have one, Skipper," said Bonnett.

Garcia had stepped across to Bonnett's side. He took the tube from the first officer.

"There should be a better way to live and a better way to die," said Sparrow. He shuddered, stabbed a glance at Bonnett. "Well, set it aside and see if there are any more!"

Bonnett appeared about to reply, but remained silent. He reclaimed the tube from Garcia, deposited it gently in a padded tray of his tool box.

Sparrow passed a hand across his forehead. His head ached strangely. *Is there a spy aboard?* he asked himself. *Is it Ramsey? Is it Les? Is it Joe? The EPs are hoping we lead them to the well.* He looked blankly at the open wiring before him. *Then why set off a tracer now? To test our alertness? The obvious time for a signal will be when we're sitting on top of the well.*

A strange vibration inside his head distracted Sparrow. He was startled to discover he'd been grinding his teeth. *When we're sitting on the well! God help me! How will I prevent it? I can't remain awake the whole time.*

"That's the last one," said Garcia. He indicated a

tube which Sparrow had automatically placed in the balance scales.

Sparrow shuddered, drew himself back to the present. "Put it back," he said.

Garcia complied.

Sparrow looked at Bonnett. "Les, start checking the spares in E-stores."

"Aye," said Bonnett.

Sparrow spoke to Garcia: "Stay on watch here."

Garcia nodded. "Are you going to rest, Skipper?"

Sparrow shook his head from side to side. "No. No, I have to go back to the shack and help Ram—" He stopped, glanced at Garcia. "We've engaged the enemy and come through." Sparrow stepped to the door leading aft. "I'm going to help *Johnny* check out the tubes in the shack."

"What about that?" Garcia indicated the tube Bonnett had left in the tray of his tool box.

Sparrow returned, picked up the tube, went back to the door, examining the tube. "We'll have a look. Maybe it'll tell us something." He glanced at Garcia. "You be thinking about how we can contact base."

He was gone through the door.

Garcia clenched his fists, turned to face the master board. His gaze fell on the sonoran chart and its marker: a red insect creeping across vastness. *Where? Where's the well?*

Ramsey looked up from his instruments as Sparrow entered. "Anything new, Skipper?"

"Les found this." Sparrow placed the tube on the felt padding of Ramsey's bench. "It's five ounces over."

Ramsey looked at the tube without touching it. "Has it occurred to you that thing could be set to explode on tampering?"

"Some of the old Salem sea captains used to attend their own funerals before embarking," said Sparrow. "Figuratively, I'm in the same frame of mind."

"That's not what I mean," said Ramsey. "A half ounce of nitrox could get us both. Maybe you'd better leave me alone with it."

Sparrow frowned, shrugged. He thumbed his chest mike: "Joe, Les—hear this. This tube may be booby-trapped. If anything happens to Johnny and me, you two drop the tow and head for home. That's an order."

*Johnny!* thought Ramsey. *He called me Johnny!* And then he remembered: *We've met the enemy. The old magic is dead. Enter the new magic.*

"We'll want a record of this," said Sparrow. He took a camera from a drawer, racked it above the bench, focused it. "Okay," he said. "You're the expert on these gadgets."

Ramsey spoke without looking up from the tube: "A half hour of just looking at this thing, studying all the angles, could mean the difference between success and failure."

"What're we looking for?"

"I don't really know. Something different. Something that hits a sour note."

Sparrow bent over the bench, grabbed a handhold as the *Ram*'s deck slanted to the upflow of an undersea current. Ramsey steadied the tube with one hand, brought up folds of the felt padding to keep the tube from rolling. The amber light of the temperature-gadget indicator on the board ahead of them flashed off, on, off.

Ramsey switched on the thermo repeater above the light: thirty-four degrees.

Sparrow nodded at the repeater. "The Arctic bottom drift. It's full of food. There'll be a sonic curtain of sea life above us." He smiled. "We can breathe a bit easier."

Ramsey shook his head. "Not with that thing to solve." He stared at the tube on the bench. "If you were going to trigger that to explode, how would you do it?"

"A tiny wire maybe. Break it and—"

"Maybe," said Ramsey. "A better way would be to set a trigger keyed to pressure change—if the vacuum breaks . . . " He straightened. "First some infra and X pictures. Then we'll rig a vacuum jar with remote controls, handle the tube in the vacuum. After that we'll break the seal."

Sparrow touched the tube with one long finger of his left hand. "Looks like standard heavy-pressure glass."

"I don't understand something," said Ramsey. He spoke as he worked, setting up the portable infra camera on the bench. "Why did this thing start when it did? That wasn't smart. The clever thing would've been to wait until we reached the well."

"My idea exactly," said Sparrow.

Ramsey focused the camera. "How much longer until we reach it?"

The casual way of the question caught Sparrow off balance. He looked up to the shack-room sonoran chart, started to say, "Well, it's on the flank of—" He froze.

Ramsey made an exposure, turned the tube to a new angle.

*He's too casual,* thought Sparrow.

"You were saying." Ramsey spoke without looking up from the tube.

"Mr. Ramsey, a subtug's destination is known only to its commander until the immediate area of that destination is reached."

Ramsey straightened. "That's a stupid order. If something happened to you we couldn't go on."

"Are you suggesting I should confide our destination in you?"

Ramsey hesitated, thought: *I already know it. What would happen if I indicated that to Sparrow? That'd confirm his opinion that I'm Security.*

"Well?"

"Skipper, I asked you a civil question. Phrased a bit loosely, perhaps. What I want to know is how much longer until we reach Novaya Zemlya?"

Sparrow held himself in rigid control, thinking: *Security? A spy trying to draw me out with a clever guess?* He said, "I don't see where it's your concern how long it takes us to get anywhere."

Ramsey returned his attention to the tube. *Is he convinced that I'm a Security officer?*

*I could ask him for the exact co-ordinates,* thought Sparrow. *But would it prove anything if he doesn't know them? Or if he does know them?*

Ramsey set up a bell jar and vacuum pump, the tube resting on the black mastic sealer inside the jar. He removed the jar, arranged a small remote-control console, replaced the jar.

Sparrow watched carefully, still undecided about Ramsey.

"This is going to be slow," said Ramsey.

*Lord in heaven, if I only knew!* thought Sparrow. *Is he a spy? How can I tell? He doesn't really act like one.*

Ramsey locked a stool in place before the bench, sat down. "Slow and easy," he said.

Sparrow studied him. *It could be a clever act. I'll get busy checking the shack tubes, watch him.* He said, "I'll start checking out your tubes." He removed a cover plate at the left, found scales, began removing tubes, weighing them.

Minutes ticked away—an hour, two hours . . . two hours and forty minutes. Inside the bell jar, the parts of the tube were laid out in rows. Sparrow long since had finished his job, was watching the work at the bench.

"No booby trap," said Ramsey. He activated a magnet arm inside the jar, lifted a grid section. "And I still don't see how they rigged this thing to go off. This looks like standard stuff." He rotated the part on the magnet. "There's nothing arranged to fuse with an overload. Nothing extra at all except that micro-vibrator and its capacitor power source." He replaced the grid section. "Our boys are going to want to see that." He picked up a cathode segment, turned it over, set it down. "No trigger. How was it done?"

Sparrow looked to the camera which had been capturing every movement of the examination, turned back to Ramsey. "We have another problem."

"What's that?" Ramsey straightened, rubbed the small of his back.

Sparrow slid off his stool. "How're we going to get word of this back to base? If the EPs get us, the things we've discovered are lost. But I have an iron-clad order against breaking radio silence."

Ramsey stretched his back. "Do you trust me, Skipper?"

Before he could stop himself, Sparrow said, "No." He frowned.

Ramsey grinned. "I'm still the one with the solution to your problem."

"Let's have it."

"Put the whole story onto a squirt repeater and——"

"Squirt repeater?"

Ramsey bit his lip, coughed. *Damn! Another Bu-Psych-Security secret.* It had slipped out.

"I've never heard of a squirt repeater," said Sparrow.

"It's something new in . . . uh . . . electronics. You code a message onto ultra-stable slow tape, then speed up the tape. You set the message to repeat—over and over—a little squirt of sound. It's recorded at the receiver end, slowed for playback and translation."

"That's still breaking radio silence."

Ramsey shook his head. "Not if the message is broadcast by a little set in a floater rigged to start transmitting long after we've gone."

Sparrow's jaw fell. He snapped his mouth shut. Then: "Could you rig it?"

Ramsey looked around him. "We have all the essentials right here."

Sparrow said, "I'll send Garcia in to help you."

Ramsey said, "I wont need any help with——"

"He'll help you anyway."

Again Ramsey grinned. "That's right. You don't trust me."

In spite of himself, Sparrow grinned back at the amusement in Ramsey's face; then wiped the grin from his features and from his thoughts. His brows drew together. *Is this all an act on Ramsey's part?* he wondered. *Amuse me. Throw me off guard. It could be.*

Ramsey glanced at the wall chrono. "My watch." He indicated the parts in the bell jar. "This'll keep."

"I'll stand your watch," said Sparrow. He thumbed his chest mike. "Joe, come to the shack. Johnny's figured out how to get a message to home base. I want you to help him."

"This shouldn't take more than a couple of hours," said Ramsey. "It's really a simple rig. I'll report in as soon as we've finished."

Sparrow pursed his lips in thought, stared solemnly at Ramsey. "There's something else. I'm instituting a new watch procedure: two men on duty at all times, never to leave actual sight of each other."

Ramsey's eyes widened. "There are only four of us, Skipper."

"It'll be rough," said Sparrow. "We'll stagger the watches, change the second man in mid-watch."

"That's not what I meant," said Ramsey. "It'll be more than rough. There are only four of us. Isolated. Under your plan, we'll obviously be watching each other. When you watch another man it tends to make you suspicious. Suspicion sets up a paranoiac situation where—"

"Your reluctance to accept an order for the general safety is being noted and will be entered in the log," said Sparrow.

Ramsey's face took on a look of watchful remoteness. He thought: *Take it easy. This is the paranoiac leaning that Obe mentioned.* He said, "Efficiency will suffer if we're—"

"I'm still the captain of this vessel," said Sparrow.

"Yes, *Captain,*" said Ramsey. He made the title sound faintly reproachful.

Sparrow's lips thinned. He whirled, left the shack, hurried aft to his quarters, bolted the door behind him. He sat down on his bunk, swung the folding desk into position. The faint whispering of the induction drive resonated through the wall behind him. The *Ram* had an uncertain, shifting motion; the bottom turbulence of the Arctic Current.

He thought: *We've a spy aboard. It's obvious someone activated that spy beam. I wish I'd had Joe checking Ramsey when he opened that tube. He says there was no internal trigger system in the thing, but he could've hidden something from me.*

From a recess in his desk, Sparrow removed his private log, opened it to a clean page, smoothed the log flat. He took his pen and, in a neat cramped hand, wrote the date, then: "This date Ensign John Ramsey made objection to a Security procedure designed to . . ."

He paused, remembering that he'd ordered Garcia to the shack. He thumbed the switch on his chest mike: "Joe, are you in the shack?"

Garcia's voice came out of the wall speaker. "Righto."

"Just checking," said Sparrow. "Would you have a look at that spy beam, see if there's anything about it we may have missed?"

"Righto, Skipper. Been doing just that."

"That's all," said Sparrow. He turned back to his log.

In the shack, Garcia looked up from the bell jar. "You're dead right, Johnny-O. No trigger."

"What's that thing look like to you?" asked Ramsey.

"Only one thing it could be," said Garcia. "A relay amplifier."

Ramsey nodded. "Right. The actual signal's coming from someplace else."

"It'd have to be close," said Garcia. "Just giving you a free-hand estimated-type guess, I'd say within ten feet."

Ramsey rubbed the back of his neck.

"What're you wearing a phone for?" asked Garcia. He nodded toward the monitor phone in Ramsey's left ear.

"Monitor on the seismo," said Ramsey. "If another spy beam goes off—"

"Good idea."

Ramsey brought his hand around to the side of his neck, passing it over the faint scar which covered the pellet.

"What'd you find in the spare?" he asked.

Garcia shook his head. "Nothing."

"Skipper checked the shack while I was dismantling that tube," said Ramsey. "Negative here, too."

"Hadn't you better get started?" asked Garcia.

"Huh?"

"Building your little gadget."

"Sure." Ramsey turned back to his bench. As he turned, the speaker above the seismoscope rasped to an upper-range sound. Ramsey's eyes snapped to the scope. The pulsing green line made a sharp upsweep, repeated.

Bonnett's voice came over the speaker from the control deck: "Skipper."

Sparrow's bass tones: "What is it, Les?"

"Seismic shock somewhere astern."

"I have it here," said Ramsey. "Torp blast. It's in the same range as the EPs' 24-K fish." He scribbled some figures on a note pad, picked up a slide rule, set it, read it. "About a hundred miles astern. Well within range of drift for that little package we left behind us."

"Would they waste a torp on that little thing?" asked Sparrow, then answered his own question. "What's the matter with me? Of course they would. All they'd see on their gear would be the signal. They'd think it was us lying doggo."

"That's the way I figure it," said Ramsey. He looked at Garcia. "What do you say, Joe?"

Garcia was trembling, face pale. He shook his head. Ramsey stared at him questioningly. He appeared extremely agitated.

Sparrow's voice boomed from the speaker: "All hands: as soon as I am finished with work here, I will relieve Mr. Bonnett." There was the sound of a throat being cleared.

Ramsey glanced at the wall chrono. "About time. Les has been on three straight watches."

The skipper's voice continued: "At that time I will post a new watch schedule in the wardroom. It is to go into effect immediately."

Garcia had brought himself under control. He said, "What's eating the skipper? He sounds angry."

Ramsey outlined the new watch schedule.

"What the bloody!" said Garcia. "As if we weren't nuts enough already!"

Ramsey stared at him. *That was an odd reaction for an engineering officer,* he thought. *For a psychologist, okay. But not for Garcia.*

In his quarters, Sparrow wrote: "I must make certain there is no opportunity for anyone to activate a spy signal when we reach the well." He penned his signature, made the final period an exclamation point, closed the log, and returned it to its hiding place.

The timelog repeater on his cabin bulkhead showed seven days, nineteen hours, twenty-three minutes from point of departure.

Sparrow stood up slowly, left his room, closing the door meticulously behind him. He turned, strode forward to the wardroom. As he passed the shack, he heard Ramsey saying: "This stabilizes the micro-timing of the take-up spool. It has to be right on."

Garcia's answer was lost to Sparrow as he stepped into the wardroom, closing the door meticulously behind him.

They dropped the signal squirter in the next watch. Sparrow noted the time—seven days, twenty hours, forty-eight minutes from departure—and entered it in the main logbook. He added the position from the sonoran chart: sixty-one degrees, fifty-eight minutes North Latitude, seventeen degrees, thirty-two minutes West Longitude. The squirter was set for a four-hour delay.

"Very good, Johnny," he said. There was no warmth in his tone.

Ramsey said, "We make do with what we have."

"Let us pray that it works," said Sparrow. He looked at Garcia. "But we won't count on it."

Garcia shrugged. "It *could* work," he said. "If anybody hears it." He stared coldly at Ramsey.

Sparrow thought, *Joe's suspicious. Oh, Lord! If Ramsey's a spy, he'd key that squirter to a wave length the EPs are listening to. It'll tell them we're onto the spy beam and they'll redouble their patrols!*

"Am I relieved now?" asked Ramsey.

"Until your watch," said Sparrow. He stared after Ramsey.

In his quarters, Ramsey brought out the telemeter box, examined the tapes. Sweeping disturbance lines hit his eyes. Now Sparrow was reacting. But what reaction! They reminded Ramsey of a feedback record. Each succeeding wave worse than the one before. The whole area from the discovery of the spy beam was a scrambled record of disturbance.

The room seemed to grow smaller around Ramsey, pressing in upon him.

*Sparrow's losing touch with reality. I'll have to do something. But what?*

He took deep breaths to calm himself, forced his mind to orderly channels.

*I've been with Sparrow a week. I've observed him in all manner of stress. The big elements should be in my hands by now: enough to make some kind of a plan of action. What do we have here?*

He made a mental list:

*We started out with evidence of rigid self-control.*

*But only after we knew that he could react.*

*There is some indication of religious paranoia.*

*A tendency to paranoiac type was Obe's earlier classification.*

*But there are things that don't fit the pattern.*

*He thinks clearly in a stress situation where you'd expect a breakdown.*

*Extremely masculine type. A leader.*

*But not totally despotic, or even nearly so.*

*And he's a brilliant submariner. At times you'd think*

*the boat was a part of him or vice versa. That he was a built-in component*: *Captain, Submariner type: Mark I. Portable.*

Ramsey's back stiffened. *Part of the boat. Mechanical. What better way to describe rigid self-control?*

He recalled his own feeling of synchronous intermingling with the boat. Fleeting as that had been—one instant in the shack. And then gone beyond recapture.

*It'd be a strong survival adaptation.*

*Captain, Submariner type: Mark I. Portable. That may be closer than I'd imagined.*

He rubbed at a burning sensation in his eyes, glanced at his wrist watch. Two hours until his next watch and he was aching with fatigue. He put away the telemeter, flopped sideways onto his bunk. Almost immediately, he was asleep and dreaming.

A giant surgeon with Sparrow's face bent over him in his dream. Little wires. Nerves. One here. One there. Soon he'll be built into the boat.

Electronics officer, Submariner type: Mark I. Portable.

It was Garcia's watch.

Timelog reading: eight days, four hours, and nineteen minutes from point of departure.

Bonnett on stand-by, dozing on a tall stool in front of the control search board.

The *Ram* at cruising speed making twenty knots.

Garcia lounged against the guardrail in front of valve master control, eyes idly taking in the gauges, now and then a glance at the auto-pilot indicator.

The search board emitted a soft buzzing.

Bonnett's head snapped up. He looked to the green face of the scope at his left, kicked the switch which automatically silenced the *Ram*'s motors.

They coasted quietly.

"What is it?" asked Garcia.

"Metal. Big. Coming our way."

"One?"

"Dunno yet."

"Is it an EP?"

His hand adjusted a dial and he looked to a gauge above it. "One. Coming fast like she owned the ocean. In these waters that means EP. Buzz the skipper."

Garcia pushed a button on the call board.

Presently, Sparrow joined them, bending his tall figure for the aft doorway. He buckled his belt as he stepped across the control deck.

Bonnett nodded toward the search board.

The *Ram*'s deck had been slowly tipping to starboard as she lost headway. Now, she was pointing by the nose and the starboard incline was steep enough that Sparrow had to steady himself on the main grab-rail. He swept his gaze across the search board, asked, "How far to bottom?"

"Too far," said Bonnett.

Garcia, one hand on the valve-board rail, turned toward them. "I hope you two decide what we're going to do before we turn turtle. We're almost at a standstill."

Sparrow's gaze again went to the search gauges. The other sub was less than three miles distant, coming fast. As he looked, the detection equipment suddenly resolved its signal into two images.

"Two of them traveling tandem," said Sparrow.

Through his mind sped a quotation from the tactical handbook: "Submarines stalking each other under the sea are like blindfolded adversaries with baseball bats, locked in a room together, each waiting for the other to strike."

"They're going to pass inside of a thousand yards," said Bonnett.

"If they hold their present course," said Sparrow. "And that could be a trick to throw us off guard."

"They must be asleep not to've spotted us before this," whispered Garcia.

"Their metal-detection gear isn't too hot," said Sparrow. He turned to Garcia. "Joe, drop four homing torps, five minutes delay, set to swing around in front of them. Then give us just enough push to get underway and take us down to absolute."

Garcia's hands moved over the control board, adjusting a vernier, setting a dial. He slapped one hand against a switch, turned to the drive controls. The *Ram* picked up speed slowly, nose pointing into the depths. The deck righted.

Sparrow and Bonnett watched the detection gear.

"Drift," said Sparrow.

Bonnett's hand swept over his drive switch. They floated downward silently.

"Give us a little more," said Sparrow.

Again the engines took up their slow turning.

Garcia whispered: "They're not blind; they're deaf!"

Sparrow held up a hand to silence him. He glanced up to the big static pressure gauge; 2790 pounds to the square inch . . . 2800 . . . 2825 . . .

Slowly, the indicator hand swept around: 2900 . . . 2925 . . .

Above the gauge, the flat bronze plate stamped with the *Ram*'s weight and specifications. Someone had used red paint to fill the indentations showing pressure limit: 3010 pounds.

The hand of the dial pointed to 2975 . . . 3000 . . .

Perspiration stood out on Garcia's face. Bonnett pulled nervously at an ear lobe. Sparrow stood impassively, feeling the boat around him. "Ease her off," he whispered. He wet his lips with his tongue.

The knowledge of the outside pressure was like an actual physical weight pressing inward against his skull. He fought against showing his feelings.

The dial steadied at 3008, slowly climbed to 3004, stayed there.

Bonnett whispered, "They're almost on top of our—"

A dial fluttered wildly and they felt the *whump!* of a detonation through the hull. Sparrow's glance darted to the static pressure gauge: it made a stately fluctuation through 3028, back to 3004.

Garcia whispered, "I heard that the *Barracuda* took 3090 before she imploded."

"There's a bigger safety factor than that," said Bonnett.

Sparrow said, "May the Lord take their souls and grant them mercy. Even as it may come to pass with us. God forgive us that we do this not in anger, but out of need."

Garcia fingered the beads of his Rosary through his shirt.

A sudden thought passed through Sparrow's mind. He looked down at his first officer. "Les, what do you do when the heat is on?"

"Huh?" Bonnett glanced up at him, back to the dials.

"What do you think about?"

Bonnett shrugged. "I remind myself I been married four times—four beautiful babes. What more could a man ask?"

"Every man to his own philosophy," said Sparrow.

Ramsey entered the control room, took in the scene, whispered, "The silence woke me up. Are we hunting something?"

"And vice versa," said Garcia. "Get in here and help me on the board."

"You were not called to duty," said Sparrow.

Ramsey hesitated.

"Get in here with Les," said Sparrow. "I'll stand by with Joe." He backed away from the controls.

Ramsey stepped into the vacated spot.

Sparrow moved up to stand beside Garcia.

Bonnett looked at Ramsey out of the corners of his eyes. "I'll clue you in on something, Junior," he said. "This is too much like playing grab-tail with a panther for me ever to become addicted to it."

Sparrow said, "We can't be traced from the track of our fish. They were on a curving course before they could've been detected."

"That second boy out there could've gotten a shock-wave echo from the blast," said Bonnett. "He's just drifting now. He's already put out his anti-torp volley and it should—"

Three shock waves washed over them in rapid succession.

"That would be our fish being knocked out," said Sparrow. "Any breaking up noises from that EP?"

"Negative," said Bonnett.

"Then they have our position now from the echo," said Sparrow. "Send out a detection scrambler and get our anti-torp volley off." He slapped Garcia on the back, said, "Evasive action. Force speed."

Ramsey standing beside Bonnett hit a series of switches with the heel of his hand. A cloud of tiny torp-homing exploders swept out from the *Ram*.

Bonnett kicked the control which sent out a dummy torpedo carrying signal equipment to scramble detection systems.

"Why couldn't I have taken a nice safe job in a nitrox factory?" Garcia moaned.

"You guys who want to live forever make me sick," said Bonnett. "Here you are in a nice perambulating sewer pipe with ple—"

"Up!" barked Sparrow. "If we get into close quarters I want a bigger pressure margin."

Garcia complied. The deck slanted upward.

Ramsey said, "What makes you think . . ."

"We're coming out of that scrambler's field," said Bonnett.

"Fire another along our forward path," said Sparrow. Again he slapped Garcia's shoulder. "Right rudder and drift."

Garcia pulled the wheel right, straightened it, shut down the drive. Slowly, the *Ram* lost headway. Again the deck tilted to starboard.

"We've gotten sloppy on our trim," said Sparrow.

Bonnett leaned toward Ramsey, whispered, "That guy's a genius. We coast along the edge of the first scrambler's field. The one we just sent out will leave a track for the other boys to follow and they'll—" He broke off, staring at the detection system, eyes widening. "Skipper!" he husked, voice hanging on the edge of horror. "They're right on top of us—force speed. Going overhead now. Not more than one hundred feet!"

Sparrow shouldered Garcia aside, kicked the *Ram*

into force speed, swerved it into the wake of the other
sub. To Bonnett, he said, "Keep us on their tail. Gently,
friend . . . gently."

Garcia whispered, "I heard of this happening once
with old *Plunger*, but I never thought I'd see it myself."

Ramsey said, "Their blind spot. They can't hear us
in the turbulence of their own wake."

Bonnett's voice came calm and steady: "Two degrees
port."

Sparrow swerved the *Ram* to follow.

Ramsey pointed to the oscilloscope.

Bonnett followed the direction, said, "Skipper, off to
starboard is a whole wolf pack. They're converging on
that last scrambler we sent out."

"Too close for comfort," said Sparrow. With one
hand he eased down drive speed; with the other he
punched the controls to arm a torpedo. "Give me minimum range," he said. "This has to be fast. As soon as
the blast reaches us, fire scramblers to the four points of
the compass."

Bonnett acknowledged. "One hundred yards," he
said. "One twenty-five . . . one fifty . . . one seventy . . ." He glanced to the secondary scope. "Any
second now that pack will be getting two signals from
us and one of the signals won't fit IFF. Two fifty . . .
two seventy-five . . ."

Sparrow fired the single torpedo, killed the drive, began counting: "One, two, three, four, five, six, seven,
eight, nine, ten, elev—"

The concussion shook the *Ram*.

Bonnett fired the scramblers.

Ramsey's ears were ringing.

Sparrow kicked on drive to force speed, brought the
*Ram* about in a tight circle, coursing upward. With one
hand, he pushed Garcia into the control position,
stepped back. "They'll be expecting us to dive," he
said. "Blow the tanks."

Garcia palmed the switches and the *Ram* bounced to
the lift.

Sparrow said, "Les, give me a fifty-foot warning on the edge of the scrambler field."

"Right," said Bonnett. "We've a way to go yet."

Bonnett caught the puzzled look on Ramsey's face, said, "They taught you things in subschool, but they never taught you this, did they?"

Ramsey shook his head.

"We're going to float up," said Bonnett. "We may be walking on the ceiling before we get there, but we're going to do it silently."

Sparrow looked to the static pressure gauge: 1200 pounds—above the 3000-foot level. He glanced inquiringly at Bonnett, who shook his head.

The seconds ticked away.

Bonnett said, "Now!"

Garcia killed the drive.

Sparrow wiped his face with his hands, looked startled when his hand came away bloody. "Nosebleed," he said. "Pressure change was too rapid. Haldane tablets, everyone." He fished a flat green pill from a pocket, popped it into his mouth. As always, his reaction was sudden nausea. He grimaced, held the pill down by will power, shuddered.

Ramsey choked on his pill, coughed, fought it down.

Bonnett spat into his handkerchief, said, "Human beings weren't meant to take this kind of a beating." He shook his head.

The *Ram* began to tip gently to the right.

Sparrow looked at Ramsey, said, "Johnny, go over to the left there."

Ramsey complied, thinking: *What a way to get on a first-name basis! I'd sooner stay a dryback.*

As he passed Garcia, the engineering officer spoke the thought aloud: "Bet you wish you were still Junior Ramsey."

Ramsey smiled faintly.

The deck's tipping slowed, but did not stop.

Sparrow nodded to Bonnett. "Hand pump. Start shifting some water. Slow and easy."

Bonnett stepped to the aft bulkhead, swung out a

crank handle. Sparrow took over the search-board position.

Slowly, they steadied on an even keel, but now the nose began to sink. Then the deck began to slant slowly to the left.

Sparrow glanced at Ramsey, nodded toward the aft bulkhead on his side. "Take over fore-and-aft stabilization. Easy does it. No noise."

Ramsey moved to obey. He looked at the pressure gauge: 840 pounds. They were above the 2000-foot level.

"We can maintain some sort of trim until we hit wave turbulence," said Sparrow. "Then we may have to risk the drive."

Gently, the *Ram* drifted upward, tipping, canting.

Ramsey found the rhythm of it. They couldn't hold her in exact trim. But they could rock her to a regular teeter-totter rhythm. He grinned across at Bonnett on lateral stabilization.

The deck suddenly stopped a leftward countermotion and heeled far right, came back again, nose rising; again she heeled to the right. A hissing sound resonated through the hull.

The screen on the forward bulkhead—tuned to the conning TV eye—showed milky green.

Sparrow stood at the controls, one hand on the rail. He stared upward at the screen.

*When's he going to give us headway?* Ramsey wondered.

This time the *Ram* heaved far over to the left.

For one frightening moment, Ramsey looked directly down into the pipe and conduit maze against the port pressure hull. *We're going over,* he thought.

But the *Ram* came back sluggishly, righting. The bulkhead screen broke free of foam, cleared to reveal fog and long, whitecapped rollers. The *Ram* pitched and bobbed in the seas.

"I agree with you, Skipper," said Bonnett. "One way of dying is as good as another. They'd have heard us sure."

Garcia worked his way along the handrail, fighting the uneasy motion of the deck. "If we could rig a sea anchor," he said.

"We already have one," said Sparrow.

Garcia blushed. "The tow!"

"Thank you, Lord, for the lovely fog," said Bonnett.

The *Ram* swung downwind from her tow in a wide, rolling arc, jerking against the lines like a wild horse at a snubbing post.

"More line on the tow," said Sparrow. He nodded to Garcia, who jumped to obey.

The motion of the deck smoothed.

Sparrow kept his gaze on the detection gear. "What's our heading, Joe?"

"Near fifty-eight degrees."

"Wind's favorable," said Sparrow. "And those boys down under haven't changed course."

"They're still snooping after our last scrambler," said Garcia.

"Time for you to go off watch, Joe," said Sparrow. "I am relieving you."

"Want me to bring up some sandwiches before I sack down?" asked Garcia.

"Ham and cheese," said Bonnett.

"No, thanks," said Sparrow. He studied the sonoscope on the search board. "We'll drift with the wind until we no longer get signals from that pack."

Ramsey yawned.

Sparrow hooked a thumb toward the aft door. "You, too. That was a good job, Johnny."

Ramsey said, "Aye." He followed Garcia down the companionway, muscles aching from the unaccustomed exercise at the ballast pumps.

Garcia turned at the wardroom door, looked at Ramsey. "Chow?"

Ramsey steadied himself with one hand against the bulkhead. Beneath him, the deck rolled and dipped.

"These tubs weren't designed for the surface," said Garcia. "What breed of sandwich?"

The thought of food suddenly made Ramsey's stomach heave. The long companionway appeared to gyrate in front of him, rolling counter to the motion of the deck. He capped his mouth with a hand, raced for his quarters. He reached the washbasin just in time, stood over it retching.

Garcia followed him, pressed a blue pill into his hand, made him swallow it.

Presently, the surging of Ramsey's stomach eased. "Thanks," he said.

"In the sack, Junior."

Garcia helped him grope his way into his bunk, pulled a blanket over him.

*Seasick! I'll never live it down!* thought Ramsey. He heard Garcia leave. Presently, he remembered the telemeter. But he was too weak, too drowsy. He drifted off to sleep. The motion of the *Ram* became a soothing thing.

*Rockaby . . . rockaby . . .*

He could almost hear a voice. Far away. Down a tunnel. In an echo chamber.

"The boat is my mother. I shall not want . . ."

When he awakened it was the call to watch and he had a scant moment in which to glance at the telemeter tapes.

Sparrow had returned to the pattern of rigid control.

It was as though Ramsey's subconscious had been working on a problem, chewing it, and these were the final data. The answers came spewing up to his conscious level.

He knew what he had to do.

Twenty-three hours the *Ram* drifted downwind, angling away from Iceland to the northeast. A gray speck on gray and foam. And behind her, barely submerged, the green surge of their tow, a sea monster escaped from the deep.

In Ramsey's second watch they passed within two miles of a radioactive iceberg, probably broken from the skerries of the northeast Greenland coast. Ramsey kept radiation snoopers tuned to the limit until they were out of range. The berg, its random contours catching the wind like a sail, was almost quartering the gale. It pulled away from the *Ram,* like a majestic ship.

Ramsey noted in the log: "Current setting easterly away from our course. We did not cross the berg's path."

Outside radiation: 1800 milli-R.

Garcia came across the control room. "Safe yet?"

"Clear," said Ramsey.

Garcia looked to the screen on the control bulkhead, the view of gray rollers. "Moderating."

"If the fog will just hold," said Ramsey.

Sparrow came through the aft door, his lank form seemingly more loose-jointed than usual.

*He's relaxed,* thought Ramsey. *That fits. What EP commander would dream of looking for us up here? We're too low in the water to show on a shore screen.*

"All quiet, Skipper," he said.

"Very good," said Sparrow. He looked to the time-log: nine days, three hours, and forty-seven minutes. "Joe, how long since you've had a signal from our friends?"

"Not a sign of them for almost ten hours."

Sparrow glanced at the sonoran chart. The red dot stood at sixty-six degrees, nine minutes, twenty seconds North Latitude, two degrees, eleven minutes West Longitude. He nodded to Ramsey. "Get us underway, if you please. Surface speed. Quarter throttle. Keep us under eight knots."

Ramsey moved to obey.

The *Ram* shuddered to a wave impact, fought up the slope of a sea. They gathered headway, sluggishly.

"She answers the helm, sir," said Ramsey.

Sparrow nodded. "Course thirteen degrees. We've drifted a bit too close to the Norwegian coast line. The EPs have shore-based listening posts there."

Ramsey brought the subtug around on her new heading.

"We'll stay on the surface as long as we have fog," said Sparrow.

"Our guardian angels are working overtime," said Garcia.

"I wonder if they have a union?" asked Ramsey.

Sparrow looked to the timelog: nine days, four hours even. He caught Garcia's attention, nodded toward the timelog and then the helm. "Take over, if you please, Joe."

Garcia took the helm from Ramsey.

"You are relieved," said Sparrow.

Ramsey felt a wave of fatigue sweep through him. He remembered what he had to do, fought down the tiredness. "We'll be there soon," he said.

Sparrow frowned.

"None too soon for me," said Ramsey. "I feel like we're living on borrowed time. I want our payment in the bank—a whole load of that sweet oil."

"That will be enough," said Sparrow.

"You afraid I'm going to give away a nasty old Security secret?" asked Ramsey.

Garcia darted a puzzled glance at him.

"Go to your quarters," said Sparrow.

"Righto," said Ramsey, copying Garcia's accent. He made his tone as insolent as possible without coming to actual insubordination, turned toward the aft door.

"I'll wish to speak with you before your next watch," said Sparrow. "We're long overdue for an understa—" He broke off as a red warning light flashed on the reactor system's scram board. The light winked green, then red, then green.

Garcia saw it, too.

Ramsey turned back to the control bulkhead, caught the last flash from red to green.

"Something's loose in the pile room," said Sparrow.

"That torpedo shock we took," said Ramsey.

"More likely the pounding we've had from these seas," said Garcia.

"That's circuit 'T' of the secondary damper controls," said Sparrow. "Right side forward. Get Les up here on the double."

Garcia pushed the alarm buzzer.

"Try the screens," said Sparrow.

Ramsey moved back to the helm, took it. Garcia glanced at him, moved to the screen controls, began hitting switches.

Bonnett entered. "What's up?"

"Something loose in the pile room," said Sparrow. "It's 'T' circuit."

"Right side forward," said Bonnett. He moved to get a better view of the screens, caught the handrail to steady himself against the rolling of the deck.

Sparrow said, "I'm going forward." He looked at the scram board. The light winked at him: red, green, red, green, red, green . . . "Les, come forward with me and help me into a suit. I'll have to crawl the right-side tunnel, use the manuals and mirrors."

"Just a minute, Skipper," said Garcia. "Look at that." He pointed at a screen.

Sparrow stepped to his side.

"Central damper controls," said Garcia. "See. When we pitch into the trough of a wave it seems to— There!"

They all saw it. The long hanging arm of the manual damper control swung free like the multi-joined leg of an insect. It exposed a break at the top elbow hinge. The upper bracing flapped outward to the sway of the boat.

"It was wedged against the hinge," said Garcia. "Now it's broken free again." He looked at the scram board. Red, green, red, green, red . . .

Each time the light flashed red, the swinging arm touched a control circuit cable. A blue arc of electricity splashed upward.

Garcia pointed to the lower half of the screen which showed the base of the control system. "There's the real trouble. The whole control base is twisted. See those sheared bolts."

Sparrow whirled to the forward hatch, undogged it. "Les, I've changed my mind. Stay here with Johnny on the main board. Joe, come with me." He glared at Ramsey, hesitated, then said, "Take us down below wave turbulence."

Ramsey's hands went to the controls: diving planes two degrees, compensating system open, hull pressure holding. He found that it was better to let his body react, to accept the results of his training, secure in the knowledge that this way he would be right.

Sparrow went through the door, out onto the engine-room catwalk. Garcia followed.

Ramsey activated the engine-room scanners to follow their movements. *What a time I picked to go into my act,* he thought. He gave a mental shrug. *But one time's as good as another.*

"We're going to make it," said Bonnett. "Nothing can stop us."

Startled, Ramsey darted a glance at the first officer.

Bonnett was staring at the screen. Ramsey followed the direction of his gaze. Sparrow and Garcia were scrambling down the ladder to the right-side tunnel. Sparrow jerked open the door to the bulkhead locker, swung out an ABG suit on its traveler rack.

"The EPs are crazy to think they can beat him," said Bonnett. "He's like a god!"

Something in Bonnett's voice . . .

Ramsey fought down a shudder.

The screen showed Garcia helping Sparrow into the bulky suit.

Ramsey turned back to his controls as the subtug steadied. He found the need to say something, said, "We're out of wave turbulence."

Bonnett looked at him. "Do tell." He turned his attention back to the screen.

Ramsey adjusted the controls, brought the deck to level.

Now, Sparrow was completely sealed into his suit. He turned clumsily, helped Garcia.

*What does the telemeter show?* Ramsey wondered. *Is Sparrow under control? Or is the wild feedback starting?*

In the heavy suit, Sparrow felt the perspiration begin to roll off him. His fingers seemed unwilling to obey him as he assisted Garcia. *Damned sweat suits! There!* The final seal went into place.

Sparrow took a deep breath, spoke into his suit mike: "Testing . . . testing. Do you read me, Les?"

The captain's voice boomed out of the speaker on the control desk. Ramsey turned down the volume.

Bonnett spoke into his chest mike: "Loud and clear."

"Joe," said Sparrow. "Are you receiving me?"

"Righto, Skipper."

"Now get this, Les," said Sparrow. "If that damper arm swings out too far it'll begin clubbing the side of the pile. Monitor me on your screen. I might not be able to see a position change soon enough."

Bonnett looked to the screen showing the reactor room. "It's quiet now, Skipper. Resting against the first-stage clamps."

"Those bolts are sheared off, though," said Sparrow. "The whole unit could fall over onto the pile."

Bonnett studied the screen. "Skipper, there's a chance you could catch the main drive bar with the grapple of the forward manuals." He bent closer to the screen. "It'll be a near thing. You'll have to snake past that broken hinge."

"How much clearance?"

"Maybe six inches. No more. The mirror's at a bad angle."

"Take me in," said Sparrow. "We can do it." He turned, undogged the tunnel hatch and snapped on his helmet light. "Joe, stay here unless I call you." He reached a hand into the tunnel, found the filter-system switch, started it. He plugged his suit hose into the traveler, tested the air.

Garcia said, "I'll time you. Have Les monitor the tunnel radiation."

Bonnett, listening to the conversation over the intercom, said, "I'll give you the time-over-radiation from here." He twisted a dial, plugged in a jack, tested the circuit.

"I'm going in," said Sparrow. He bent, slid into the tunnel. "I'll give you a running commentary when I reach the manuals, Les. Get everything on tape. Base will want a complete record of this."

"Take it slow and easy, Skipper," said Bonnett.

Sparrow said, "Joe, dog that tunnel door behind me. If that base falls to the right it'll smash the end-plug. There'd be hot stuff all over the place."

"Righto."

A faint thump behind Sparrow and a feeling of pressure change told him when Garcia had complied. Sparrow felt the isolation like a physical band tightening on his forehead. Perspiration rolled down his cheeks, down his nose. His clothes were damp with it, clinging to him.

Garcia's voice came over the phones like a sound from another world. "What do you see, Skipper?"

"Tunnel's clear. Nothing hot yet." His helmet light cut a bright path through the metallic darkness.

*It's another birth canal,* he thought. And he remembered all the times he had crawled the mock-up tunnel at training school without ever encountering that thought. *There's a first time for everything: a first time to be born, a first time to die.* He longed to wipe the perspiration from his forehead. *Lest ye be born again ye shall not enter . . .*

The light picked up the safety door near the end of the tunnel. This was the limit of the bulkhead. Beyond that was the lead soda straw jutting into the pile room. And at the end: the manuals. He undogged the door, swung it back into its recess.

Pile-room floodlights cast their blue glare onto the tunnel floor ahead of him, reflected through the mirror system in a weird splotching of brilliance and shadows. Sparrow inched his way into the glare.

"I am at the manuals," he said. He turned onto his back, fighting against the terror that threatened to overwhelm him. Out there in the blue glare of the pile room was . . . what? The world and all its threats.

Garcia's voice came over the intercom: "Are you okay, Skipper?"

Sparrow took a deep breath. "Yes."

*I'll pretend I'm still in school,* he thought. *This is a test. I have to pass or take a black mark. They've yanked the control units free of their base and I have to make repairs under simulated action conditions. Old Lieutenant Maurey is back at the tunnel mouth hoping I'll fail. That's not really a reactor out there; it's just a mock-up. They wouldn't risk an unimportant student with the real thing. They have to wait until you've had all that expensive training and it's cost something to lose you. Then—*

"Skipper," Les's voice, metallic in the phones.

"Yes?"

"Are you ready?"

"Just a moment, Les."

"Right."

Sparrow slipped his hands into the fitted grips of the manual controls, pulled the stud which hooked him into the grapple. He pulled back with his right hand, watched in the mirror as the grapple came into lift position.

"Les?"

"I see it, Skipper. Bring it up about three feet. Line it up with the spring bar, but keep it back away from the broken hinge."

Sparrow pulled down on the right grip, turned it slightly to bring the hydraulic booster into play. The grapple darted upward. *Too fast!* Sweat popped out on his forehead.

"A little slower," said Bonnett.

Sparrow whispered, " 'Lord, I am like David. I am in a great strait: let us fall now into the hand of the Lord; for his mercies are great: and let me not fall into the hand of man. Stay now thine hand. I have sinned and I have done wickedly: but these sheep, what have they done? Put thine hand over mine, Lord. Guide me.' "

Steadiness came to him.

"Did you say something, Skipper?" asked Bonnett.

"I'm all set, Les. Guide me in."

"Okay. You have to come up about six inches and to the left about an inch. Take it slow."

Sparrow lowered the thrust of the hydraulic booster, put his muscle into the grip. The manual arm went up slowly, paused, shifted to the left.

"Right on, Skipper. Bring it forward three feet and lock it while you lift the rear hinge section into place."

The grapple moved as though it were a part of his body. He twisted his left grip to lock the end section, eased the next element of the grapple arm into alignment.

"How's that?"

"Perfect. Now, can you lift the whole arm about an inch? You're a little close to that broken hinge."

"I can't see the end of the grapple and the next element at the same time, Les. I'd better watch the element."

"Okay. Fine it down and bring the grapple end up a quarter of an inch at a time."

Sparrow grunted as he made the first lift.

"That was a half inch, Skipper. One more exactly like it."

Again Sparrow grunted as he moved the grip.

"A hair over, Skipper, but you still have clearance."

"Do you want me to fine it down?"

"No. Let it stand there. Now bring the grapple end past the hinge. One straight push about three feet."

Sparrow twisted his head to get a view of the grapple in the mirrors. It looked as though it would smash directly into the broken hinge. *Poor angle of view,* he thought. *How'd a piece of bad planning like that get by?* He lifted his right hand grip. The grapple surged forward, stopped.

"Hold it right there a second, Skipper."

Sparrow heard mumbling over the phones.

Bonnett's voice returned: "You'll have to get three elements of the grapple arm past that break before you can drop the tip. Better align the next element."

Sparrow brought up the next hinged section, straightened it. "How's the alignment?"

"Right on. Bring it forward."

He complied, his hands moving the controls with increased sureness. The next element came up, was aligned, sent forward.

"Another foot forward, Skipper."

He moved the grapple arm.

"Now comes the ticklish part. Drop the end at number-three joint. Take it down slowly and stop when I tell you."

Sparrow bent the end elements downward. He thought that it was almost as though he could feel the moving part as he could feel his own arm. He sensed the position and stopped it while Bonnett was forming the order on his lips. The grapple end now was out of sight below the control base. It would take four adjustments of the mirrors to bring it back into view.

"You're about ten inches above the main drive bar. To reach it, you'll have to angle down with that section spanning the broken hinge."

"I don't dare jar that hinge," said Sparrow. "There's a lot of leverage that far up. I could break it right off."

"I've used the calipers on the screen," said Bonnett. "You'll have about an inch to spare."

Sparrow felt the fatigue in his wrists and forearms, whispered, "Just a little longer, Lord, We're making it."

"You ready?" asked Bonnett.

"Yes. Talk me down."

"Okay. Take the tip toward you about four inches."

Sparrow moved the grapple.

"Now down six inches."

Sparrow eased the tip downward, felt the sureness of his control, said, "How's the lateral alignment?"

"Half inch to the right."

He shifted the descent angle, continued down with the tip. "How's the upper clearance?"

"You still have two inches."

He felt the grapple jaws touch the drive bar, lowered them onto it, gripped the bar.

"Skipper, you couldn't have done that better if you'd had your own hand out there."

Sparrow locked the grapple into position, brought up secondary grapples to brace it. He slid backward down the tunnel until he could reach the manual controls at number-two position, reached up with a short grapple and clamped it onto the broken unit. The control shivered.

"Lordy," said Bonnett. "It would've gone right over without the bracing on that drive bar."

Sparrow swung an extension torch into place above the broken hinge, locked it into position, lifted the broken end until the sheared sections touched. He started the torch.

"Fuse it solid at the hinge. Only thing I can do now. There's enough play in the other elements to almost compensate for the lost mobility. We'll be able to cover more than eighty percent of this pile face. The manuals will cover the rest."

"What're you going to do, Skipper?"

"What about the base?"

"I'm going to knock the sheared bolts right on through into the catch basin." He lowered the torch, playing its flame onto the sheared hinge. At the molten moment, he cut the torch, crushed the broken elements together. The repair formed a wedge-shaped cup. He sprayed the inside with brazing flux, brought up the brazing rod, and filled the cup.

"That looks like it'll hold," said Bonnett, "I've been examining the base. It doesn't appear to be warped, but it's out of alignment. You'll need a spreader jack at the aft end."

"Right. What's the inclination?"

"About one degree. Put the replacement bolts along the inside face first. They'll hold it while you drop the drive bar."

"I've a better idea," said Sparrow. "Watch closely and tell me if anything starts to go wrong."

"What're you going to do?"

"Drop the bolts into place along the inner face, then throw a little torque into the drive bar. The thrust against the grapple will push the base back into position."

"That's risky."

"No worse than thrusting a jack against the base of the pile to horse that thing into position. This way we don't touch the pile."

Sparrow continued to speak as he worked. "Rule one of pileroom repair should be: Don't touch the reactor unless you absolutely have to."

"You have nine minutes, Skipper," said Bonnett. "You should be on your way out in five minutes."

"That's another reason for doing it my way," said Sparrow.

"Couldn't Joe finish it?"

"Only if he has to. Best not to have two of us on the cooling-off list."

He touched the drive-bar switch. The control base rocked against its grapple braces. Metal protested. Two of the bolts dropped into position. Sparrow slipped nuts onto them, drove them tight with a motor wrench. Again he rocked the base with the drive bar. The remaining bolts slipped home.

Sparrow's fingers flew over the manual controls as he completed the job. He disengaged the grapples, swung the repaired control arm out of the way, clamped it.

"Two minutes, Skipper. On your way, right now!"

Sparrow released the last temporary brace, dropped it, slid backward down the tunnel, closed and dogged the door at the bulkhead limit. His helmet light was a pale flame after the blue glare of the tunnel end. He crawled backward, heard Garcia undog the door behind him, felt the other man's suited hands on his legs helping him the last few feet.

Bonnett's voice came over the phones: "You went

about a minute over. Get down to the sick bay and take your shots."

Sparrow grinned: It was good for Les to give orders, eased his tensions.

"On the double, Skipper," said Bennett. "Every second's delay means that much more time cooling off for you."

Sparrow fought down a feeling of irritation. Under Rule Ninety, Bonnett was technically in command when his superior officer had taken an overdose of radiation. But one minute!

Garcia ran a snooper over him, working silently, gesturing for Sparrow to turn. The engineering officer straightened, racked the snooper. "Into that decon chamber." He unhooked Sparrow's hose from the tunnel system, closed the door and dogged it.

Sparrow climbed into the decontamination chamber, felt the surge of foaming detergent around him.

"Joe, what's the delay?" Bonnett again.

"He's in decon now, Les. Thirty seconds more."

"Cut it short, Joe. Ramsey is on his way down with the needles to give him his shots there. It'll save a couple of minutes."

Ramsey came out on the catwalk above them, carrying a radiation-first-aid kit under his arm. He dropped down to their level, helped Garcia break the seal on his suit.

Sparrow came out of the chamber without his suit, frowned at the kit in Ramsey's hand.

"Bend over, Skipper," said Ramsey.

Sparrow obeyed, dropped his trousers, winced at the needle. "Just don't enjoy yourself, Johnny," he said.

Ramsey extracted the needle, wiped the bare skin with disinfectant. "That does it and I hope you never have to do the same for me."

The lifting of tension about Sparrow was an almost physical thing.

Ramsey replaced the hypodermic in the kit, sealed it.

"Let's go," said Sparrow.

Garcia hung his ABG suit in its locker, followed them up the ladder.

Ramsey thought: *What's on the telemeter? Lord, I thought he'd never come out of that tunnel.*

They stepped out onto the center catwalk, headed for the control room. Abruptly, the giant motors around them fell silent. Sparrow broke into a run, ducked through into the control room. Ramsey sprinted after him, went through the door on Sparrow's heels.

Bonnett stood at the search board, one hand on the drive controls. His eyes were on the oscilloscope of the limit sono-finder. He spoke without turning: "Signal. At extreme range. We've lost it."

"By now they must have a rough idea of our course," said Sparrow. "They're quartering the area. What's the depth?"

"We're over the sub-arctic shallows," said Bonnett. "Bottom's about 350 fathoms."

"Too shallow for us to lie doggo," said Sparrow. "They would range too close for—"

"There it is again," said Bonnett. He nodded toward the scope, adjusted two flanking dials. "Northeast. A pack by the noise. Damn! Lost them again. That's probably a school of fish between us."

"Head for the Norway basin," said Sparrow. "We need deep water." He glanced at the sonoran chart. "Course nine degrees."

Bonnett engaged the drive, swung the helm to the left until they were on the new course.

Sparrow stepped to his nav-plot board, bent over it, figuring. Presently, he straightened. "Estimating time of arrival two hours and six minutes." He turned. "Johnny, stay with search here. We've the range on them, but not so much that we can afford to get careless."

Ramsey moved to the search board.

Garcia stepped through the door from the engine room. "The real danger is an EP that lies doggo until we're in range," he said.

"It's a big ocean," said Sparrow.

"And a small world," said Garcia.

Sparrow looked at the radiation kit which Ramsey had placed on one of the control-board stools. He glanced at his wrist watch. "Does someone have a timer set for my next shots?"

"I have," said Ramsey.

"Get what rest you can, Skipper," said Bonnett. "I'll have a look at you as soon as we find a sitting spot."

"I can do it," said Garcia.

Bonnet nodded. "Okay."

"Timer's in the kit," said Ramsey.

Garcia picked up the sealed box, gestured for Sparrow to precede him aft.

*They're worried about me,* thought Sparrow. *But one minute over isn't that important.*

Ramsey noted the proprietary attitude of Garcia and Bonnett toward Sparrow, realized abruptly that he shared it. *He's our skipper,* he thought.

Sparrow and Garcia went aft.

The *Ram* crept onward.

"It's a little deeper," said Ramsey. "We're over the hump."

"Sill depth across here runs 400 to 600 fathoms," said Bonnett. "When we reach 600 we'll be close to the basin slope."

"It's 450 now."

"A bad stretch," said Bonnett. "You'd expect the EPs to be ranging this area in net formations."

Garcia slipped into the control room. "Les."

"How is he?"

"Are you sure it was just one minute over?"

"Certainly I'm sure. What's wrong?"

"Very low white count. It looks like closer to half an hour over."

"Any burns?"

"No indications yet."

"It could be that he didn't recover well from handling that Security lieutenant," said Ramsey.

"That's what I was thinking," said Garcia. "I gave him a sedative and a booster shot of de-sulph and de-carb."

"Good." Bonnett turned to Garcia. "Stick by him until I call you."

"Righto." Garcia ducked back through the door.

*Bonnett's in command,* thought Ramsey. *We never thought of that. Can he adjust to the job?* And then another thought: *Good Lord! What if he's the sleeper?* He studied the first officer covertly out of the corners of his eyes.

The *Ram* sped onward.

"Depth 550 fathoms," said Ramsey.

Bonnett shifted the *Ram*'s diving planes, took them down to 500 fathoms in a low glide. He brought the deck level when the pressure gauge read 1300 pounds to the square inch.

"Twenty minutes," said Ramsey.

"Give or take a few," said Bonnett. "What's wrong with Joe? Why doesn't he let us know how the skipper is?"

"You didn't tell him to," said Ramsey.

"Yes, but—"

"There's most likely nothing to report. It's too soon."

"Get him on the intercom."

Ramsey shrugged, thumbed the switch on his chest mike: "Joe?"

"Here."

"How's the skipper?"

"Still sleeping. I'd give a pretty to know what the overdose actually was."

"Did you check his suit dosometer?"

"Right after he got out of the tunnel. Slight overage, just as Les said. You know, I'm no medical chap, but I'd bloody well swear that he'd gotten contaminated atmos."

"How?"

"I don't know, really. I saw him check suit pressure before going in. It was still holding when he came out. I'm certain there were no leaks."

"Did you snoop the tunnel filter system?"

"That's what I'm worried about, Johnny. I naturally assumed—"

Bonnett interrupted, speaking into his own microphone: "Can you leave the skipper?"

"Yes. He's resting quietly."

"Get forward and snoop that filter."

"I'm on my way."

Bonnett turned to Ramsey. "There's a lesson for you and I'm ashamed to say it of Joe: Never assume anything. You have to know!"

"Couldn't he assume that the tunnel's filter system was okay?"

"Well . . ."

"We assume a lot of things about our little world."

"The perfect ecology," muttered Bonnett. "Self-sustaining."

Garcia slipped into the control room, went out the forward door without speaking.

"If that filter system is leaking," said Bonnett, "I'll—"

"Signal!" Ramsey slapped the cut-off switch, silencing the drive. The *Ram* drifted. "Quartering to the east." He narrowed down the tuning band. "Pack. There's more behind us!" He rotated the finder band. "More at 340."

"Boxed!" said Bonnett. "Have they spotted us?"

"Can't be certain. No collision courses."

"What's the depth?"

"Reading now 680 fathoms. We're on the edge of the basin."

Bonnett engaged the drive, eased them forward at minimum speed. "Tell me the instant you detect a change of course from one of those signals."

"Aye."

Garcia's voice came over the intercom. "Les?"

"What is it?"

"Filter's cool, but the inner hose line shows a slight leakage."

"How much?"

"Sixty m-r. I make it a thirty-eight minute overdose."

"Where's the leak?"

"Inside somewhere. Maybe that broken control arm slapped something. I can't tell from here."

"Dog the hatch and come up here. We're ranging an EP signal."

"Righto. I heard you slip the drive."

Bonnett turned to Ramsey. "Depth?"

"Something over 7200 feet. Shelving off rapidly. Les! That pack behind us has changed course." Ramsey worked over his dials. "They've closed the angle, but they're not headed for us."

"It could be a trick! We can't chance it." He fed more power to the drive. The *Ram* picked up speed.

"Theyre on us! They've altered course, increased speed."

Bonnett pushed the drive control to its limit. They felt the straining of the giant engines.

Garcia stepped into the control room, wiped a spot of grease from his hand, looked at the searchscope. "Have we had it, chaps?"

Bonnett ignored him. "Depth?"

"A little over 1500 fathoms. I'd make it about 9100 feet." Ramsey reset a dial beside the searchscope. "The pack to our east has changed course. They are now on collision heading."

"It was nice knowing you, gentlemen," said Garcia.

"We can't turn east or south," said Bonnett. "Bottom is 2000 feet below our limit."

"I'm getting an interference reading at 8400 feet," said Ramsey. "Seamount. Heading 215 degrees."

"It might just as well be 84,000 feet," said Garcia. "That'd be something like 3600 pounds to the square inch, almost 600 over our limit."

"They'll be in firing range within a half hour," said Ramsey. He glanced at Bonnett. "What happens to the pressure hull coefficient if we boost internal pressure beyond ten atmos?"

"We wouldn't be alive to enjoy it," said Garcia.

"Maybe," said Ramsey. He slipped his vampire gauge from its belt case, locked it onto his wrist, shot the needle into his vein. "How long would it take to draw everything but the oxy out of our atmos?"

"Pure oxy?" Garcia appeared startled.

"What's on your mind?" asked Bonnett.

Ramsey said, "Put the anhydrase generation on manual and balance it by sight." He nodded toward the gauge on his wrist.

"What do the medics say about that?" asked Garcia.

"Nothing certain," said Ramsey. "I've heard it argued both ways." He glanced at the scope in front of him. "I think it may be our only chance."

"Joe, take over here," said Bonnett. He stepped away from the controls as Garcia took hold of the helm.

"What're you going to do, Les?"

"Unhook the governor from the anhydrase generator system."

Garcia's head jerked around. "You're not paying serious attention to this punk's suggestion!"

Bonnett already was removing the cover plate from the atmosphere controls. "I am."

"That's suicide."

Bonnett looked to the scope in front of Ramsey. "We're already dead. What do we have to lose?"

He put the cover plate carefully on the deck, returned to the maze of wiring which had been revealed.

"It's those red primaries at the top," said Garcia.

"I know," said Bonnett. He reached in with cutter pliers, snipped the wires. "Do you think the skipper's all right?"

"This is no time to worry about that."

Bonnett nodded, adjusted a pump control. "Johnny, what's the helium reading?"

"Point four."

Bonnett took out his own vampire gauge, adjusted it on his wrist. "Joe, take us down. Heading 215 degrees. Johnny, how far to that seamount?"

"Six minutes."

Bonnett's head snapped up. "You been working time-over-distance in your head?"

Ramsey busied himself with the search controls as the *Ram*'s deck slanted downward. "Yes."

"We'll make a submariner out of him yet," said Garcia. He looked at Bonnett. "Are you sure it wouldn't be better to try floating up again?"

"They're too close," said Bonnett. "Besides, I'm afraid to take another chance on rolling. We sheared off the damper-control base in there." He nodded toward the bow. "No telling what we did to the pile base."

Garcia wet his lips with his tongue.

"Won't they hear us go down?" asked Ramsey.

"They know our depth limit," said Bonnett.

"This was your idea," said Garcia. "Are you getting cold feet?"

Ramsey swallowed.

"Their metal detection is poor," said Bonnett. "I'm counting on their thinking we've taken the deep six rather than risk their fish."

"They won't hear any breaking up noises," said Garcia.

"We hope," said Ramsey.

Garcia paled.

Ramsey looked to the big static pressure gauge. "Outside pressure 2900 pounds." He glanced at Bonnett. "Skipper."

"We have only one skipper," said Bonnett. "He's aft in sick bay."

"No, I'm not!"

They whirled. Sparrow stood in the aft doorway, hand on the metal rim, face pale and beaded with perspiration. "What is the situation, Les?"

Bonnett told him.

Sparrow turned a searching look on Ramsey. "This was your idea?"

Ramsey nodded. *How long was he standing there?* he wondered.

"What are your orders?" asked Bonnett.

"Carry on," said Sparrow. "You are in command."

Bonnett turned back to the pressure controls. "Helium below detection range," he said. "Shall we go sit in the mud, Joe?"

"The medics say it's theoretically possible for the human body to take 400 pounds under pure oxy and carbonic anhydrase conditions," said Ramsey.

"Do all of them say that?" asked Bonnett.

"No, only some of them."

"I can see it, now," said Garcia. "An account of the reactions of four human bodies to 400 pounds atmospheric pressure in a Hell Diver Class submarine, with technical commentary on the autopsies."

Ramsey shivered, looked at the red center dial on the static pressure gauge showing the *Ram*'s internal pressure: 297 pounds to the square inch. He glanced at the vampire gauge on his wrist, said, "$CO_2$ diffusion is now .266. We have .054 to go under present conditions."

Bonnett said, "I'll give us 350 pounds internal as a starter." He opened a valve, increased the anhydrase pump setting.

"Two minutes to bottom," said Ramsey. "It's a long thin seamount, ridge running parallel with our course. About ten miles."

"Pressure is holding," said Bonnett. "'How long until that pack ranges us?'"

"Fifteen minutes."

Behind them, Sparrow said, "Now we're going to find out how well these Hell Divers are built."

"I'm more interested in how well I'm built," said Garcia.

"I'd say the good Lord did an excellent job, all things considered," said Bonnett.

Ramsey thought: *Now that was a strange remark from him. More what I'd have expected from Sparrow.*

"Lord, we beg your indulgence upon us," said Sparrow. "We who have no right to ask it. Amen."

"Flatten the glide angle," said Bonnett.

Garcia brought up the nose.

"Give us the nose eyes and two searchlights."

The main screen above them came alive, showing a path of light through green water. Pale phosphorescent shapes ranged beyond the limits of the light.

Ramsey looked at the internal-pressure reading: 400 pounds even.

"Ease her down," said Bonnett.

The deck tipped.

Outside pressure passed through 3400 pounds . . . 3420 . . . 3440 . . .

Ramsey found himself unable to tear his gaze away from the dial.

3500 . . . 3520 . . . 3540 . . .

"Diffusion is normal," said Bonnett. "Is anyone feeling ill effects?"

"I feel silly," said Garcia.

"Steady," said Bonnett.

"Be alert for oxygen intoxication," said Sparrow.

The pressure dial passed 3600 pounds . . . 3620 . . .

"Flatten the glide," said Bonnett.

Garcia complied.

"How far to the bottom?"

Ramsey forced himself to look at his instruments.

"Fifty feet."

"Down," said Bonnett.

Again the deck tipped.

Now, they watched the big screen below the pressure gauge.

"There!" said Garcia.

It seemed to come at them out of a green fog; a long pie cut of red ooze slashed from the darkness by the searchlights. A uniform ripple pattern stretched diagonally across the ooze. It showed not a sign of sea life.

Garcia eased up the bow planes and the *Ram* grounded gently, stirring up a fog of the red ooze which clouded the screen.

"Kill the drive," said Bonnett.

Garcia's hand already was on the switch. The motors fell silent.

Ramsey whispered, "It's 8460 feet."

"A new world's record," said Garcia.

Sparrow stepped forward onto the control deck. "Thank you, Lord," he said.

"I've come to a decision," said Ramsey. "I'm just a natural-born coward. Nothing ever came so easy to me in all my life."

"Is anybody feeling ill effects from the pressure?" asked Sparrow.

"I'm still feeling silly," said Garcia.

"Anybody else?"

Ramsey shook his head, studied the search instruments in front of him.

"Diffusion is .214," said Bonnett. "We're still rid of it faster than we take it in."

Ramsey said, "Great God in heaven!"

"Where else would you expect him to be?" asked Garcia.

"There's a cold current moving in," said Ramsey. "Right over us."

"God spreads his cloak upon us," said Sparrow.

"Pack ranging over us to the south," said Ramsey. "Eight thousand yards."

Bonnett said, "Any indications that they smell us?"

"No."

"They won't look where they don't believe we can be," said Garcia. He grinned. "And that's not strange. I don't believe I'm here, either."

"I'm losing 'em through that cold layer," said Ramsey.

"Skipper an' God are buddies," said Garcia. "Good close buddies. Do favors for each other alla time." He staggered slightly.

Ramsey grabbed Garcia's wrist, looked at his vampire gauge. "Diffusion normal. What's—"

"Oxygen reactions vary," said Bonnett.

"What's wrong with you chaps?" Garcia's head wobbled. He peered at them owlishly.

"Take it easy, Joe," said Sparrow.

"Easy?" He squinted up at Sparrow. "I know you, Skipper. You're King David all over again. I've heard you." He shook his head loosely, lifted his right hand. " 'In my distress I called upon the Lord, and cried to my God: and he did hear my voice out of his temple, and my cry did enter into his ears.' "

"All right, Joe. Let's go back and hit the sack." Sparrow took Garcia's elbow, urged him toward the aft door.

"Leggo me," said Garcia. He shook off Sparrow's hand, staggered, caught his balance, turned, and stared deliberately at Ramsey. "I know all about you, Mr. Long John Ramsey. You look down your long nose at me! Think you know somethin' bout me. You don't know nothin'. Nothin'!"

"That will be quite enough, Mr. Garcia." Sparrow's voice had iron in it, a harsh note of command.

"Sorry, Skipper." He turned toward the door. "Le's go. 'M tired."

Sparrow stared at Ramsey, then turned, urged Garcia out the door.

In the control room there was silence for a moment broken only by the faintest murmuring of stand-by machinery. Then Bonnett said, "Long John? How'd you get a nickname like that?"

Ramsey studied his instrument before turning toward Bonnett. *That damned nickname! It could mean only that Garcia knew about his past—his real past.*

Bonnett said, "I asked—"

"Yes, I heard you. A supply officer christened me. Said I was a worse pirate than the original Long John Silver. That's all."

"Pirate? Why?"

"For scrounging extra equipment. Moonlight requisition."

Bonnett smiled. "I don't see why that'd put Joe on his ear. Unless he's jealous of someone better at it than he is."

And Ramsey was thinking: *Garcia will tell the skipper. Sure as hell he will.*

"Is it extra hot in here?" asked Bonnett.

Ramsey looked at the beads of perspiration on Bonnett's face, glanced at his vampire gauge. Blood temperature normal. He looked at the dial of the thermosystem monitor on his board, said, "Seventy-one degrees."

"My skin feels itchy," said Bonnett.

Ramsey resisted the impulse to scratch at his own forearm, said, "I've been noticing the same thing."

Bonnett glanced at the exposed wiring of the atmosphere controls, checked a dial setting. "Anhydrase generation is double the normal. Gas volume twenty cc.'s per cubic meter."

"We're off in a wild unknown," said Ramsey.

"We shouldn't be," said Bonnett. "We've had carbonic anhydrase for forty years."

Ramsey reset a kick-out meter on his sono-board, looked up at the primary oscilloscope.

"Hear anything?"

Ramsey shook his head. "This C-A is funny stuff, Les. We've pushed chimpanzees to 400 pounds with it for extended periods. Some lived. Some didn't. A few of the bright boys think they know why."

"Why?"

"Well, the theory is that C-A acts on a rather nebulous central nervous system thing called the 'metabolic governor' in such a way as to keep us from burning up when available oxygen is increased. They think sometimes the governor gets a little bit off— out of timing kind of—and the organism gets caught in a feed-back situation: oscillates to death."

"Why?"

"That they don't know. Maybe the 'metabolic governor' gets tired."

"What're the chances one of us'll get caught that way?"

Ramsey shot a sharp glance at him, looked at the search board. "That's a stupid question, Les."

Bonnett colored. His jaw set.

"If you're trying to get me to reassure you, no dice," said Ramsey. "All I know is we're still alive, even if we are a bit uncom— Signal!" He slapped the switch on the ranging computer read the dial. "Five hundred yards. They're quartering southwest."

"Do we still have God's cold cloak over us?"

Ramsey caught a jibing cynicism in Bonnett's voice he had never noted before. He glanced at the thermo-couple dial. "It's been over us periodically. Gone now. I think this seamount acts like a barrier to the Arctic Current. Probably sets up complex whorl patterns." He looked back to the ranging dials. "The EPs are holding course. They're drawing away now."

"Was there any doubt that they would?" asked Bonnett.

"What do you mean?"

"You've some things to learn yet about our skipper," said Bonnett. "Joe wasn't joking. There's an unca—"

The *Ram* gave an abrupt lurch and the deck tipped two degrees left.

Ramsey caught the rail in front of his board. "What the—"

"The tow," said Bonnett. "Current's playing with it."

"I felt it nudge us when we sat down," said Ramsey. "But the bumpers—"

They lurched another degree to the left.

"Just pray it doesn't drag us off this mountain," said Bonnett. "We couldn't take the extra 500 feet."

"How do you know?" asked Ramsey. He studied the search board.

"I feel the mountain under my feet all foggy."

Ramsey looked up. "What'd you say?"

"I feel all foggy in the head," said Bonnett. He leaned against the grab-rail. "Fall off the mountain. Hate the fog." He forced himself upright. "Not thinking straight. Take over, Mr. Ramsey. I'm . . . I'm—" He sat down on the deck, one hand above him still clinging to the rail.

An abrupt correlation interlocked in Ramsey's mind. He glanced one more time over his search board, turned away, forced himself to walk calmly across to Bonnett. He bent over the first officer, checked Bonnett's vampire gauge. $CO_2$ diffusion .228. Above normal by .016. He dropped Bonnett's wrist, stood up and made a minute micro-meter-gauge reduction in anhydrase generation.

"What's wrong with Les?" Sparrow stood in the aft door, gaze sweeping over the control deck. He stepped through the door as Ramsey turned.

"Take it slow," said Ramsey.

"Wha—" Sparrow hesitated in mid-stride.

Ramsey bent over Bonnett, again checked his vampire gauge, compared it with the one on his own wrist. No change. Too soon. He said, "I've just formed the Ramsey Theory on why some chimpanzees died and some didn't."

Sparrow again moved forward, bent over Bonnett. "What chimpanzees?"

"The chimps Med. I put under 400 pounds with peak anhydrase. My advice is for you not to overexert, get excited, nervous, or—"

"I know about the chimps," said Sparrow. "Do you think—" He hesitated.

"Some kind of glandular upset," said Ramsey. "What's more likely than an emotional trigger, maybe coupled to physical activity?"

Sparrow nodded.

Ramsey noted the vampire-gauge needles sinking toward normal. He began massaging Bonnett's left arm. "You're okay, Les. Just relax and take it easy. The crisis is over. Take it easy . . . take it easy . . . take it easy . . ."

Bonnett's head rocked groggily.

"We have to avoid excitement," said Ramsey. "Our

bodies are walking a tight wire down here. An uneasy balance."

Sparrow stood up, went to the search board. "I gave Joe a sedative. He was crying, raving. Maybe I—" He fell silent.

Bonnett opened his eyes.

"Remain calm," said Ramsey. "Do you hear me, Les?"

The first officer nodded.

"There's no danger if you relax.

"You can't force a man to relax," said Sparrow.

Ramsey reached around Bonnett's head, found the nerve line on the back of his neck, massaged it. "You're feeling better already."

Bonnett wet his lips with his tongue. " 'M okay. Get back to your board."

"Breathe slow and easy," said Ramsey. He stood up.

Bonnett swallowed, spoke as though past a thickened tongue. "It was like quicksand. Feelin' better now."

Ramsey turned toward Sparrow. "He'll be okay now."

Sparrow glanced down at Bonnett. "Stay where you are Les, until you feel like getting up." He turned to Ramsey. "I've been on the eyes. The current has pulled our tow to a forty-five-degree angle across our stern. If we slack off the top towline we'll right but that might free the tow for a further shift."

"Best leave well enough alone," said Ramsey.

"How near the edge of this seamount are we? The eyes don't show it."

"Maybe seventy-five yards. For the tow, that is. We were angling away from the edge when we sat down."

Sparrow looked at the ranging computers. "Intermittent signal near extreme range."

"That cold layer is waving over us like a fan," said Ramsey.

Sparrow backed away from the board, looked around him, brought his attention back to Ramsey. There was something in the way he looked at Ramsey of the same attention he gave to his boat's instruments.

"What's this 'Long John' business? Joe doesn't make sense."

Ramsey repeated what he had told Bonnett.

"Did the *Ram* benefit from this acquisition propensity of yours?"

"Not this trip, Skipper."

Sparrow glanced upward to the row of reactor-room telltales. "Maybe next trip."

Bonnett spoke from his position on the deck. "We're gonna have a next trip, too. If we don't crack up like poor Hepp."

"We won't," said Sparrow.

Bonnett heaved himself to his feet. "I'm glad we have God's word on that."

Sparrow gave him a searching stare, said, "I'm reassuming command, Les. The circumstances warrant it. I'm in no immediate danger from that radiation overage."

"Of course, Skipper." There seemed a sigh of relief in Bonnett's voice.

Sparrow said, "I'm going back now and have another look at Joe. I'm leaving Johnny on the search board. All clear?"

"All clear, Skipper."

Sparrow turned his angular form slowly, went out the aft door.

"He's an automaton," said Ramsey, addressing the empty air where Sparrow had stood.

"He's under more pressure than the submarine," said Bonnett. He took a deep breath. "Let's you pay attention to that board."

Ramsey frowned, returned his attention to his gauges and dials.

Silence hung between them.

Presently, Bonnett said, "Thanks, Johnny. Maybe you saved my life."

Ramsey shrugged, remained silent.

"I heard what you told the skipper. It feels right. Come to think of it, maybe you saved all of our lives."

"Be damned lonesome down here all alone," said Ramsey.

"You'd probably prefer three well-stacked blondes," said Bonnett. "Come to think of it, that'd get my vote, too."

"Another signal at outer range," said Ramsey, "Six subs in net-search spacing. They'll pass out of range in the south-east quadrant."

"They just ain't looking where nobody could possibly be," said Bonnett. "Can't say that I blame them. I still don't believe I'm here." He glanced up at the static pressure gauge, looked quickly away.

"No need for two of us here," said Ramsey.

"Nothing except the skipper's double-team orders."

"Stupid orders," said Ramsey.

"Take it easy, lad,' said Bonnett. "You can't fight the Navy chain of command and you can't fight God." He shrugged. "And when the two are on the same team—"

"What makes you believe that nonsense?" asked Ramsey.

Bonnett froze. "I make jokes, boy. That's one thing. What you just said is another thing." He shook his head. "I've been forty missions with the Savvy Sparrow guy. Don't talk to me about nonsense. I know what I've seen."

*And you know what you want to believe,* thought Ramsey.

Somewhere a faint dripping caught his attention: condensation on the pipes. The *Ram* suddenly assumed a cold empty feeling around him. *We're not going to make it,* he thought. *A thousand alert enemy subs ranging across our track. It was crazy to send us out. A desperation move.*

The lights of his thermocouple monitor winked blindly on the instrument board.

*God's cold cloak waving over us! Maybe that's the best thing to believe. Knowledge is the course of our lives. We eat the apple and we learn just enough to make us afraid.*

The *Ram* shuddered briefly as the current tugged at her tow. The deck tilted back toward level.

"If we raise a big mud patch on the surface—stirring up the bottom like a mud pie—they'll spot it," said Bonnett. "They'll have a sky full of buzzards this close to their own shores."

"How'll they see it in the fog?" asked Ramsey. He felt a sudden lightening of his spirits.

"Fog topside? How can you tell?"

"Skipper arranged it with God," said Ramsey.

"You think you're joking," said Bonnett. He looked at Ramsey. "You do, don't you?"

Ramsey reset the ranging computer in front of him. "A man has to live with his boat—be a part of it," he said, speaking lightly. He felt the sudden undertow pull of thought below the words. It was like stepping outside his body and watching it function. "This boat believes in God," he said.

The counter hands of the timelog swept around . . . around . . . around . . . The watches changed as the *Ram* snuggled into the mud of the seamount.

Eleven days, thirty-two minutes from point of departure.

Sparrow stood at the control board with Ramsey, sharing the last half of the electronics officer's watch. The sense of excess pressure outside their hull had become a thing accepted.

"How long since you've heard one of their packs?" asked Sparrow.

"Over six hours."

"How's the tow?"

Ramsey checked the line telltales, switched on the stern eyes one by one. "Laying to starboard about thirty degrees. Towlines clear."

Sparrow tested the drive controls, switched on the motors. A humming sense of expectancy came over the subtug. Ramsey felt it tingle through his body, starting in his feet against the deck.

"Let's go get that oil," said Sparrow. He threw in the drive switch, threw it off. "Just to stir up the mud around us. Drop four waist torpedoes, Johnny. We'll need buoyancy."

"What about the tow? It's not carrying enough pressure to blow at this depth."

"We're going to jerk it off the bottom. Pay out line until we get a good run on."

Ramsey pushed down the flat black toggles which dropped the torpedoes from the waist belt.

The *Ram* bobbled upward. Sparrow again threw power into the drive. The subtug slanted upward, towline reeling out behind them.

"Snub it," said Sparrow.

Ramsey locked the magnetic brakes on the outside reel drums. The tug came almost to a full stop, motors straining. Slowly they struggled ahead.

"Line stretching," said Ramsey. "That's slug's in solid."

Sparrow shook his head. "How much more line?"

"Eight hundred feet more or less."

"Give us some more."

The *Ram* again angled upward. Sparrow circled left, came back to the right in a snake track, barely moving.

"Operational depth," said Ramsey. "Outside pressure 2994 pounds."

"Snub towlines and blow number-one tank," said Sparrow.

Again Ramsey stopped the outside reels. His right hand went out to the red handle marked "high pressure air." He set it over number one, flicked on the safety toggle, started bleeding air into the number-one tank.

"Give it everything," said Sparrow.

Ramsey turned the valve two revolutions.

Sparrow put full power into the drive. The *Ram*'s bow tipped up to almost ten degrees. By inches, they climbed, twisting soggily.

"She's off," said Ramsey.

"How's the slug's compensator system?"

Ramsey looked to the tow board. "Following the pressure curve."

"Blow the slug's bow and stern tanks," said Sparrow.

"She's not at—"

"Blow them anyway. Water pressure will hold the air until we reach operational depth. We're going to need all the help we can get and as soon as we can get it."

Ramsey's hands moved over the tow board carrying out his orders.

They inched upward. Ramsey stared at the red dials of the slug's pressure system. "Bow tank's beginning to bubble."

They could feel it in the deck: a return to normal climb gradient, speed picking up.

"Bow tank just blew," said Ramsey. "There goes the stern." He wiped perspiration from his forehead.

"That was the thing Les should have considered," said Sparrow. "Now we know we can get off. As long as we have external weight which we can drop for the initial buoyancy."

"How do you know that Les didn't—"

"I know my shipmates," said Sparrow. "Learn something from this, Johnny, and you'll make a good submariner. Never head into anything with a sub unless you have already worked out a plan for coming out the other side."

Ramsey chose his words carefully. "What's your plan for making the big come-out on the other side—with the oil?"

"Not just one plan," said Sparrow. "I have plans for every contingency I can think of. And for some maybe I shouldn't have thought of."

"Like for instance?"

Sparrow turned and looked full at him. "Like for instance my crew going psychotic, one by one."

Ramsey's eyes widened. The words leaped out before he could stop them. "And what about yourself?"

Sparrow's eyes glittered. "That's one of the ones

maybe I shouldn't have thought of," he said. He swung back to the controls.

*He's like a piece of machinery,* thought Ramsey. *Great God in heaven, what went into making a man like that?*

Bonnett entered carrying a hypodermic, its needle covered by a sterile pad. "Time for your shot, Skipper."

"In my left arm?" asked Sparrow.

"Well—"

"Don't I get to keep any dignity?" asked Sparrow.

Ramsey grinned.

"I swear you guys take a perverse delight in this," growled Sparrow.

"It's really too much for your arm," said Bonnett. He glanced up at the static gauge. "Six thousand feet! What're we doing up here in the shallows?"

Sparrow chuckled. "Okay, take my mind off my troubles." He backed away from the board. "Take over here, Johnny.

Ramsey stepped into control position. Behind him, he heard Sparrow grunt. "Easy, Les!"

"Easy as I could, Skipper. There. Have Joe check you on his watch. You seem to be coming along okay."

"I should be. I've three nursemaids."

Sparrow moved up beside Ramsey. "Hold us on course sixty-four degrees, forty-five minutes."

Ramsey turned the helm, looked up at the sonoran chart. "That'll bring us around Nordkapp." He did some mental figuring, glanced at the shaftlog counter. "About twenty-six and a half hours."

Sparrow looked startled.

"He's good with figures," said Bonnett.

"He's also too interested in where we're going to be and when," said Sparrow.

"That Security pap is for the birds," said Ramsey.

"I wish to remind you that we found a dead man aboard this vessel, that we've been sabotaged right and left, that—" He broke off, staring at Ramsey.

It was Bonnett's turn to look startled.

*And now I'm in over my head,* thought Ramsey. *My plan had better be right or I won't . . . come out the other side.*

Sparrow looked at the timelog. "Time for Les to go on watch now." He gestured for Bonnett to take the helm. "Put us on auto-pilot. Steady as she goes."

Ramsey went to the aft door, found Sparrow staring at him. The captain turned deliberately away, moved closer to Bonnett. "Stand by the search board as soon as we're on auto-pilot."

"Aye, Skipper."

Ramsey went out the door, swung it almost closed behind him, stood there with his ear to the crack.

Bonnett said, "How's Joe?"

"He's all right. He'll stand his regular watch."

"What's with this Long John Ramsey? Skipper, could he be a phony?"

"No doubt of it," said Sparrow. "The only question in my mind is: What kind of phony?"

"Could he be a—"

"He very definitely could be. Someone loaded us with spy beams and trapped that Security officer."

"But Ramsey wasn't aboard then."

"That's what bothers me. Unless there was something wrong with the Security man's timing. That would explain it."

"I'll watch him, Skipper."

"You do that. I'm also alerting Joe."

Ramsey tiptoed away from the door. *Well, I did it,* he thought, *I'd better be right.* He shuddered, turned at the end of the companionway, dropped down to his cabin level. He paused in front of Garcia's cabin, looked at the blank metal of the door. Again the thought passed through his mind: *I'd better be right.*

He went into his cabin, closing the door softly behind him, locking it. Then he brought out the telemeter, unreeled the tapes.

There was response for Sparrow's time in the tunnel

repairing the pile controls, but now Sparrow was under rigid control. The wave patterns on the tapes were like the path of a rubber ball bouncing between two walls.

*I have to be able to crack that control at will,* thought Ramsey. *He has to fail—just once. At the right time and at the right thing.*

And another part of his mind said: *That's a helluva way to make someone well.*

He fought down that thought. *It has to be. It's accepted practice. It works.*

*Most of the time.*

Sparrow's advice came back to him: *"Never head into anything unless you have already worked out a plan for coming out the other side."*

Ramsey sat down on his bunk, reset the telemeter, sealed it, slid it back beneath his desk.

*What if my plan doesn't work? What's my alternative for that contingency?*

He lay back on his bunk, staring at the rivet pattern overhead. Around him, the muted throbbing and humming of the subtug took on a fantasy life. As though it knew where it was going and how to get there.

Ramsey fell into a troubled sleep, awoke for his next watch to find his body soaked in perspiration, a disturbing half memory of a dream—no, a nightmare —which he could not bring to consciousness.


The automatic timelog read twelve days, seven hours, and five minutes from departure. Last half of Garcia's watch, first half of Bonnett's. The red dot on the sonoran chart stood well into the shore off Nordkapp: shallow water with the *Ram* creeping along the bottom in one hundred fathoms.

In the control room, a brightly lighted sweep of bulkhead, telltales flashing, heavy shadows on the undersides of levers and valve wheels. Wavering admonitions of dial needles. The two men bent over their work like laborers in a metal cave.

Bonnett looked up to the static pressure: 260 pounds

to the square inch. "What's the skipper thinking of, coming in close like this?"

"Don't ask so many questions." Garcia made a minute adjustment in the bow planes, watched the depth repeater. "We're twenty feet from bottom."

Sparrow ducked through the door from the aft companionway. "Anything showing on the search board?" His voice was husky with a sense of fatigue. He coughed.

"Negative," said Bonnett.

"This is their water," said Sparrow. "They've no shore stations along the north coast; only along the Norway reaches."

"This is still awful close," said Bonnett. Again he looked to the depth gauge. "And awful shallow."

"You don't think this is a safe place for us?" asked Sparrow.

"No."

"Good. That means they don't either. They know this is a *deep* tug. They're out scouring the Norwegian basin. The sill depth there is right on our known limit."

"So?"

"So we're going to shoot right across the shallows." He glanced at Garcia, then up to the sonoran chart. "Course seventy degrees, Joe."

Garcia swung the helm, watched the compass until they were heading true, then he, too, looked at the chart. "Novaya Zemlya," he whispered.

"We're shallow enough to start taking outside samples," said Sparrow. "Les, look for an isobaric surface running almost parallel with our course. We could use the shielding of some cold water."

Bonnett pulled down a density-gradient chart for the area, checked the isobaric differences, ran a siphon sample of the exterior water. "Give us sixty-nine degrees for five minutes," he said.

Garcia touched the helm. They watched the thermocouple repeater. Suddenly, it dipped fifteen degrees. "Resume course," said Sparrow.

The *Ram* returned to seventy degrees, cruising under the sheltering mask of the cold current which spilled down around them.

"Steady as she goes," said Sparrow. "Push search to limit. It's a straight run from here on in."

"It's Novaya Zemlya, isn't it?" asked Garcia.

Sparrow hesitated, then: "It's obvious anyway. Yes."

"That's an EP rocket-testing base," said Bonnett. "It'll be bristling with buzzards and snoopers."

"We dug the well right under their noses," said Sparrow. "If we could dig without their hearing us, we ought to be able to drain it dry undetected."

"Are they tapping the reservoir, too?"

Sparrow grinned wolfishly, his long face glistening in the multihued lights of the control board. "That's the beauty of it. They don't even know it's there."

"Lord," whispered Bonnett. "A fresh well. What're we looking for in the way of landmarks?"

Again Sparrow hesitated while his eyes sought out the red dot on the sonoran chart. *It wouldn't even be a secret from the EPs if they spotted us here,* he thought. *Now, we're in God's hands for sure.*

"We're looking for a narrow fault fissure," he said. "It's called the gut and it slants right up into the island shelf. You can't miss it once you range across it. Depth down to 3600 feet and only 400 feet across."

"Fissure is right," said Garcia. "Do we go down into that thing?"

"No. It's our trail. We track it in." Again he looked at the chart. "Thirty-three hours at this rate." He turned to the aft door. "Call me if anything develops."

And he was gone down the companionway.

"If anything develops," muttered Bonnett. "We're sitting ducks. The only development we'll get is a fish in our belly. That'll wake him!"

"I think he's right," said Garcia. "They're all out in the deeps looking for us. This is going to be a milk run."

"I'm curdled already," said Bonnett. He fell silent, watching the search board.

The *Ram* drove onward, headlong across the shallows like a frightened fish. The hands of the timelog swept around, around.

"Relieving Mr. Garcia on watch." Ramsey spoke as he ducked through the door into the control room. He could sense the immediate stiffening of the two men on the board, the mounting tension.

Garcia made an attempt at casual banter. "Look who's gone all Navy formal on us."

Ramsey took up his position beside Garcia. "What course?"

"Seventy degrees." Garcia surrendered the helm.

"Busting right across the shallows," said Ramsey. "If we make this, I'm going to burn a candle to St. Cuthbert."

"That's not good talk," said Bonnett.

"Have you heard what the EPs have done now?" asked Ramsey. "They've put engines in Novaya Zemlya. When we get close they're going to move it right out of our way, let us go lumbering off into Siberia."

"Clever chaps," said Garcia.

"Skipper's going to run us right into an EP trap net," said Ramsey. "We'll spend the rest of the war in a prison camp being brainwashed while they take the *Ram* apart bolt by——"

"Button your bloody lip," said Garcia. "We're going to pull this one off. And when we set foot on that blessed dock I'm going to take an obscene pleasure in pushing you——"

"That will be enough!" said Bonnett. "This is no time for fighting among ourselves."

"You wouldn't say that if you knew all about this wise guy," said Garcia. "The superior brain: knows all, sees all, tells nothing!"

"Hit the sack, Joe," said Bonnett. "That's an order."

Garcia glowered at Ramsey, turned away, went out the aft door.

"What're you trying to prove, Johnny?"

"How do you mean?"

"Baiting Joe like that."

"He baits easy."

Bonnett stared at him. "One way to wreck a ship is to destroy crew morale," he said. "There will be no more such actions from you on this cruise."

"You sound like one of the old ladies of Security," said Ramsey.

Bonnett's face darkened. "Knock it off, Mr. Ramsey. This won't work with me."

*It's already working,* thought Ramsey. He said, "This is going to be a really gay bunch when we get to Novaya Zemlya. All of us looking over each other's shoulders."

"How do you know where we're headed?" gritted Bonnett. "You weren't here when Skipper announced our destination."

"I read tea leaves." Ramsey nodded toward the depth-gauge graph tape. "Are we looking for that?"

Bonnett snapped his attention back to the tape. A sharp line broke off the tape, came back on after a brief interval.

"That a *development*," said Bonnett. "Buzz the skipper."

Ramsey depressed the black toggle of the number-one call button. "Shall I hold course?"

"No. Quarter back on— Signal!" He slapped the button for the range computer, shut off the drive. "Eighteen miles. Intercept course."

Ramsey whirled the helm to the right. "Have they heard us?"

"There's no telling," said Bonnett. They coasted silently while he watched the pipes on his screen.

Sparrow entered the control room. "Signal?"

"Heading 270 degrees," said Bonnett.

"What's the depth here?"

"Four hundred feet, give or take a few."

"You're forgetting something," said Ramsey. He pointed to the tape record of the deep fissure.

"Hide in that thing?" Bonnett's voice rose half an octave. "We couldn't maneuver. Straight down the alley and they'd have us bottled up."

The *Ram*'s deck began to tip to the left as they lost way.

"Give us headway," ordered Sparrow.

Ramsey eased in the drive. He watched the pulse-reader showing bottom depth below them. Abruptly, it fell off beyond the meter setting. Without being told, Ramsey brought the helm up to left until they were over the fissure.

"Down into it," said Sparrow.

"What if it narrows down to nothing?" asked Bonnett. "We couldn't back out without fouling our towlines. We'll be—"

"Watch your board," ordered Sparrow.

The oscillations on the screen damped down, then blanked out.

"Full speed," said Sparrow. "Down farther, Johnny!"

Ramsey felt the excitement gripping his stomach. "The walls of this fissure are hiding our sound!"

"If we hit something, we've had it," said Bonnett.

Sparrow glanced at the big static pressure gauge: 1240 pounds. "Give us a pulse sweep on those walls—fifth-second intervals."

"Whatta you think I'm doing?" muttered Bonnett.

Sparrow grinned. He put a hand on Ramsey's shoulder. "Ease her up."

"Speed?"

"No, depth. Set us level."

Ramsey brought up the bow planes. The *Ram*'s deck came up to level.

"One degree right," said Bonnett.

Ramsey swung the helm.

"We're doing twenty-two knots," said Sparrow. "If we can just put—"

"Two degrees right," said Bonnett.

"Coax a little more speed out of her," said Sparrow.

Ramsey fined down the setting on the magnometer for the induction drive.

"Open the silencers," said Sparrow.

"But—"

Sparrow's fingers dug into Ramsey's shoulder. "Do it!"

Ramsey's hand went out, jerked down the big red handle above the helm. They could feel the added surge of power.

"Twenty-eight knots," said Sparrow. "There's life in the old girl yet."

"Two degrees left," said Bonnett.

Ramsey complied.

"An EP subcruiser can do forty-five knots," said Bonnett. "Are you trying to run away from them?"

"How fast were they closing us at our last known position?" asked Sparrow.

"Estimated search speed of twenty knots," said Bonnett. "Say forty-five or fifty minutes unless they were on us and upped speed when we went out of sound. Then maybe only a half hour."

Sparrow looked at the timelog. "We'll count on a half hour." He waited silently.

"Two degrees left," said Bonnett.

Ramsey brought the helm over, straightened them out on the new course.

"She's narrowing down," said Bonnett. "No more than 300 feet wide here." He reset the ranging computer. "Now it's down to 250. Here's— Two degrees left!"

Ramsey swung the helm.

"We're all right if we don't scrape the slug off on the walls of this hole," said Sparrow.

"Three degrees right."

Ramsey obeyed.

"Two hundred feet," said Bonnett. "Minus . . . minus . . . 185 . . . 200 . . . 215—Two degrees right."

The *Ram* tipped to the rudder response.

"Give us the silencer planes," said Sparrow.

Ramsey pushed up the big red handle. They could feel the drag.

"Half speed," said Sparrow. "How far to the canyon rim?"

"I can only guess," said Bonnett. "Too sharp an angle to get a difference reading."

"Well, guess then."

"Eighteen hundred feet."

"Hear anything behind us?"

"Negative."

"Motors off," said Sparrow.

Ramsey silenced the drive.

"Now, do you hear anything?"

Bonnett fussed with his instruments. "Negative."

"Full speed," said Sparrow. "Two degrees on the bow planes."

"Two degrees on the bow planes," acknowledged Ramsey. He brought up the planes, eased in the drive, sent them surging upward.

"One degree left," said Bonnett.

Ramsey swung the helm.

Sparrow looked at the pressure reading: 860 pounds. They were above 2000 feet. Still the *Ram* coursed upward.

"Half speed," said Sparrow.

Ramsey brought back the throttle control to the mid-notch.

"I can give you a rim reading," said Bonnett. "About ninety fathoms."

"Five hundred and forty feet," translated Sparrow. "Are you sure of that sill depth?"

Bonnett rechecked his instruments. "Reasonably sure. I can give you a better reading in a minute."

Again Sparrow looked to the pressure gauge: 600 pounds.

"Make it eighty fathoms," said Bonnett. "I was getting angular distortion."

"Four hundred and eighty feet," said Sparrow. "Less than a thousand to go. Quarter speed, if you please."

Again Ramsey brought the throttle bar back a full notch.

"Hear anything, Les?"

"Negative."

The pressure gauge climbed past 400 pounds to the square inch: above 1000-foot depth.

"I make that canyon rim in 460 feet of water," said Bonnett.

"Anything on the phones yet?"

"Still quiet."

"Give us full power until we reach maximum speed," said Sparrow. "Then shut everything down and coast up onto the rim. Set us down gently as you can."

Ramsey's eyes widened.

"Now," said Sparrow.

Ramsey shot the throttle forward. The subtug leaped ahead. They watched the pitlog sweep through twenty-three knots.

"Now!" barked Sparrow.

Ramsey killed the drive, freed the induction system to allow the propeller to spin free. He jockeyed the planes to keep them on an even keel with the least drag.

"We're over," said Bonnett.

Ramsey watched the pitlog, began counting off the time-over-distance until he was certain the tow had cleared. Then he brought the bow planes down.

They grounded in mud with almost no headway.

"I'm hearing them, Skipper," said Bonnett. "About ten miles behind us and to the—"

"What's wrong?"

"Lost 'em."

"They've gone into the gut after us," said Ramsey.

"Lift us," said Sparrow. "Force speed!"

Ramsey jerked into motion, fed power into the drive, eased them off the bottom, pushed the throttle to the final notch.

Sparrow watched the timelog. Five minutes. "Kill the drive."

"Still silent," said Bonnett.

"Five minutes more," said Sparrow.

Ramsey again sent them shooting ahead. Five minutes. Drift and listen. Five minutes. Drift and listen. Five minutes. Drift and listen.

"Set us into the mud again, Johnny."

The *Ram* slanted down, grounded on a ripple surface of black manganese pebbles.

"We've come eight miles from the gut," said Bonnett. He looked at the pressure gauge: 300 pounds. "It's only 700 feet deep here."

"What do we care?" asked Ramsey. "They think we're in that slot. They'll be scraping the bottom of it."

Sparrow said, "And there goes the whole shooting match."

Ramsey looked at him sharply. "What do you mean?"

"They spotted us too close to target. And right on the trail leading to the well."

"How do they know it wasn't a feint?"

"No. They know we were hiding. They know—" He fell silent.

"You mean we're going to slink home empty-handed?" It was Bonnett, voice bitter.

"I wouldn't give them the satisfaction." The voice came from the aft door: Garcia.

The three in the control room whirled.

Garcia stepped fully onto the control deck. "We've *got* to thumb our noses at them, Skipper."

"How long've you been there?" asked Sparrow.

Garcia frowned. "Maybe ten minutes. I heard the shift in speed and felt—" He broke off. "Skipper, we've come too far to—"

"Relax," said Sparrow. "We're going through."

"How?"

"We're going to sit here."

"How long?" asked Ramsey.

"Maybe a day; maybe longer. Until they get tired of looking or decide they've missed us."

"But they're sure to leave a stake-out around here on just that chance," protested Bonnett.

"Let's just pray that they do," said Sparrow. "Les, take over the controls and stand-by search. Johnny, you and Joe come with me." Sparrow led the way across to the chart board. He swept his earlier work aside, pulled out a fresh sheet of scratch paper, began drawing cyclic curves across it. He took a second sheet, repeated the performance.

Ramsey watched, puzzled, Garcia bent close to the work.

Presently, Sparrow straightened. "What do I have here, Johnny?"

"It could be a sonic curve, but—"

"It's the modulated beat of one of our A-2 fish," said Garcia.

Sparrow nodded. "Now watch this." He lifted one of the sheets, placed it over the other, held both to a light and adjusted them. He clipped the sheets together, still holding them up to the light, began to draw a new free-hand curve, a broken scrawl on the surface. "That's rough," he said, "but it gives the idea."

"A silencer-damped screw beat from the *Ram*," said Ramsey.

"Two of our A-2 fish hooked in tandem and their screws set to resonate," said Sparrow.

"It might fool an EP until he got close enough to detect the difference in mass," said Ramsey.

Sparrow nodded. "And what if our pair of fish carried a scrambler set to go off before they could detect mass difference?"

Ramsey stepped back from the board, stared at Sparrow.

"These are shallow waters," he said. "The EPs would blanket the distortion area and flood it with seeker fish and—"

"And they'd get a very satisfactory explosion," said Sparrow.

"This is all very well, but how're we going to rig our fish out there when we're in 700 feet of water and unable to start our engines?" asked Garcia.

"We've a perfect stabilizer," said Sparrow. "The slug. We bleed air into our tanks until we gain enough buoyance to lift; then we pay out towline until we reach 300 feet where we can go outside and do our work. The slug anchors us."

"Balance on the four points of the towlines," muttered Garcia. "It'll bloody well work. It will." He looked up at Sparrow. "Skipper, you're a genius."

"Can you two rig those fish to fake the sound of our screw?" asked Sparrow.

Ramsey grinned. "Just let us out there."

"One more thing," said Sparrow. "I'll want you to alter the drive speed controls like this—" Again, he bent over the chart board, scribbling on the scratch pad.

Ramsey shook his head. "Just a minute, Skipper."

Sparrow stopped, looked up at Ramsey.

The electronics officer took the pencil from Sparrow's hand. "To the devil with speed only. That's too complicated. What you want is a sound variation: first the *sound* of a Hell Diver subtug under quarter speed, then half speed, and then full speed to simulate flight." He sketched in a series of matched harmonics. "We'll just change the resonating factor and—"

"The adjustments to change resonance won't give it much increase in speed," said Garcia.

"It'll be enough," said Sparrow. "They won't be looking for refinements. Johnny's plan is simpler, less likely to break down." He put a hand on the sketch pad. "Can you two do it?"

Garcia nodded. "Get us up there."

Sparrow turned back to the control board, strode across to Bonnett. "You hear that, Les?"

"Enough to get the idea." He tilted his head toward the search board. "Still no sounds of those boys."

"Let's hope they run right up onto Novaya Zemlya," said Sparrow. "Give us a half a percent buoyancy in the bow tank."

Bonnett stepped to his left, turned a valve wheel a fraction of a degree, watched a dial above it, closed the valve.

"Joe, play us up on the towlines," said Sparrow.

Garcia moved to the tow controls, released the magnetics clutch on the big master reel. Slowly, almost imperceptibly, the *Ram* lifted off the bottom, slid upward.

They watched the static pressure gauge climb through 200 pounds to the square inch, 180 . . . 160 . . . 140 . . .

"Slow us down," ordered Sparrow.

Garcia fed a little power into the magnetic brakes. 130 . . . 120 . . . 115 . . .

"Snub us," ordered Sparrow.

The needle stopped on 110 pounds.

"That's close enough to 250 feet," said Sparrow. "Joe, Johnny, this is your show."

Garcia secured the tow board. "Better watch the balance on these lines," he said. "If the current shifts—"

"That's our worry," said Sparrow. "I'd blow tanks before I'd pull you two down into high pressure."

Garcia smiled wanly. "Sorry, Skipper. You know how I feel about—"

"You've a good electronics man with you," said Sparrow. He nodded toward Ramsey, looked significantly at Garcia.

"I'm with you, Skipper," said Garcia.

Ramsey thought: *Why doesn't he just say, "Keep an eye on this suspicious character?"* He looked at Garcia. "You afraid of the water?"

Garcia's dark features paled.

"That will be enough," said Sparrow. "You've a job to do."

Ramsey shrugged. "Let's go swimming," he said, turned toward the forward door and led the way out onto the engine-room catwalk, up the ladder to the escape hatch.

The sea suits and aqualungs were in a slide locker beside the hatch. Ramsey yanked one set out, stepped aside for Garcia, fitted himself for the sea. Finished, he undogged the hatch, climbed inside, and leaned against the ring rail.

Garcia followed, checked his mouthpiece, pulled it aside, and glared at Ramsey. "Somewhere, someday, someone is going to thump your head for you."

"Yeah, head thumper."

Ramsey stared at the engineering officer. "What do—"

"You psycho boys are all alike," said Garcia. "You think you're the custodians of deep, dark knowledge . . . sole custodians."

"I don't—"

"Come off that," said Garcia.

"But I thought you—"

"Yes?" Garcia grinned at him—a mirthless expression.

"Well, I—"

"You thought I had you pegged for a spy, a jolly old sleeper," said Garcia. He shook his head. "None such. I'm quite certain you're not."

"What gives you the idea I'm a psych man?"

"We're wasting time," said Garcia. He jammed his mouthpiece into place, pulled up the hatch, and dogged it.

Ramsey put the cold rubber of the mouthpiece between his teeth, tested the air. It tasted of chemicals, bitter.

Garcia spun the sea valve.

Cold water rushed in around them, spewing upward onto the circular walls, whirling in swift currents.

A kick of fin flippers took Ramsey to the open hatch. Outside was utter blackness broken only by the glow from the escape compartment and the small hand lamp carried by Garcia. The long Arctic night on the surface and the cover of water conspired to create an utter absence of light. In spite of the reflecting layers of his sea suit, Ramsey could feel the chill of the water begin to bite into him.

Garcia held to the hatch guard with one hand as he rigged a safety line onto his belt. The hand lamp clipped to his wrist pointed down toward the waist rack of torpedoes: thin deadly shapes stuck through the metal guide slots like bullets in a belt.

Ramsey fastened his own belt clip to the safety line.

Garcia pointed his hand lamp back into the hatchway, indicated another line snaking out of the green gloom of the escape compartment. Ramsey pulled on the line, brought out a tool kit.

A current caught at Ramsey, pulled him away from the hatch. He was snubbed short by the safety line, swam back and caught up the kit.

Garcia kicked off the hull, swam down toward the torpedo rack. Ramsey turned for one look upward toward the night-cloaked surface, followed. The engineering officer stopped at a torpedo low down on the rack, keeping well clear of the finned arming rotor on the torpedo's nose. Yellow stripes behind the arming rotor identified it as a short-range, low-blast model for infighting.

Row on row of the deadly metal fish extended upward around the *Ram*'s waist.

Garcia patted the torpedo, looked at Ramsey.

Ramsey shook his head, pointed to one below it: red stripes—a long-range seeker.

Garcia nodded.

They dropped down to the torpedo, cautiously disarmed it. Ramsey noted the number: fourteen, pointed to it. Garcia nodded.

Ramsey unhinged the side plate, motioned for the light. Its beam shone into the torpedo. He had already figured out the changes necessary: disconnect seeker circuit, reset for level course; drive-timer coupling racked back to new control order—400 revolutions, 600 . . . 800. He forgot to worry about Garcia in the concentration of work.

Presently, it was done. They dropped down to another torpedo of the same model, repeated the changes except for the calculated resonance factor. Then it was time to disconnect the upper torpedo, lower it down beside the second, link the two carefully with swivel bolts.

Below the altered torpedoes, Ramsey sought out the solid yellow and red nose of a scrambler model, inserted the seeker capsule from the first unit they had changed. He tied this torpedo to the other two with a length of light cable.

Toward the last he found himself working in less and

less light. He seated the final cable clamp, looked up the hull.

Garcia floated high along the rack; now he was swimming toward the escape compartment. Swimming fast. The sea's darkness swept down around Ramsey.

*Is he going to trap me out here? Close the hatch against me?*

Panic washed over him. He flailed the fin flippers, swept up toward the receding light.

*Garcia could wait in the compartment until he was almost out of air, knowing I'd be in the same fix. Then he could go inside to safety. I'd drown before they could come back out. Hed' have a plausible story about me disappearing.*

Garcia's light sank into the escape compartment, leaving the darkness behind.

*I'm not going to make it!*

The safety line abruptly snubbed him up short. Ramsey tugged at it. Fouled on something! He fought the belt connection, freed it, resumed his flailing progress toward the hatch, a faint glow from Garcia's light against the blackness.

Now, he was over the hatch. Ramsey grabbed the rail, felt a hand take his, pull him inside. Garcia! Ramsey felt a wave of relief. The light in the compartment showed that Garcia had been reeling in the safety line. It stretched taut between reel and hatch. The snag. Garcia pointed toward the hatch.

*He wants me to go out and free it,* thought Ramsey. He shook his head.

Again Garcia pointed toward the hatch.

Again Ramsey shook his head.

Garcia hesitated, then swung up the line and out the hatch, taking the portable light with him. Presently, he returned and the line sagged. He reeled it onto its drum, sealed the outside hatch.

Ramsey opened the high-pressure air valve. The water level began to lower.

When it reached their shoulders, they unhooked the

face connections of the aqua lungs. Garcia's mouth held a subtle hint of amusement.

*He knows he frightened me,* thought Ramsey. *He did it deliberately.*

The last of the water swished out of the sea cock. Garcia undogged the inner hatch, led the way out onto the upper catwalk of the engine room. Silently, they stripped the suits from their bodies, returned to the control deck.

Sparrow met them at the door. "Well?"

"All done," said Garcia. "Fourteen is linked to twenty-two. They'll both fire on twenty-two's stud. They'll seek a northerly course and hold about ten fathoms off bottom."

Sparrow looked at Ramsey, who nodded. The skipper turned back to Garcia. "Run into any trouble?"

"Johnny's the electronics man. He did all the work."

Sparrow turned to Ramsey.

"It was fairly easy."

Garcia said, "Johnny's safety line snagged on the way in, but I freed it. Outside of that, it was a quiet swim."

"All quiet in here, too," said Sparrow. He nodded toward a cot on the far side of the control room, Bonnett stretched out on it. "Les is getting some shut-eye. You two had better do the same. We're going to sit here for a while."

"Righto," said Garcia. "The swim made me tired. Let's go, Johnny boy." He ducked through the door, went down the companionway, Ramsey following.

Garcia stopped at the door of his room, turned and smiled at Ramsey. "Pleasant dreams . . . head thumper."

Ramsey brushed past him into his own room, locked the door behind him, and leaned against it. He could feel his heart thumping heavily.

*Damn that man!*

He fought himself into a semblance of calmness, went to the telemeter box, examined the new lengths of tape.

Sparrow was still locked in icy control.

Ramsey reset the box, turned off his lights, fell into his bunk and into a restless sleep. It seemed that he had just closed his eyes when he was aroused by the buzzer. He got up stiffly, went forward to the control deck. The others already were there.

"Take over the search board," said Sparrow. He waited for Ramsey to comply, depressed the firing-board stud at number twenty-two.

Immediately, Ramsey picked up the beat of it on his instruments. He felt Sparrow move into position beside him. Together, they stared at the scope.

"Good job," said Sparrow. "Looks just like our pip."

Ramsey rotated the outside bell-detector of the ranging system. "No sign of a stake-out," he said.

"That would be a bitter one," said Garcia. "All of our yeoman efforts out there gone for nought. I'd almost ra—"

"There he is," said Ramsey. "Northeast and coming fast."

"Interception course," said Sparrow.

"And there's the first speed increase in our decoy," said Ramsey.

"Couldn't have been better timing," said Bonnett.

"Another signal to the west," said Ramsey. "Our stake-out has called his pals."

"And there's full-speed simulation," said Sparrow. "Wonderful job, Johnny!"

"And waited, watching the signals merge. Abruptly, the instruments gyrated wildly as the decoy's scrambler system was activated.

Again they waited.

A distant double thump resonated against the *Ram*'s hull and simultaneously, the scrambler signal stopped.

"Now track every one of them," said Sparrow. "If those EPs all leave, we've made it."

Ramsey watched the signals. "Pack quartering over the explosion area. Four departing." He waited. "Two more. Courses southwest. There go the last ones."

He tracked them until they went off his instruments,

turned with a triumphant smile and looked at Sparrow. "Just as you planned it, Skipper."

"Ummmm, yes." He turned away. "We'll wait here another four hours before going on into the well area."

The *Ram* crept up the fissure at quarter speed, lifted out in six hundred feet of water and slid upslope like a giant fish seeking its dinner in the bottom mud. Inside, Sparrow stood at the helm, Garcia with him.

"There's the ledge," said Sparrow. He nodded toward the screen above them. It showed a pie slice of illumination cut from the dark waters by the bow lights, a rocky outcropping.

"Shall I call the others?" asked Garcia.

"Yes."

Garcia pressed the call button. Ramsey acknowledged from the electronics shack.

"What are you doing in the electronics shack?" asked Sparrow.

"I couldn't rest, so I—"

"My orders that we were to work only in double teams didn't interest you?"

"Skipper, I had an idea about—"

"Just a moment." Sparrow pointed to the screen above him, a starfish-shaped mound. "Right on, Joe." He disengaged the drive, drifted up on the mound, past it, grounded.

"Two hundred and five pounds even, Skipper."

Sparrow nodded, plugged in the side-eyes, examined the bottom, "Plenty of mud for ballast."

Bonnett entered. "Skipper, are we—"

"We've arrived," said Sparrow. "Les, will you go aft to the shack and check on Johnny?"

"Isn't he—"

"He's been in the shack for some time . . . alone!"

Bonnett whirled around, disappeared down the companionway.

"I will not be responsible for revealing the site of this well," said Sparrow.

"What do you mean?" asked Garcia. "You don't think I—"

Sparrow froze him with a look. "Mr. Garcia, we've been shipmates since you were a chief machinist and I was a dryback ensign; but right now I wouldn't trust you as far as I could see you. One of Security's men was trapped and killed aboard my ship. The EPs got spy beams aboard us. Someone did it. Do I make myself clear?"

"Yes, sir." Garcia turned back to the search board.

In the electronics shack, Ramsey held up the tube on which he had been working. *This has to be how they set off their spy beam,* he thought. *And it means they could have another one ready to go any second.*

His hand trembled as he reached out to plug the tube into a test socket. The hand was abruptly knocked aside and a fist crashed into the side of his jaw.

"You dirty spying bastard!" growled Bonnett. Again his fist crashed into Ramsey's jaw.

Ramsey— bent backward over the bench—tried to dodge aside. "Les, wait! I—"

"Gonna save us the price of a trial," gritted Bonnett. He crashed an elbow into Ramsey's mouth, lifted a knee to the groin.

*My God! He means to kill me!* thought Ramsey. He fought back desperately, chopping an arm at Bonnett's throat. Nausea from the groin blow clutched him.

Bonnett dodged Ramsey's blow, sent another fist into the electronics officer's mouth.

"For God's sake!" screamed Ramsey. "I'm no spy!"

"You dirty, lying, sneaking—" Bonnett stepped back, chopped the side of his hand into the curve of Ramsey's neck, sent a fist crashing into Ramsey's jaw.

Ramsey felt himself going blank, waved his arms futilely in front of him. Something crashed against the side of his head. He felt a sledge-hammer blow over his heart and blacked out.

Voices.

They came to Ramsey from somewhere at the top of

a long black hole. He tried to ignore them, moved his head. Pain shot through him.

"I think he's coming around." Garcia.

"Here. Make him drink this." Sparrow.

"Why waste it?" Bonnett.

"I'm not satisfied that you're correct." Sparrow.

"I tell you, Skipper, I saw him putting that spy-beam tube into a socket and—"

"How do you know it was a spy beam? One of you stepped on it and crushed it during that fracas."

"It looked damned suspicious, Skipper."

"Looked . . . schmooked." Garcia.

Hand under his neck. Something acid and biting in his mouth, burning his throat.

Choking, coughing.

Ramsey gagged, retched.

Again the liquid was forced past his lips. He shuddered, managed to keep it down. His body felt like one large ache.

"Can you talk, Johnny?" Sparrow.

Ramsey opened his eyes. Sparrow bent over him, supporting his shoulders.

Bonnett and Garcia stood beyond.

Ramsey's eyes focused on the rest of his surroundings: rec room, cot, table, and first-aid kit.

Back to Bonnett and Garcia.

Bonnett glowering, perhaps a bit uncertain.

Garcia faintly worried.

Ramsey groped toward his jaw with one hand, felt a lance of fire shoot through his head. "I c'n talk a li'l," he said.

Sparrow brought some pillows up behind Ramsey, eased him back onto them. "What were you doing in the shack?"

The tube! Spy beam!

Ramsey forced the words past his thickened lips. "Think I found out how spy beam triggered."

Sudden interest in the eyes of Sparrow and Garcia. More uncertainty in Bonnett's expression.

"By someone on board?" asked Sparrow.

"No. This's urgen', Skipper. Don' raise th' peri-box."

"Why?"

"Piping in a signal."

"The air's full of stuff. What—"

"This's special. You gave me idea." Ramsey passed his tongue over his thickened lips, forced himself to speak clearly. "Go'to un'erstan'me," he said. "Resonance. EPs are sending out a harmonic on th' plate frequency of our L-4 tubes. Eventually, it breaks 'em down so they become microphonic. Th' tubes we found were just amplifiers. Spy beam actually comes from th' L-4s."

"But if we've taken out all the amplifiers—"

"Enough L-4s sending and they'd interact in feedback," said Garcia. "Wouldn't need an amplifier. They'd set up a howl that could be heard anywhere."

"Why the peri-box?" asked Sparrow. Then he said, "Of course: they have to get a clear strong signal into us and the peri-box is the only road that isn't damped by a plasteel hull."

He shook his head. "Granting that you're telling the truth and that this is so, how can—"

"Rig a substitute for the L-4s," said Garcia. "That's the weak spot in the system."

"That's what I was testing when Les jumped me," said Ramsey.

Bonnett scowled. "This could be a trick, Skipper."

Garcia said, "Can it, Les?"

"Dammit all!" shouted Bonnett. "Yesterday you were both telling me how suspicious—"

"We'll discuss it another time," said Sparrow. He turned to Garcia. "What do you think, Joe?"

"It sounds right, Skipper." Garcia held up a hand, ticked off items on his fingers. "It has the advantage of simplicity: all they'd have to know is the plate frequency factor of a suitable tube and they could channel all their efforts toward breaking down that one unit. If the actual signal originates with them and is merely rebroadcast from our system, they'd have the essential elements of a sonoran system: pin-point accuracy in locating us. And what would be harder to detect? Their broadcast would be a constant sound in the ether; so every time we raised our peri-box, our board filters would automatically cut out that signal as nondangerous and we wouldn't be listening at all on the wave length that would be likely to give us away!"

Even Bonnett was nodding in agreement as Garcia finished.

Garcia looked at Ramsey. "Is that the way you had it figured?"

"Yes."

"I could probably figure out a substitute system to eliminate the L-4s," said Garcia, "but you're the electronics expert. How?"

"Schematic on shack workbench," said Ramsey.

"Les, check that," ordered Sparrow. "If it's true, it's one more item to confirm his story."

Bonnett went out the door.

Ramsey shut his eyes, tried to slide off the pillows and stretch out flat on the cot.

"Better not," said Sparrow. He held Ramsey upright. "Joe, steady him here a moment while I look at that nose."

Garcia held Ramsey's shoulders.

Sparrow touched Ramsey's nose gently.

"Ouch!" Ramsey jerked back.

"Doesn't appear to be broken," said Sparrow. He reached out, put a thumb on Ramsey's left eyelid, held up the lid while he flashed a hand light into the eye. "Maybe a slight concussion."

"How long was I out?" asked Ramsey.

"About an hour," said Sparrow. "You—"

Bonnett entered carrying a grease-stained sheet of note paper. He passed the paper to Garcia, who removed one hand from Ramsey's shoulder to take the paper.

"What do you say, Joe?" asked Sparrow.

Garcia studied the paper silently, nodded once, passed it to Sparrow. "A clever adaptation. Simple. It'll work and it uses a tube with a different plate frequency."

"What does this mean?" asked Bonnett.

"It means you batted out, old chap," said Garcia. "In the vernacular, you goofed."

Bonnett's voice was dangerously low. "Is that so?"

"As a matter of honest fact, we've all goofed," said Garcia. "You were the overt instrument of our dereliction."

Bonnett looked down at Ramsey. "If I made a mistake, I apologize." He glanced at Sparrow, who was still studying Ramsey's schematic diagram. "But I reserve the right to my own opinion."

Sparrow straightened from beside Ramsey's bunk, looked at Garcia. "Keep him awake for a couple of hours, Joe." He turned away. "Come along, Les. We've a slug to fill and some tube-jockeying. No time to waste."

"Do you want me to do the electronics work?" asked Garcia.

"You stick with him," said Sparrow. He pushed in the doorway, stared speculatively at Ramsey, turned and left, followed by Bonnett.

"Do you think they could break down those L-4s without piping through the peri-box?" asked Garcia.

"In time," said Ramsey. "But they'd have to increase signal strength by several factors to get a return signal unamplified unless our box were on the surface."

"Clever devils," muttered Garcia. "How'd you spot it?"

"Skipper gave me the idea with his scheme for faking the sound of our screw."

"Got you thinking about resonance," said Garcia.

"About building signals with harmonics," corrected Ramsey.

"Same thing." Garcia came around in front of Ramsey. "Boy, he really worked you over."

"I guess he did."

"Your own fault, though."

Ramsey jerked his head up to stare at Garcia, winced at the sudden motion. "Why do you say that?"

"For some reason, you've deliberately set out to make the skipper suspicious of you. But you forgot one thing: suspicion is contagious."

"The pressure's cooking your brains," said Ramsey.

"I wish I knew what you were trying to prove," said Garcia. "Maybe you're trying to beach the skipper."

"Nuts! You have too much imagination."

"We're alike there, Johnny. And time drags in a sub-tug. There's time for a good imagination to run wild." He stared at the bulkhead a moment. "That's the skipper's problem, too, really."

"That's a rare piece of insight," said Ramsey.

Garcia acted as though he had not heard. "Imagination is a weakness when too much responsibility hangs on your shoulders."

They felt the *Ram* move, stop.

"We're seating the pump onto that well cap," said Garcia. "It'll take us a couple of days to fill the slug, then home we go."

"If it were only that easy," said Ramsey.

Garcia turned, strode across to the rec-room bookshelf, found a book, searched in it for a moment, and brought it back to Ramsey. "I think you'd better read this, Johnny. It's Savvy Sparrow's favorite passage."

He handed Ramsey a Bible, pointing to the beginning of a chapter, said, "Isaiah, twenty-seven, one and two."

Ramsey read it through silently, then reread it aloud:

" 'In that day the Lord with his sore and great and strong sword shall punish leviathan the piercing serpent, even leviathan that crooked serpent; and he shall slay the dragon that is in the sea.' "

Garcia continued the quotation from memory:

" 'In that day sing ye unto her, A vineyard of red wine.' "

Ramsey stared at the passage, shook his head. "What's it mean to him?"

Garcia said, "And he shall slay the dragon that is

in the sea." He reached down, took back the Bible. "To Savvy Sparrow, we're the dragon in the sea."

"Here, let me have that," said Ramsey. He took back the Bible. "Think I'll read for a while."

"Look out, or you'll get religion," said Garcia.

"No chance," said Ramsey. "My teachers always said if you want to understand a subject, study the basic source. This is it for our captain."

"For a great many people," said Garcia softly. "And a psychologist who does not have an intimate knowledge of that book is a doctor without instruments. And blind, to boot."

Ramsey looked at Garcia over the top of the book. "When are you going to give up that line?"

"When you wake up," said Garcia.

Ramsey hid a frown behind the Bible, opened it again to the passage Garcia had pointed out, soon lost himself in the fury of Isaiah and the woe of Hezekiah and the thundering messages of prophecy.

In the cold Arctic waters outside the *Ram,* pumps turned, hose nozzles sought out bottom muck for ballast. The plastic slug began to swell with its cargo of oil—like a live thing drinking at a jugular in the earth.

The hands of the timelog swept around, around. Fifty-one hours at the well.

Full slug. It stretched out on the bottom behind the *Ram,* turgid with its cargo, now almost a mile long, held in delicate hydrostatic balance so that it would tow beneath the surface.

Ramsey and Garcia entered the control room together. Sparrow and Bonnett already were there.

Garcia nodded at something Ramsey had said. "You're right. We'd better—"

"Right about what?" asked Sparrow.

"Johnny was just saying that the slug's compensator system would drop ballast if we try to pull that deep-dive maneuver on the way home."

"He's right," said Sparrow. "And if we don't compensate, we'll rupture the slug."

"And bleed oil all over the surface," said Bonnett. "Wouldn't that be lovely, now."

"There might be a way to pull it off," said Sparrow. "But let's hope we don't have to try it." He turned to the control board. "Les, lift us off. Minimum headway. Take us right down into the gut. We're going to use it for cover as long as we're able."

"Aye." Bonnett's hands moved over the controls.

"Wouldn't they be likely to lay for us in a place like that?" asked Ramsey.

"We're dead, remember?" said Garcia.

Sparrow said, "Joe, take over auxiliary search and keep us down the center of that canyon. Johnny, get on standard search and watch for enemy pips." He folded his arms in front of him. "The Lord has been kind to us, gentlemen. We're going home."

"A milk run," said Garcia.

"For mad dogs and Englishmen," said Bonnett.

The *Ram*'s deck tilted upward, hung there for a moment. Slowly, the slug lifted behind them, followed. They slanted down into the gut.

"One degree right," said Garcia. "Steady as she goes."

"Steady as she goes," sang Bonnett.

"Here's where we thank our lucky stars that the slug will track us in sections of hull length," said Ramsey. "If we scrape the side wall—"

"Two degrees left," said Garcia.

"Two degrees left," acknowledged Bonnett.

Sparrow glanced at Ramsey. "You were saying."

"I was just making talk."

"Let's save the talk for rest camp," said Sparrow. He turned back to the board in front of Bonnett. "We will take fatigue shots in three hours and at four-hour intervals until we've cleared the Arctic Circle. Let me know immediately if any of you show a Larson reaction from them."

Bonnett said, "They tell me those shots lop the sleepless hours off your life expectancy. Wonder if there's anything in that?"

"I once heard the moon was made of green cheese," said Garcia.

"Shall we pay attention to business, gentlemen?" asked Sparrow.

Ramsey smiled. He could sense the increased vital drive in the crew like a strong outpouring of elation. He rubbed at the sore spot on his jaw where Bonnett had hit him, thought: *It came at me from an unexpected angle, but Catharsis Number One has come and gone. AND I'm still alive. And Sparrow's still functioning.*

The captain cleared his throat. "As soon as we've cleared the Norwegian basin we should be out of immediate danger. Their search packs should be ranging the Iceland passage now and they won't be expecting someone from behind them. Our chief worry is picket tugs, line replacements moving up: the chance passerby."

"I've decided I'm going to die of old age," said Garcia. "That's my chief worry."

"You're getting old before your time," said Bonnett.

"One degree left," said Garcia.

"One degree left," acknowledged Bonnett.

Deep in the underwater canyon, the *Ram* coursed generally westward. At the sill of the Norwegian basin, they lost the gut as it shoaled, crept along the basin rim, course 276 degrees. The bottom depth crept upward. They were in 200 fathoms when they swung south to parallel the Norwegian coast line, course 201 degrees.

Eighty-one hours, fifty-eight minutes from the well, still two degrees above the Arctic Circle. Ramsey said, "Signal!" and slapped the switch which silenced their motors.

I'm just getting them on the outer limits of the long-range system: say thirty-five miles."

"Resume speed," said Sparrow. "They have nothing that'll reach that far."

"They'll be off my board in a minute at present course," said Ramsey.

"Southeast, ranging westerly and maybe a bit south."

"We'll play it safe anyway," said Sparrow. "Ten minutes run due east, then resume course."

Garcia at the helm, acknowledged. The *Ram*

"Course, distance, and direction?" asked Sparrow. changed course.

"Lost them," said Ramsey.

"Resume course," said Sparrow.

Again they came around to parallel the Norwegian coast. South they went, and then west-southwest to gain greater distance from the shore stations along the southern reaches of Norway. And again bearing to the south, and again westerly to give the Faeroes a wide berth. Now they were at the edge of the deeps southeast of Iceland. Watch and stand by: Ramsey and Sparrow on the control deck.

"You certainly called the shot," said Ramsey.

"Don't brag your luck," said Sparrow. "It'll change."

"What makes mariners so superstitious?" asked Ramsey.

"Awareness of the limits of our knowledge," said Sparrow. "And experience with the reality of luck."

"It's a wonder we don't have government-issue rabbits' feet."

"I'll suggest it when we—"

"Pack!" Ramsey slapped the silencer switch. "They're onto us, Skipper! They were lying doggo!"

Sparrow kicked the alarm buzzer, brought the engines to life.

"They're right in our path," said Ramsey. "Range fifteen miles."

"Sure-kill range," said Sparrow. He brought the sub-tug and tow around to the northeast, pulled the power bar to its last notch.

Bonnett and Garcia hurried into the control room.

"A pack on us," said Ramsey.

"On the controls, you two," said Sparrow.

Bonnett and Garcia moved into their battle stations, Bonnett at the helm, Garcia on the torpedo board. Sparrow stepped to Ramsey's side.

"There's bottom at 8800 feet," said Ramsey.

"We'll have to chance it," said Sparrow. "Les, take us down. Johnny, monitor the atmosphere."

Ramsey opened the control valve on the anhydrase generator one notch.

The subtug's deck slanted downward.

"Joe, call the depths," said Sparrow.

"Sixty-eight hundred feet and 2880 pounds . . . 7000 feet and 3010 pounds . . . 7500 and 3235 . . . 8000 and 3440 . . . 8500 and 3655—"

"Coast in," said Sparrow.

Bonnett silenced the drive.

Garcia's voice continued: "—8600 and 3700 . . . variation, Skipper—"

"—8700 and 3750 . . . that's nine pounds over normal, Skipper—"

"Noted."

"—8750 and 3780 . . . that's eighteen pounds over . . ."

"Noted. Les, flatten the glide angle and give us the bow eye on the main screen."

"Bottom is forty feet," said Ramsey. "The pack is closing fast. Range about eleven miles."

The big screen above their heads showed its pie slice of light and, abruptly, bottom mud.

"Drop the slug in first," said Sparrow.

Bonnett brought up the bow planes until they felt the drag of the slug behind them. The *Ram* settled onto bottom mud in 8800 feet. The big static pressure gauge read 3804 pounds even: Twenty pounds above normal for the depth.

"Pack range nine miles and fanning out," said Ramsey. "I count sixteen of them."

"Fanning out," said Sparrow. "That means they're confused by our—"

"Two breaking away toward the surface," said Ramsey. "They think we've floated up."

"Over normal pressure," said Sparrow. "There's a cold density layer above us confusing our sound pattern. Unless they detect metal, we're safe."

"Unless we implode," said Bonnett.

"If we had some ham we'd have some ham and eggs, if we had some eggs," said Ramsey.

Garcia chuckled.

"The important thing is for us all to relax," said Sparrow. "We don't want the same complications we had last—"

"Complishmashuns," said Garcia. "Alla time talk-talk-talk-talk. So he can psycho . . . psy—So he can find out what makes us go tick-tick-tick-tick-tick-tick. Don't y', Johnny boy?"

Ramsey raised his eyebrows, looked at Sparrow. Sparrow shrugged, said, "Come along, Joe. You need a shot."

"Need a whole bottle," said Garcia. "Need a shy-coan'lyst like Johnny boy here. Don' I, Johnny boy?"

"I'm ordering you to come with me, Joe," said Sparrow.

Tears welled up in Garcia's eyes. "I need a conscience," he sobbed. "I wanna confess, but no one—"

"Come along!" Sparrow grabbed Garcia's arm, jerked him toward the aft door.

"Easy, Skipper," said Ramsey.

Sparrow took a deep breath. "Right."

"I'll come quietly," said Garcia. "No need get excited. I don' wanna be any trouble. I been enough trouble. I been terrible trouble. Never forgive me. Never."

He allowed himself to be led out the door, still mumbling, "Never . . . never . . . never . . . never . . ."

"Quoth the raven," said Ramsey. He rubbed absently at the still-sensitive bruise on his jaw where Bonnett had hit him.

"That figures," said Bonnett.

"Huh?"

"Head thumper. BuPsych rang you in on us."

"Not you, too, Brutus," said Ramsey.

"Sure, it figures," said Bonnett. "Hepp went loco, so they rang you in on us to find out why."

"What?"

"Sure. You want to see which of us is next."

"Me, if I hear any more of this nutty talk. I've—"

"Otherwise you're a spy," said Bonnett. "I guess you're not that."

"Of all the—"

"I'm trying to apologize," said Bonnett. "It isn't easy. Basically, I don't like head thumpers. You screw-doctors are all alike. Superior . . . know-it-all. Explanations for everything. Religion is a manifestation of deep-seated anxieties which—"

"Oh, knock it off," said Ramsey.

"What I'm trying to say is that I've felt better ever since I pounded you. Call it a cathartic. For a minute I had the enemy in my own hands. He was an insect I could crush."

"So?"

"So I've never had the enemy in my hands before." He held up his hands and looked at them. "Right there. I learned something."

"What?"

"This may sound asinine."

"Say it anyway."

"Maybe I'd better not."

"Nothing was ever more important than for you to focalize that thought," said Ramsey. And he thought: *No matter what I do, I'm cast in the role of analyst!*

Bonnett rubbed his hands against his shirt, looked at the control board. "When you meet your enemy and recognize him and touch him, you find out that he's like yourself: that maybe he's part of you." He shook his head. "I'm not saying this right."

"Try."

"I can't do it." Bonnett lowered his head, stared at the deck.

"What's it like? Try a comparison."

In a low, almost inaudible voice, Bonnett said, "It's

like when you're the youngest and weakest kid on the playground. And when the biggest kid smacks you, that's all right because he noticed you. That means you're alive. It's better than when they ignore you." He looked up at Ramsey. "Or it's like when you're with a woman and she looks at you and her eyes say you're a man. Yeah, that's it. When you're really alive, other people know it."

"What's that have to do with having the enemy in your hands?"

"He's alive," said Bonnett. "Dammit all, man, he's alive and he's got the same kind of aliveness that you have. Each of us is the enemy"— Bonnett's voice grew firmer—"to the other and to himself. That's what I mean: I'm the enemy within myself. Unless I master that enemy, I always lose."

Ramsey stared at Bonnett in amazement.

"Not the kind of thinking you'd expect from me," said Bonnett.

Ramsey shook his head.

"Why not? I feel things just like anybody else. So I hide it most of the time. Who am I hiding it from?" He sneered. "Me. That's who."

"What set you off?"

"I found someone I could talk to, someone who had to keep his professional mouth shut because—"

"Just a minute." Ramsey's gaze, never off the search-board instruments for more than a few seconds, had caught a sharp needle deflection. "Sonic search blast. There's another. If they're spaced on us, our hull will stick up like a sore thumb: a fat metal finger."

"They won't look for us down here."

"Don't count on it. There's anoth—"

"What's going on?" Sparrow ducked through the door into the control room.

"Sonic search bombs," said Ramsey. "The EPs are looking for a metallic bounce labeled *Fenian Ram*."

Sparrow moved closer to stand at Ramsey's shoulders. "And here comes one ranging over us."

"Fast," said Ramsey. He put his hand on the anti-torp volley switch.

"Leave that alone," said Sparrow. "They won't use a fish on an unidentified bump."

"He's inside of a mile," said Ramsey. "In the six-thousand foot level. There goes another search bomb."

They felt the dull bump of it through the hull.

"If one of our external fittings implodes, the shock wave'll crack us like—"

"We've all read the manual, Les," said Sparrow. He turned away from the board, bent his head. "Lord, we who have no right to ask it, do plead for your mercy. Thy will be done. . . . Whatever."

"He's turning away," whispered Ramsey.

"Lord, turn not away from thy—"

"That EP sub," said Ramsey. "He's turning away."

Sparrow lifted his head. "Thank you, Lord." He looked at Bonnett. "Joe's under sedation. Go back and stay with him."

Bonnett went out the aft door.

Sparrow again moved to stand beside Ramsey. "That was a good thing you did for Les."

Ramsey stiffened.

"I stood outside the door until he'd shed the load on his chest," said Sparrow. "You're a much deeper man than I'd suspected, Johnny."

"Oh, for Heaven's sake!"

"Yes, for Heaven's sake," said Sparrow. "You're a devious one."

Ramsey closed his eyes in exasperation, opened them. *I'm the father-confessor whether I like it or not,* he thought. "Garcia is off his rocker," he said.

"I've shipped with Joe for quite a number of years," said Sparrow. "I've seen him drunk before. Pressure drunkenness is no different. He's not the kind to make false accusations. That would be bearing false witness against—"

"He's just talking to—"

"He's troubled in the spirit," said Sparrow. "He needs

someone like you—a confessor. Did you ever stop to think that you boys are like priests in the way—"

"I've heard it mentioned," said Ramsey, and realized he had made a confession of identity.

Sparrow smiled. "Always have a way out the other side, Johnny. Have your safe line of retreat prepared. Joe hates you right now because he doesn't want to admit he needs you."

Ramsey thought: *Who's the doctor and who's the patient here?* He said, "Are you suggesting I copper my bets in the religious gamble?"

"No bet-coppering there," said Sparrow.

"Yeah, I guess you're right," agreed Ramsey. His mouth twisted into a wry smile. "That's like telling your psychoanalyst, 'I'm going to get married as soon as my analysis is finished.' You'll never finish." And he thought: *Well, the mask is off. Why do I feel relieved? That's suspicious. I shouldn't feel relieved.*

Sparrow studied the search board. "They're almost out of range." He began to hum, then in a low voice sang, "You'll never get to heaven on roller skates! You'll roll right past those pearly gates."

" 'I ain' gonna grieve my Lord no more,' " said Ramsey.

"What?" Sparrow turned away from the board.

"That's what you were singing: 'I ain' gonna grieve my Lord no more.' "

"So I was." Sparrow cocked his head toward the search board. "They're going out of range in the northeast quadrant. Surface currents set northeast here. That means they've decided we floated up. Give them an hour out of range."

Ramsey checked the sonic pickup monitor on the board, said, "All accounted for in that quadrant, Skipper. No stakeouts."

"Certain?"

Ramsey nodded toward the monitor tape.

"They're flustered and that means bad judgment every time," said Sparrow. "Remember that, Johnny. Keep calm no matter what and you'll—"

"Skipper!" It was Bonnett at the door behind them. They whirled.

"Joe's blood pressure. It's going up, then down, wider and wider. He acts like he's in shock and—"

Sparrow turned back to the board. "They're beyond range. Slide off, Johnny. Take us to 6000 feet. Fast!" He hurried toward the door. "Les, come with me."

"What about the slug?" called Ramsey.

Sparrow stopped in mid-stride, turned back to Ramsey. "I should listen to my own advice. Les, do what you can for Joe. Johnny, free the clutch on the tow cables." Sparrow moved to the main controls. "We'll have to lift the *Ram* and leave the slug on the bottom until we reach cable limit."

"Then try to jerk it off," said Ramsey.

"If we can get it started up, the compensator system will keep it coming," said Sparrow.

"If," said Ramsey.

"Drop two of our fish," said Sparrow.

Ramsey depressed two of the red-banded torpedo switches.

The subtug shifted, remained on the bottom.

"Two more," said Sparrow.

Again Ramsey selected two matched torpedo switches, depressed them.

The subtug's nose lifted gently, seemed to hesitate, resumed its rise. The tail came up. Ramsey fed power into the drive, raised the bow planes.

The *Ram* slid upward. They could feel the faint rumbling of the giant cable reel into the outer hull.

At 1700 feet, Sparrow said, "Try the brake."

Ramsey put pressure on the reel hub. The *Ram* strained against the lines.

"Five hundred feet more cable," said Ramsey.

Sparrow threw full power into the drive. "Lock the reel."

Ramsey closed the switch on the magnetic brake.

The subtug came almost to a full stop, then slowly resumed its climb. Ramsey watched the tow board. "That freed her, Skipper. Now, how much mud are we going to lose out of the compensator system?" He leaned to the right to adjust the atmosphere controls. "If we lose ballast, it'll be—"

"Skipper." In was Bonnett at the aft door.

Sparrow spoke without turning away from the controls. "How is he?"

"Resting easier." Bonnett looked at the big static pressure gauge. "It's only 2790 pounds now. We got off okay."

"Not okay yet," said Sparrow. "Take over the helm." He turned the wheel over to Bonnett, moved across to Ramsey's station.

"What course?" asked Bonnett.

"Steady on 197 degrees."

"Steady on 197 degrees," acknowledged Bonnett.

"We need some more luck," said Ramsey.

"St. Christopher is already getting overtime on this trip," said Bonnett.

"She seems to be maintaining hydrostatic balance," said Ramsey.

"Stay with that board," said Sparrow. "It's too soon to tell."

"Compartment twenty-seven is fluctuating a little," said Ramsey.

"How much?"

"Maybe five percent."

"Keep an eye on it." Sparrow went back to Bonnett's station. He stared up at the sonoran chart. "That pack left us in the corner of the northeast quadrant."

"They made a bad guess," said Bonnett.

Sparrow said, "Are you sure Joe is all right?"

"Everything was back to normal when I left him."

"Mmmm, hmmm." Sparrow nodded. "Don't sell that enemy commander short. He had inadequate information. The surface currents set that way." Sparrow pointed to the lower portion of the chart. "That's radioactive water to the south—contaminated by the British Isles. He knows we wouldn't turn east into the range of their shore station. *Ergo:* We went with the current."

Bonnett pointed to the red-outlined radioactive area

west of the British Isles. "There are deep cold currents setting south into that area, Skipper."

"You're reading my mind," said Sparrow.

"They wouldn't be as hot as the surface layers," said Bonnett.

"It depends on how well we're able to follow the thermal layer," said Sparrow.

"It'd be like nosing into a one-way pipe," said Ramsey, "We'd have to follow the thermal current of uncontaminated water. And what would happen if we had to come up through all that hot water? Uh, uh."

Sparrow said, "Let me figure this." He took a sheet of paper from his pocket, scribbled on it, stared at it, scribbled some more, again examined his work. "Steady as she goes on 197 degrees," he said. "It's our best chance."

Bonnett said, "What about Joe?"

"I'll go back and check him now. Stay here with Johnny. Let me know if outside water goes above 1000 milli-R."

"Aye."

The *Ram* coursed southeast, moving closer and closer to the blighted Scottish coast, rising to shallower and shallower waters. The relatively radiation-free thermal current thinned until it was not quite twice the *Ram*'s hull diameter from top to bottom: about 120 feet.

Sparrow returned from the rec room. "He's okay now. No residual effects." He stepped across to the tow board. "Any more fluctuation in compartment twenty-seven?"

"Negative. We haven't been in one depth long enough for me to get a check on the pressure constant." Ramsey looked at the search board, watched the green face of the ranging scope. "Not a pip out of those EP packs." He turned to Sparrow. "Could we risk a slave pulse inside the slug? I'd like to get something positive on the relative densities."

Sparrow pulled at his lower lip, looked at the ranging scope. "Okay. Just one."

Ramsey set up the recording dials on the tow board, pushed the sonar-pulse button. Dial needles surged: the time-over-density counter buzzed.

Sparrow said: "Ballast compartment's slow forward."

Ramsey compared the outer and inner time recordings. "Oil in the ballast," he said. "There's a pressure break on the inside."

"And we're painting an oily path on the surface!" barked Sparrow. "If the EPs have an air patrol over this area they'll spot the slick. They might just as well have an engraved chart of our course."

Ramsey turned to the timelog. "Four hours to daylight topside. What's the Security word on EP air patrols over these hot waters?"

"Dunno. I wish they'd —"

"What's wrong?" Garcia stood in the aft door.

Sparrow said, "You're not supposed to be up. Get back to sick bay."

"I'm okay." He stepped onto the control deck. "What's going on?"

"We're leaking oil," said Bonnett.

Garcia's gaze darted to the sonoran chart. "Holy Mother! What're we doing down here?"

Sparrow said, "Les, take us up. Johnny, monitor the outside radiation. Mark each 1000-milli-R increase. Let me know immediately if that ruptured oil compartment starts to blow." He turned toward Garcia, studied him for a minute. "Joe, do you feel up to rigging us for slug repair?"

Garcia shrugged. "Why not? I've just had a good rest. What'd I do this time?"

"A cheap drunk," said Bonnett. "Where'd you hide the bottle?" He bent to turn the wheel on the bow planes.

"Two degrees! No more," barked Sparrow.

"Two degrees," acknowledged Bonnett.

Garcia moved forward, went through the door onto the engine-room catwalk.

"Reading 2200 milli-R," said Ramsey. "Pressure 690 pounds to the square inch."

Sparrow said, "Oil loss?"

"Fifty-five gallons a minute. Constant."

Sparrow said, "I'll take over here, Johnny. Go forward and help Joe."

"Aye." Ramsey surrendered his position, went to the forward door, stepped through onto the catwalk. The electric engines were four droning hives around him, the gray metal of their casings gleaming dully in the stand-by lights. Through the webwork of girders, catwalks, and ladders, Ramsey could see Garcia high above him near the escape hatch unreeling a safety line, readying it for the outside spools.

Ramsey mounted the ladders, came up behind Garcia. "Looks like I'm going swimming again, Joe."

Garcia glanced back, returned his attention to his work. "This one's on me."

Ramsey bent over, steadied the spool. "Why?"

"I'm the best swimmer aboard. It stands to—"

"Somehow I got the idea you might be afraid of the water."

Garcia grinned, then frowned. "I was responsible for a man dying in a water-polo game. Broke his neck. That was supposed to be a game. This is business."

"But you just got up from pressure sickness."

"I've had a good rest." He straightened. "Hand me down that patching kit from the bulkhead rack. That's a good fellow."

Ramsey turned to the bulkhead, found the underwater patch kit, removed it. Behind him, he heard Garcia on the intercom.

"Is it compartment twenty-seven?"

"Yes. Why?" Sparrow's voice impersonalized by the speaker system.

"How'm I going to fix—"

"I'm doing this one, Joe. That's—"

"I'm rested, Skipper, and I feel fine. Remember me? Swimming champ?"

Silence. Then: "Are you sure you feel okay?"

"Tiptop, Skipper. Never better."

"Ramsey."

Ramsey turned, then grinned at the reaction, pushed the button on his chest mike. "Here, Skipper."

"How's Joe look?"

Ramsey looked at Garcia. "Same as ever."

"Okay, Joe. But if you start feeling funny, come back in immediately. That's an order."

"Righto, Skipper. How much oil we losing?"

"It's been going down as we climbed. Now it's about thirty gallons a minute. Have Ramsey rig you in a detergent suit. That oil is mucky stuff to work in."

Garcia said, "Remember in refresher school when your suit system failed? You looked like a—"

"All right, Joe. Some other time."

"How hot is it out there, Skipper?"

"You can take it for about one hour, Joe. That means you would be starting back within forty minutes."

"That's cutting it close, Skipper. Is there a margin?"

"I don't think so. Watch your suit counter. We're stabilized now at 150 feet. We'll slip down and balance on the pumps. Outside pressure is sixty-six pounds to the square inch. Milli-R . . . 9050. You're on, Joe. Be careful."

Ramsey said, "Shouldn't I go out with him, Skipper?"

"I don't want two of us on the radiation-limit list if I can help it," said Sparrow. "Get yourself rigged and stand by for an emergency call."

"Aye." Ramsey pulled a detergent suit from its locker, helped Garcia into it, tested the seals.

Garcia spoke over his suit system. "Make sure I'm tight. The suit will give me a little margin."

Again Ramsey went over the seals. "You're tight."

"Control deck, do you read me?"

"Loud and clear, Joe."

"I'm going into the hatch now."

"We'll follow you on the eyes. Be careful."

"Righto." Garcia swung open the escape hatch, clambered through, closed the hatch behind him.

Ramsey heard the water pouring into the locker chamber. He turned, pulled out another detergent suit, donned it. His own suit seals came in for a double

check. He could hear Bonnett's voice over the intercom: "Lock pressure equalized. Outer door open . . .
closed."

Sparrow's voice: "Johnny?"

"Aye."

"Into the lock as soon as the water's out of it. Seal
the hatch and stand by to flood it."

High pressure air roared and the green light beside
the hatch flashed clear. "In I go," said Ramsey. He
worked the outside dog controls, breached the hatch,
climbed inside the escape chamber, sealed the hatch
behind him. The flood-valve release light blinked on.
He leaned against the ring rail within reach of the
valve, settled down to wait.

"Keep an open talk switch," said Sparrow.

"You mean me?" asked Ramsey.

"Yes. Joe's out of range of the stern eyes now."

Ramsey watched the water dripping from the damp
flood-valve control, glanced at his suit snooper. Some
residual radiation: about twenty-three-hour dosage.
He looked around the oval compartment, up to the egg
dome of the outside hatch. Garcia was out there, probably through the stricture valve by now and into the
viscous crude of compartment twenty-seven. Ramsey
could imagine the patient search by feel in the black
muck of oil. His eyes began to get heavy and he opened
the oxy regulator of his lung suit a crack.

The hands of the timelog swept around: fifty-five
minutes.

"Ramsey!"

He snapped up, realized he had been dozing. "Aye,
Skipper."

"We've given Joe all the time we're able. Really too
much. Go see what's wrong . . . and be careful."

"Right." Ramsey spun the big wheel of the flood
valve, felt the gush of water around his ankles. It
surged up about him, tugging at his suit. The warning
light and buzzer of his snooper came on simultaneously.
The red needle swung into the seventy-minute zone.

Compartment pressure equalized. Ramsey undogged

the outside hatch, swung it clear, and locked it in open position. They could free the magna-lock inside if they had to and this would save time. He pulled a hand light from its wall rack, kicked his fin flippers, and drifted out the hatch opening. Immediately, he felt a wave of aloneness. No intercom out here where signals could be heard by the enemy.

The hand light picked out Garcia's safety line snaking away in the darkness. Ramsey hooked his suit ring to it, struck out along the line. The water had an inky quality that swallowed the glow of the light. He sensed the bulk of the slug ahead and above him before he could actually see it and was struck by the oddity of the feeling. The line ran aft along the plastic wall, looped upward onto an external knob.

Ramsey tugged at the line. No response. He swam up to the knob. A coil of the line was caught in a half hitch around the projection, the end disappearing into a tiny hole through the slug's surface.

Fouled control on the stricture valve. Ramsey freed the half hitch, again tugged on the line. He grabbed the projection, felt the valve control through it, pulled downward and turned.

A gush of oil shot out around the safety line as the hole expanded. The oil diffused upward, leaving a darker shape within its cloud. The darker shape moved toward Ramsey's light trailing an oily smudge. Ramsey closed the stricture valve, reached out and touched the moving shape. A hand gripped his shoulder through the suit: once, twice, three times.

All well.

They turned together, swam back with the safety line. The hatch light glowed out of darkness and they followed it in. Ramsey unhooked the safety line while Garcia was entering the compartment, dragged the coil in behind him. Garcia brought the hatch down, dogged it. Ramsey cracked open the high pressure air line, turned to face Garcia.

"Are you okay in there?" Sparrow's voice over the intercom.

Ramsey said, "Apparently, Skipper."

"Joe's had a twenty-five minute overdose," said Sparrow.

Ramsey looked at the oil-dripping shape across from him. The last water swept out of the compartment with a sucking roar. Ramsey opened the detergent nozzles, felt the hard thudding of the pressure streams. The oil swept off their suits, disappeared down the flushout.

"Okay, Joe," he said.

Garcia remained motionless.

"Come on, Joe, let's go."

Still he remained motionless.

"Something's wrong with him, Skipper."

No answer.

Ramsey motioned toward the hatch between their feet.

Garcia nodded, stepped aside. Ramsey undogged the hatch. It swung back with an assist from outside and Ramsey saw Sparrow peering up at him. Sparrow motioned toward Ramsey's throat.

Then Rmasey recognized the silence. Dead mike switch. He fumbled for it with his suited hand, caught Sparrow in mid-roar. ". . . sickbay on the double, Joe!"

"Detergent spray turned off my mike," explained Ramsey.

"You've got to watch that," said Sparrow. "Come down out of there."

Ramsey followed Garcia, helped Sparrow strip the suit from the engineering officer. The skipper helped Garcia up onto the catwalk mounting, peeled off the flipper sections. Ramsey stepped back, pulled off his headgear.

"Tired," said Garcia. "Knew somebody'd come for me. Coulda cut my way out in 'mergency." He slid off the catwalk mounting, led the way down the stairs.

Ramsey stripped off his own suit, put both suits away, went down the stairs; Garcia and Sparrow had disappeared through the control-room door. The motors came to life as Ramsey dropped to the control room.

Bonnett stood at the helm, alone in the maze of control arms and dials. He spoke without turning. "Get on the board and help me find that thermal."

Ramsey moved to his station, checked the outside temperature reading. The radiation counter caught his eye. "Who shut off the alarm?"

"Skipper. He had his eyes glued to it."

"Were we in that?"

"No. You had the hatch sealed before the count went up."

Ramsey shivered, stared at the dial: 42,000 milli-R. "That's almost at a self-sustaining level. Would be if it weren't for current diffusion."

"Where's that thermal?" asked Bonnett.

Ramsey tried a short-range pulse, checked the back wave. "Try two degrees starboard . . . right."

"My, we're salty," said Bonnett.

"We're in it," said Ramsey. "Radiation dropped, too." He looked at the big pressure gauge: 262 psi.

The *Ram*'s deck remained tilted downward.

"We're in it," repeated Ramsey. "Let's level out."

"Buoyancy in the tow," gritted Bonnett. He flicked the button on his chest mike: "Skipper, buoyancy in the tow."

Back came Sparrow's voice: "What's our depth?"

"We're in the thermal—about 600 feet."

"Bring us around to westward—make it 260 degrees even."

"What if we lose the thermal?"

"Just see that we don't."

"How's Joe?" asked Ramsey.

"Full of needle holes," said Sparrow.

Bonnett spun the helm, brought up the bow planes, dropped them, found the stabilizing point. The deck inclined forward at an uneasy three degrees.

"She wants to coon dog on us," said Ramsey.

"Why couldn't oil be a nice heavy substance like lead?" asked Bonnett. He changed the pitch on the rear planes, readjusted the bow planes, glanced at the pitlog. "The drag's cutting our speed in half."

Sparrow ducked through the door into the control room, looked to the rear plane setting, swept his glance across the control reading dials.

Ramsey abruptly realized that in the one sweeping glance Sparrow had familiarized himself with the facts of his vessel's life.

*He's part of the machine,* thought Ramsey.

"The tow's riding stern-heavy," said Bonnett. "We lost ballast from the bow. What we need is some nice non-radioactive bottom muck to replenish ballast."

Ramsey looked at the sonoran chart. The red dot on their position stood north of the blighted Scottish skerries, course line pointing toward Newfoundland. "Seamount Olga is right in our path," he said. "Its west slope would be scoured by clean currents and—"

"It may be hotter than our damper rods," said Sparrow. "But it's a good chance. That's why we changed course."

"Outside radiation's up a few points, Skipper. The thermal's thinner than our diameter here."

"Steady as she goes," said Sparrow. "The tank hull took a near-limit dose back there. It'll have to go through decon anyway. Our concern now is to get that oil home."

"It's hot, too," said Bonnett.

"But usable," Ramsey reminded him.

Sparrow said, "The immediate problem is how to get that ballast off the bottom when we can't go down to it. I think we're going to have to waste another fish." He turned to Ramsey. "Johnny, do you feel hot enough on the remotes to snag our ballast hose in the fin prongs of one of our Con-5 fish?"

Ramsey remembered Teacher Reed at the torpedo base on Boca Raton. He had patted the agate-smooth skin of a thin torpedo. *"This is the Con-5. Those buttons in the nose are radar and TV eyes. Through them, you sit right in the nose of this baby while you guide her into the target."* And he had turned then to a black radio case with stub antenna protruding from it. *"Here*

*are the controls. Let's see what you can do. This one's*
*a dud, so you can make lots of errors."*

"Well, what do you think?" asked Sparrow.

"Once that baby's out of her rack, she's charged and
ready to blow. If I smack the pin into something near
the hull, we've had it."

"You don't think you can handle it?"

"I didn't say that." Ramsey looked at his hands.
They were steady. "I can do it if anybody can but——"

"Youth is what it takes," said Sparrow. "Les and I
are growing old."

"Howdy, Grandad," said Bonnett.

"I'm serious," said Sparrow. "The end of that ballast
hose sticks out only about a foot. The Con-5 will have
to be moving better than fifteen knots to snag the hose
tightly. That means——"

"That means I'd better be right," said Ramsey.

"Right the first time," said Bonnett.

Ramsey shrugged. "Well, at Boca Raton they said
I took to the Con-5 like it was——"

"Boca Raton?" asked Sparrow. "What's at Boca Raton?"

And Ramsey realized he had made another error.
Boca Raton was a torpedo school . . . for Security
specialists.

"Isn't that a Security school?" asked Bonnett.

"I missed out on my regular class because of illness,"
said Ramsey. "So they sent me there." He said a silent
prayer that his lie would be believed.

"We'll be over Olga in twenty minutes," said Bonnett.

"I'm going back for another look at Joe," said Sparrow. He turned, went out the aft door.

"Garcia's trying for homestead rights on the sick
bay," said Ramsey.

"I hope he's okay," said Bonnett. "I don't think the
skipper should've let him make that slug repair. I
could've done it."

"Even I could've done it," said Ramsey. "But I
guess the skipper had his reasons." He frowned. "Only

I'd like to know his reason for picking me to do this snag job."

"Did you ever get into a Con-5 game?" asked Bonnett.

Ramsey suddenly grinned. "Sure. My instructor thought he was a hotshot. So he said we'd take these two Con-5s, him controlling one, me the other. It was a touch match in the bay, first nose-hit the winner. You know, I took—"

"All right, all right," said Bonnett. "I'm just trying to make a point. I don't want a blow by blow. That's a young man's game, or at least a school game. We've been a long time out of school. You haven't."

"Oh."

Bonnett chuckled. "I used to be pretty good at it, too. Tell you what: when we get back let's hunt up a fish school and I'll challenge you to a snag match. There's the fun."

Ramsey sobered. "The skipper doesn't make mistakes, does he?"

"Not about people," said Bonnett. "Or about machines, either." He stopped to correct the setting on the bow planes. "And when we get back home they'll have him on the carpet for wasting too many fish. And what about all those spare parts?"

Ramsey thought: *A first-year psych man knows the leader of a group is the integrative force . . . the logos. Of course this crew has the top rating. Sparrow is—*

"It makes my blood boil when I think about it," said Bonnett.

Sparrow came through the doorway onto the control deck. "What makes your blood boil?"

"All the stupid red tape back at base."

"It's supposed to make your blood boil. That's why it exists. How far to that seamount?"

"Five minutes."

"Okay, Johnny. Let's see how good you are at Contag." Sparrow gestured toward the torpedo board at Bonnett's left.

"How's Joe?" asked Bonnett.

"I just shot him full of de-carb. If that hot stuff settled in his bones, he's a cooked engineer."

Ramsey approached the torpedo board slowly.

Bonnett said, "We caught him in time. He'll be as good as new in a couple of days. No calcium, no carbonate, no—"

"Just call him rubber bones," said Ramsey. "Now how about a little quiet?"

"The maestro is about to perform," said Bonnett.

Ramsey stared up at the banks of red-handled switches, the guide screens, arming triggers. And there in front of him was the little blue stick that made a Con-5 perform. He chose one off the top of the rack, keyed it to the controls, said, "Standing by. How far is down?"

"Twenty-two hundred feet," said Bonnett. "You can go any time now. It's directly under us." He slowed the engines until they were barely moving.

"We'll have hose to spare," said Sparrow.

"Shall I make a recon down to that bottom to see if I can get some muck for our hull snooper?" asked Ramsey.

"No. We have to make this one fast. An EP may pick up our control pulse. If the bottom's hot, then we'll have hot oil and they can use it to lube atomic engines."

"Now?" asked Ramsey.

"Take her away," said Sparrow. "Les, put the side lights on that hose reel."

"They're already on," said Bonnett.

Ramsey turned the guide screen to the nose eye in his Con-5, activated the multi-wave projector beside the nose eye. The screen showed a pattern outline for the hull of the *Ram,* picked up in waves beyond the normally visible spectrum. Superimposed was the faint glow of the side light illuminating the hose reel. A second super-imposition showed the relative positions of the *Ram* and the tiny Con-5.

"A little more ship speed, please," said Ramsey. "It'll steady us."

Bonnett moved the throttle bar forward a fractional notch and the *Ram* picked up speed.

Ramsey brought the deadly torpedo in closer. He could not see the fin prongs on his torpedo, but he knew where they were—forward projecting edges of the stabilizing fins, designed for hydrostatic balance and set just back of the needle curve of the torpedo's nose.

"Blink the side light," said Ramsey.

Bonnett winked the light switch off, on, off, on.

The glow on Ramsey's guide screen went on and off to the movement of the switch.

"Wanted to make sure that was the correct light," said Ramsey. He flashed the Con-5 in close and hovered it over the light. The hose projection was visible ahead, jutting at a forty-five-degree angle from the reel base.

"Okay," he said. "Here goes." He dropped the Con-5 back ten feet, threw full power into the torpedo's drive. It surged ahead, swooped down onto the hose, seemed to hesitate, then ranged away from the *Ram*.

"You got it," said Bonnett.

"What else?" asked Ramsey. He slacked off the speed of his torpedo, looked at the counter dial which showed how fast the hose was unreeling. Abruptly, the dial showed a showling down, slacked off to zero.

"Lost it," said Sparrow.

Ramsey brought the Con-5 around in a sweeping curve. The snaky line of the hose was the superimposed outline now. He brought the little torpedo in fast, tipped it at the last minute like a hungry shark and again had the hose in tow. "Got a better hold on it that time."

"I'm bringing us around on that seamount," said Bonnett. "I have you on the search board. I'll warn you one hundred feet from bottom. You can take it in visually from there."

"I picked up the hose about ten feet from the end

that last time," said Ramsey. "Get the pump going the minute I touch the nozzle into the muck; that'll hold her there. I don't want to hold that firing pin any closer to a target any longer than I have to."

"Pump ready," said Sparrow.

Ramsey glanced sideways, saw Sparrow at the tow board. Sparrow's hands moved over the controls. "Line checks clear to the ballast compartment," he said.

Ramsey visualized the ballast connections running aft, through the tow controls and into the web mesh which linked *Ram* and slug. If that linkage remained sound . . . if he could plug that hose end into ballast muck . . . if . . .

"One hundred feet," said Bonnett. "You're bearing along the east face of the seamount."

"I have its outline," said Ramsey, eyes on screen.

He maneuvered the torpedo closer to the bottom.

"Ledge," he said. "That'll have muck."

"Pray it's cool," said Sparrow.

"Pray it's ballast," said Ramsey.

He edged the torpedo and its hose end closer to the bottom, closer, closer . . .

"She's in!"

"Pump on and . . . holding," said Sparrow.

Ramsey tipped the Con-5, freed it from the hose, brought it up away from the bottom.

"Stand by with that thing," said Sparrow. "We may have to move the hose."

They waited.

"The slug's bow is coming down," said Sparrow. He hit the switch of a ballast snooper. "It's cool."

Slowly, as the *Ram* circled over the seamount, the slug came to hydrostatic balance. Presently, Sparrow said, "Okay, Johnny, find some deep bottom for that Con-5, set it down, disengage and leave it. Don't let it blow."

"Aye." Ramsey took the little torpedo down along the flank of the seamount, found a deep ledge and set the deadly metal fish down. He shut down the remote-control system, stepped back.

"Hose coming in," said Sparrow. "Take us down into that thermal, Les. Course 260. Johnny, how about looking in on Joe?"

"Aye, Skipper." He felt suddenly exhausted, but buoyed by an inner nervous exhilaration.

"Then get some rest," said Sparrow.

Ramsey turned aft, went to the door, stepped through, and went to the rec room-sick bay.

Garcia lay on the sun-lamp cot clad only in a pair of shorts. He was on his back, one brown arm thrown across his eyes. Dots of perspiration glistened on his dark skin. As Ramsey entered the room, Garcia lifted the arm from his eyes, peered from under it.

"Oh, it's you."

"Who'd you expect? The surgeon general?"

"Aren't we funny!"

Ramsey put the back of his hand against Garcia's forehead. "Fever?"

Garcia cleared his throat. "Some. Those damned decalcification shots."

Ramsey glanced at the chart Sparrow had taped to the bulkhead above the cot. "You're due for another shot right now. De-carb and de-phos. Another de-sulf in an hour." He turned away, went to the pharmacy locker across the room, saw that Sparrow had set out the hypodermics in sterile seals, labeled them.

"What have we been doing?" asked Garcia.

Ramsey turned with the hypo for the shot, said, "Getting a new cargo of ballast for the slug. Turn over."

"This one in the left arm," said Garcia. He held out the arm, watched while Ramsey swabbed the area, administered the injection, returned the hypo to the pharmacy rack.

Garcia spoke behind him. "Have you and your little black box finally got the skipper figured out?"

Ramsey's muscles locked. He took a deep breath to quiet his nerves, turned. "What do you mean?"

Garcia's face bore a twisted smile. "Don't play it innocent, Johnny. Remember me? I'm the guy who's capable of taking over the electronics shack if you crock out."

"But—"

"My hobby is breaking and entering," said Garcia. He put his hands under his head, winced as he moved his left arm. "You've heard about Pandora's box?" He managed a shrug by lifting his eyebrows and making the slightest movement of shoulders. "You shouldn't put temptation like that in front of a guy like me."

Ramsey wet his lips with his tongue. "You mean the test equipment for the long-range—"

"Really, old boy, don't you know when the jig's up?" He stared at Ramsey, a calculating look. "The gear in that box is tied to the skipper someway. I don't know how, but—"

"Oh, come off that," said Ramsey. "You—"

"I put it to the acid test," said Garcia.

"Acid test?"

"You're a deuced reluctant type, Johnny. If I didn't—"

"Start at the beginning," said Ramsey, tiredly. "I want to know what you think."

"Fair enough," said Garcia. He wriggled into a more comfortable position on the cot.

Ramsey brought up a stool, sat down.

"In the first place," said Garcia, "you didn't offer to introduce me to the intricacies of your little black box. That was a mistake. Any normal E-man would've been all eager to share his gadget with another man aboard who could talk shop." The smile tugged at the corners of Garcia's mouth. "You, by the way, don't talk shop."

"So?"

"So there's nobody else aboard who talks your particular brand of shop."

"Is that when you figured me for a spy?"

Garcia shook his head. "I've never figured you for a spy." He frowned. "Sorry about that. Maybe I could've saved you a bad time with Les. I've been certain all along that you weren't a spy."

"How could you be?"

"Too inept." Garcia hesitated. "And besides, my wife is a cousin of Commander Gadsen of the *Dolphin*. Gad was very impressed by a fellow named Long John Ramsey from BuPsych who pulled them out of a nasty spot when their oxy system went sour. He says this man Ramsey improvised a special vampire gauge and pulled some stunts with anhydrase that weren't in the books. Seemed to think this Ramsey saved their lives."

"So you figured me for this same Ramsey."

"Gad was *extremely* impressed by this Long John Ramsey except one thing: he said the redheaded bastard got on your nerves with his know-it-all attitude!"

"The world's full of redheaded—"

"Uh, uh!" Garcia shook his head. "You're BuPsych. Two things on this floating sewer pipe interest you more than anything else: the skipper and the black box in your room. So I opened the box."

Ramsey forced himself to remain impassive. "And?"

An enigmatic grin captured Garcia's features. "There's a separate set of recording instruments in it keyed to the timelog. I copied four of your tapes, checked back on what we'd been doing."

"What'd that prove?"

"Whenever the skipper's asleep, your graphs flatten. Every time."

Ramsey shrugged, remained silent.

"But I needed the clincher," said Garcia. "Two times when the skipper hurt himself—a barked shin and one electric shock—I logged the exact time. The squiggles on a couple of your tapes go wild at exactly those moments."

Ramsey recalled the tape gyrations, his own cautious questioning to elicit the reasons. "Clever."

"Thank you, old chap. I thought so myself."

"What's all this prove?"

Garcia raised his eyebrows. "It proves you're making some kind of record of the skipper's internal chemistry. Only one type of fellow is that interested in why people tick."

"Yes?"

"He's vulgarly referred to as a head thumper."

In spite of himself, Ramsey grinned. *So I'm all washed up,* he thought. *So I'm in good company.*

"I don't believe I'm going to give you away yet," said Garcia. "This show hasn't played itself out. I must remember to thank BuPsych, too, for one of the most entertaining cruises I've ever had."

"I suppose you want into the act," said Ramsey.

"Good heavens, no! I already have my part to play. Just one thing, old fellow. Don't sell our Captain Savvy Sparrow short."

"Oh?"

"He's the director of this show. Whether you know it or not, he controls the script."

Ramsey fought down the vague tuggings of disquiet. "Is that why you're not giving me away?"

"You obviously mean well," said Garcia. His voice went lower, more harsh. "Now, give me my other shot and get the hell out of here! Your air of superiority is beginning to wear on me."

Ramsey felt the hot blood suffusing his features. He took two quick breaths, surged to his feet.

Garcia deliberately turned over, spoke with his mouth muffled slightly by the pillow. "Left buttock this time, old thing. Try not to work your temper out on me while you're about it."

Ramsey went to the pharmacy locker, returned with the hypo, administered the shot, replaced the hypo in its rack.

"That was very gentle," said Garcia. "Good control."

Ramsey walked across the room, stood over the cot. "What air of superiority?" he demanded.

Garcia rolled onto his back, grimaced, said, "I don't mind your dislike of me, or Les, but by Heaven, you owe your life to—"

"That's enough!" barked Ramsey. "You talk about

superior! Every damned one of you has been so superior it—"

"Oh, I say!" Garcia stared up at him. "We all have our soft spots. Evidently the junior ensign—"

"You've had your inning," gritted Ramsey.

"So I have." Garcia nodded. "Maybe you've just wanted to be one of the gang. In spite of—" He fell silent.

"In spite of what?"

"Your other job."

"Maybe because of it," said Ramsey.

Garcia digested this. "I never thought of that. But it makes sense. You psych boys must be pretty lonely. All your friends—outside the profession, that is—always on guard lest you pounce."

Ramsey shoved his hands into his hip pockets. "Where'd you get this low opinion of psych?"

"Watching you operate, Doctor."

Ramsey sniffed. "You've never seen me operate." He kicked the stool closer to Garcia's cot, sat down. "You're going to talk shop."

Garcia raised on one elbow. "Now see here, old thing, I really—"

"Your secret's showing," said Ramsey.

Garcia's face went blank. "What . . . did . . . you . . . mean . . . by . . . that?"

"You act like a man under some contra-survival threat greater than the fear of death. You keep making sacrificial gestures, as though you were seeking to excuse—" Ramsey fell silent, staring at Garcia.

"Well?"

"I never brought it into concrete focus before, Joe. Did you have anything to do with the death of that Security lieutenant?"

Garcia sank back onto his pillow. "No."

"Even indirectly?"

"I didn't know a thing about him until we found him!"

Ramsey started to nod, then thought: *Wait a minute! That's not a direct answer. A clever evasion phrased like an answer*. He said, "Wouldn't an outright lie be preferable?"

Garcia stared at the ceiling, mouth held in a harsh line.

"Okay, we'll talk about something else, Joe."

"Why don't you go talk by yourself?"

"You're such pleasant company I can't bear to leave. Tell me, Joe, outside of psych men who look through your sham wall of inadequate defenses—"

"Look, fellow!" Garcia turned his head on the pillow until he was staring directly at Ramsey. "So you came out after me when I was caught in the slug. That was your boy-scout good deed for the say and I thanked you nicely when we got back, but—"

"Thanked me?"

"Oh, I forgot, you goofed with the detergent jet and had your hearing aid turned off. No matter. I was about to say that your gesture wasn't necessary. I could've cut myself out of the slug if the need arose. So we're—"

"What with?"

"Huh?"

"You stripped your pockets before getting into the lung suit. Your knife was right there on the suit ledge when I got ready to go out. What were you going to cut yourself out with—the patch scraper?" Garcia's dark features grew pale.

"You're welcome," said Ramsey.

"You've suddenly built your part up greater than it first appeared, Johnny. Who does your scripts?"

"It's just that you've never really seen me operate," said Ramsey. "Now, I started to ask you a question. I'd like a straight answer and we'll call it even. Okay?"

Garcia smiled thinly. "Righto."

"What is it about this service that really gripes a submariner?"

"Nothing gripes us," said Garcia. "We love our work. There's really nothing in this whole wide world to compare with the subtugs. It has playing grab-tail with a panther pushed completely off the jolly map. Now, you take—"

"I'm serious, Joe. I'm looking for something that's bottled up way inside you. I think I know what it is, but I want to hear it from someone else. Someone like you who knows people and submarines. I think we've been looking in the wrong direction."

"What do you want to know?"

"I'm not going to put the words in your mouth. I want to know what it is about this service that really burns your country ass—the thing you don't even talk about among yourselves?"

Again Garcia lifted himself on one elbow. He grimaced as he moved the arm which had received the earlier shots. "All right, Johnny boy. You deserve a straight answer for being such an observant chap—about knives and such. You saw how we shoved off?"

"Yes."

"Sneaking off. You know—just routine."

"That's Security."

"Stuff Security. Do these fatheads imagine the EPs are ignorant of the location of our bases?"

Ramsey shook his head. "Well, Security can be sure the EPs know where *our* home base is. They can be sure if they got our squirt message, that is."

"They should be sure without our message! This cops-and-robbers routine is an ache in the bustard. Air cover and sea patrol are the real reasons there aren't wolf packs waiting at the outlets of all five of our—"

"Five?"

"Five bases, Johnny. Every submariner knows about 'em. The sub skippers know; so the men know. That's survival and Security can go blow that out its bloody bum—"

"I don't get you, Joe. Sorry."

"Johnny, let's say you're the only man aboard able to operate the boat. The rest of us are all gowed up somehow or other. Say a pile flare-up. It's survival, Johnny, for you to know that the radiation medical center is at the other end of the Charleston short tunnel and that the tunnel opens into Charleston harbor just inside the mole and a hundred feet left."

"I see what you mean. So we have five bases."

"We used to have six. Then the EPs sabotaged one of our subcruisers and it blew while going down tunnel —like we almost did. That's the Corpus Christi crater you've—"

"Wait a minute!" Ramsey shook his head. "That was an EP war rocket. It was aimed at—"

"Swamp mud! It won't wash, Johnny. That doesn't explain how the alleged war rocket pierced our 'perfect' robo-slave defenses and hit smack on that tunnel."

"What tunnel?"

"Johnny, I've been up that tunnel. So've a lot of other fellows in the sub service. Security may peddle its pap to somebody else, not to us. You can't tell me a rocket launched in Siberia can center on a hole in the ground in Texas—even by accident. That's stretching probability or accuracy." He sank back onto his pillow.

"Let's grant your argument," said Ramsey. "What's that have to do with my original question?"

"You still want to get way inside my head?"

"I'd like an answer to my original question."

Garcia stared at the ceiling. "Right, Johnny. The answer you want goes something like this: there are men all through the services—not just the subs—who are so sick of war—year after year after year after year of war—so sick of living with fear constantly that almost anything else is preferable. Death? He's an old friend—a neighbor just beyond the bulkhead there. Lots of things become preferable. Fouling up the works, for instance, to let the other side win. Just so somebody wins and that puts a stop to the thing— the bloody, foolish, never-ending thing." His voice trailed off and he turned, stared emptily at the bulkhead behind Ramsey.

"That's insane," whispered Ramsey.

"Certainly it is," said Garcia faintly. "But you're not going to argue that war is sane. We're human beings, whatever that means. If insanity is the pattern, that's us and you'll find damned little that's contradictory. Just little scratches of sanity where the blood runs through a different color."

"Oh?"

"Like the skipper. You've seen him pray for the souls of the men he kills. That's a scratch of sanity. You can feel it." He turned a fierce glare on Ramsey. "Do you ever wonder what they're like—those other fellows? Perdition! They can't be so very much different from us. They have wives, kids, sweethearts, hopes, fears. I know as certainly as I know I'm here now that there are people over there who feel the same way about this stupid war as we do." His voice rose. "Anything! Just to get this damnable thing over with! It's like a pain that's way inside your chest and it won't stop. It goes on and on and on and—"

"Easy, Joe."

Garcia relaxed. "Okay."

"That's battle pressure," said Ramsey. "I was thinking of something else." He hesitated. "No, maybe you were talking about the same thing."

"Such as?"

"It has to do with death instincts, Joe."

"Oh, and it's too deep for the likes of me."

"I didn't say that."

"You implied it, Johnny. Some more of your esoteric nonsense. I've had a normal amount of psych study. I've read the old masters and the new: Freud, Jung, Adler, Freeman, Losi, Komisaya. I went looking for answers and found double-talk. I can speak the jargon."

"So you know what a death instinct is."

"Sure, Johnny. The EPs and us—we're moving blindly toward our mutual destruction. Is that what you want me to say?"

"I guess not. I had something else in mind. Maybe I'm wrong."

"Or maybe I like to be blind, too."

"Yes. We were on another track earlier, Joe. You

didn't answer. Are you ready to tell me if the EPs have ever approached you to do their dirty work?"

Garcia looked at him coldly. "I hope to see you in hell," he said, enunciating the words precisely.

Ramsey got to his feet. "You've been a big help, Joe. But you're really supposed to be resting." He pulled a light blanket from a wall hanger, threw it over Garcia, turned away and went to the door.

Garcia said, "Do you think I'm a sleeper?"

Without turning, Ramsey said, "Would a sleeper have taken an overdose of radiation to keep us hidden from the EPs?"

"Maybe," said Garcia. "If he didn't like his job and was as tired of this war as I am."

*And that,* thought Ramsey, *is precisely the answer I was afraid of.* He said, "Get some rest."

"Bit players hamming up their parts," said Garcia.

Ramsey stepped out into the companionway and it was a cold gray corridor suddenly—leading nowhere in either direction. He thought: *My world's gone completely schizoid. Security! Its job is to make us even more schizoid—to break down as many lines of communication as possible.* He turned and looked back at Garcia on the cot. The engineering officer had turned on his side, facing the bulkhead. *That's why it's so important to belong to Savvy Sparrow's group. That's the scratch of sanity.*

And he remembered Heppner, the electronics officer who had gone mad. *If you can't belong and you can't leave; What then?*

The shape and substance of things began to reform in Ramsey's mind. He turned up the companionway, went to the control deck. The room seemed to greet him as he stepped through the door: warmth, flashing of red and green lights, a sibilant whispering of power, a faint smell of ozone and oil riding on the background of living stink which no filters could completely eliminate.

Sparrow stood at the helm, an almost emaciated figure with rumpled clothes hanging loosely upon him.

Ramsey was suddenly startled by the realization that Sparrow had lost weight when there didn't seem to be any place from which he could lose it.

"How's Joe?" Sparrow spoke without turning.

*Saw my reflection in the dive-board glass,* thought Ramsey. *Nothing escapes him.*

"He's going to be all right," said Ramsey. "His vein-counter shows negative absorption. He may lose a little hair, be nauseated for a while undoubtedly."

"We ought to set him into Charleston," said Sparrow. "The vein-counter doesn't tell you what's happening in the bone marrow. Not until it's too late."

"All the signs are good," said Ramsey. "Calcium leaching out and being replaced by non-hot. Sulphate's negative. He's going to be okay."

"Sure, Johnny. It's just that I've sailed with him for a long time. I'd hate to lose him."

"He knows it, Skipper."

Sparrow turned, smiled, a strangely plaintive gesture. "I guess he does at that."

And Ramsey thought: *You can't tell a man you love him—not if you're a man. That's a problem, too. We don't have the right word—the one that leaves out sex.*

"He said, "Where's Les?"

"Getting some rest. We hit the Arctic stream twenty minutes ago."

Ramsey moved up to the search-board station, rested a hand on the wheel to external salvage air beside the board. His mind was full of moving thoughts. It was as though the conversation with Garcia had tapped a well—or had dropped head pressure and allowed what was underneath to come to the surface.

"Les will take the next watch in an hour," said Sparrow. I can handle her now. You come on in three hours. We'll need a tighter schedule without Joe."

"Aye, Skipper."

He turned, went aft to his quarters, and was suddenly aware of a bone weariness. It was too much trouble to get out the telemeter and inspect its tapes. Besides, he knew what it would show: the iron-hard inner control that simulated normality. Or maybe it *was* normality. He fell asleep on the bunk without undressing.

The *Ram* bore southwest toward home waters, and the timelog reeled off the days. A monotonous succession of watches amidst the cold pipes, dials, wheels, levers, blinking lights, and telltale buzzers. The same faces and the same danger.

Even peril can grow boring.

A distant sound of propellers in an area where all such sounds mean *hunter*.

Wait and listen. Creep ahead a few knots. Wait and listen. Creep ahead a few knots. Wait and listen. The distant sound is gone. The *Ram* picks up speed while red-rimmed eyes watch the ranging and sonar gear.

Garcia was up and about on the fourth day—a man grown strangely morose and sullen when Ramsey was present.

Still the subtug moved steadily nearer to safety, towing the turgid slug: a prize wrested from death itself.

And a special tension—a new pressure—crept into the actions of the *Ram's* crew. It was a tension that said: "We're going to make it . . . We're going to make it . . . We're going to make it . . ."

"Aren't we?"

Ramsey, asleep in his bunk, wrestled with a silent nightmare in which Sparrow, Garcia, and Bonnett suddenly turned to face him—all with the features of mad Heppner.

Slowly, the nightmare lifted and left him peaceful in the womblike stillness of the boat.

Stillness!

Ramsey sat bolt upright in his bunk, wide awake, every sense crying out against the strange new element: quiet. He reached behind him and snapped on his bunk light. It was dim—showing that they were on emergency batteries.

"Johnny!" It was Sparrow's voice over the wall speaker.

"Here, Skipper."

"Get up to your shack on the double. We're having pile trouble."

"I'm on my way!"

His feet hit the deck, fumbled into shoes. He snapped off his bunk light, ran out the door, up the ladder two steps at a time, down the companionway and into his shack station, talk switch open. "On station, Skipper. Is it serious?"

Bonnett's voice came back. "Full-scale flare-up."

"Where's the skipper?"

"Forward with Joe."

"Joe shouldn't be anywhere near that! He's still on the hot list!"

"It was Joe's watch. You know how——"

"Johnny!" Sparrow's voice over the intercom.

"Here."

"Secure the shack for minimum power drain and come forward."

"Right." Ramsey found that his hands knew automatically which switches to hit. He blessed the long hours of patience with the mock-up board. This was what Reed had meant: *There is no such thing as a minor emergency aboard a submarine.* He made the conventional glance-around double check; stand-by light glowing amber, jacks out, main switch up, relay circuit to control room plugged in and green. He thumbed his chest mike: "Les, she's all yours."

"On your way."

He ran out the door, turned right up the companionway, through the control room without glancing at Bonnett, and out onto the central catwalk. The laboring hum of one engine turning slowly on battery power to give them headway permeated the engine room.

Garcia stood beside the tunnel hatch down forward to the left, his hands fumbling with the zipper of an ABG suit.

Ramsey's first thought was: *What's wrong with Sparrow? He can't let Joe go in there!* Then he understood the significance of the scene.

The nozzle of a detergent hose was racked beside Garcia. Sparrow stood about twenty feet away on the lower catwalk. The space between them showed raw splashes of detergent spray. As Sparrow took a step forward, Garcia stopped working with the zipper, put a hand on the nozzle.

"Stay where you are, Skipper!"

Garcia's voice was metallic and seemed to echo in the engine room and Ramsey realized the man was talking into the open mike of his ABG suit.

Garcia lifted the hose nozzle, pointed it at Sparrow. "One step more and I'll let you have another taste of this."

Ramsey went to the left hand-ladder, dropped down to Sparrow's level. He saw that the front of Sparrow's uniform was dripping with detergent, and winced at the thought of what that high-pressure jet spray could do to a man.

"Shall we rush him, Skipper?" he asked. "I could drop down to—"

"Well, if it isn't the head thumper," said Garcia. The zipper on his suit suddenly unjammed and he pulled it closed, reached back and folded the hood forward over his head, sealed it. The quartz-plate front gleamed at them like a malignant Cyclops eye.

Sparrow glanced at Ramsey, turned back to Garcia. "We couldn't move an inch against that hose. We have to reason with him."

"Let the head thumper reason with me," said Garcia, his voice booming from the bulkhead speaker above them. "That's his department."

"He's only four days from a radiation overdose," said Ramsey.

"This is my show," said Garcia. "This is my big scene. I'm going to crawl that tunnel and there's nothing you can do to stop me. Besides, I know this end of the ship better than any of you."

Ramsey looked down at the open door to the tunnel, realized abruptly that it was the same tunnel in which they had found the dead Security officer.

Garcia half turned toward the door.

"Joe, stop!" barked Sparrow. "That's an order!" He made a sudden dash forward, was bowled over backward by a hard stream of detergent spray.

Behind him, Ramsey caught part of the spray, slipped to his knees. By the time they had scrambled to their feet, Garcia had disappeared into the tunnel, closing the door behind him.

Sparrow said, "He took a wrecking bar with him. He's going to jam the hatch dogs inside so we can't follow him."

They heard metal banging on metal.

Garcia's voice came over the bulkhead speaker. "That's right, Skipper. Can't have you fellows trying to steal my scene. You have front-row seats; enjoy the show."

"Has he gone off his rocker?" asked Ramsey.

Sparrow slipped down to the tunnel door, tested the dogs. "Jammed!"

"Has he gone psychotic?" asked Ramsey.

"Of course not!" barked Sparrow. "There's a full-scale flare-up in that pile room. He's gone in to do what he can."

Ramsey looked at the snooper above the tunnel door, saw that its needle was jammed in the red. "Skipper! It's hot here!"

Sparrow slapped the snooper with one hand and the needle swung back into the seven-hour-limit zone. "Jammed when he opened the door." He turned to the tool rack beside the door. "Joe! Do you hear me?"

"Sure, Skipper. No need to shout. I'm almost at the tunnel curve."

"Joe, defiance of orders is a serious offense."

Garcia's laughter roared from the speaker. "So sue me!"

"What happened in the pile room?" asked Ramsey.

Sparrow began pulling tools from the rack. "Our repairs didn't hold. Tie bolts sheared. The whole reactor slipped to the left, jammed the remote-control bank." He glanced at his wrist watch. "The batteries will give us steerage control for about another thirty minutes. When we lose steerage, the planes won't be able to hold us level and over we go. Over goes the pile. If we're lucky it'll reach critical mass. If we're unlucky, the whole boat will be contaminated and us with it. That'll be the slow way out."

"And if Joe lives through this, you'll have his hide," said Ramsey. "Even though he's risking—"

"You blasted idiot!" shouted Sparrow. "What do you mean *if he lives?* Don't you know there's only one way to get that pile back onto its base?"

All Ramsey could think was: *I did it! I cracked through that iron control! Now his emotions can take a normal—*

"Skipper!" It was Bonnett's voice over the intercom. Sparrow spoke into his chest mike. "Yes?"

"I'm tuned to the portside pile-room eye over the tunnel plates. They're moving toward— Good God! Joe! Get out of there! Skipper! He's in the pile room!"

"That's what I meant," murmured Sparrow. "Our Father, protect him." He stared at the tunnel door. " 'The Lord is my shepherd; I shall not want. He maketh me to lie down in green pastures: He leadeth me beside the still waters. He restoreth my soul: He leadeth me in the paths of righteousness for His name's sake. Yea, though I walk through the valley of the shadow of death, I will fear no—' "

"Now hear this!" It was Garcia's voice from the bulkhead speaker. "I can last maybe fifteen minutes. When I get the remote-control bank cleared, be ready to take over."

"Sure, Joe." whispered Sparrow. He swung open a panel on the forward bulkhead, revealing the direct controls to the left-side bank. The telltale lights glowed red when he threw in the switch.

"He's a dead man already," said Ramsey.

"Quiet!" barked Sparrow. "Tune that bulkhead screen above us to that pile-room eye."

Ramsey jumped to obey. The screen came to life. It showed Garcia's figure bulky in an ABG suit. He was bent over, rigging jacks to force the reactor onto its foundation. As they watched, Garcia began to turn the screws. Slowly, the deadly block inched toward its proper position. They could feel Bonnett adjusting the planes to accommodate for the shifting weight.

Sparrow bent over the tools he had removed from the bulkhead rack, hefted a big Stillson wrench. "Let's try one of those dogs," he said.

"The only way he could've jammed it is from the bottom," said Ramsey. "If we force it down, break it off and—"

Sparrow fitted the wrench to the upper dog, said, "They drilled you well for your little job."

*Now, what's he mean by that?* thought Ramsey.

"Here, give me a hand," said Sparrow.

Ramsey took hold of the wrench.

Together, they bore down on the handle. Abruptly, the dog twisted, snapped off. Ramsey took a punch and hammer from the stack of tools, knocked the fitting through the door into the tunnel.

Sparrow had the wrench fitted to the other dog.

Ramsey glanced up at the screen. The reactor was back on its foundation, and Garcia was securing it with new lag bolts.

"Let's go," said Sparrow.

They snapped off the other dog, heard a clatter of metal in the tunnel as Garcia's wrecking bar fell away. Sparrow pried the door open, swung it wide.

The snooper's needle jammed in the red.

"Suits," said Sparrow. He motioned toward the locker.

"Skipper." It was Garcia's voice from the speaker. "Tell my wife she doesn't have to be afraid any more. She'll understand."

"Sure, Joe."

"Tell her to go someplace and change her name."

"Why?"

Ramsey passed him an ABG suit, began scrambling into his own.

"Johnny'll understand."

Sparrow slipped into the suit, looked at Ramsey. "Well?"

Ramsey shook his head, unable to speak.

Sparrow spoke into his mike as he sealed the hood in place. "Joe, we've forced the door. I'm bringing in the detergent hose and a cool suit. Come out of there."

"I'm too hot," said Garcia. "Leave me here."

"Come out or I'll come in after you," said Sparrow.

Ramsey handed Sparrow a fresh ABG suit, glanced up at the bulkhead screen. It showed Garcia's squat-suited figure, standing beside the tunnel plates. Above him, one of the giant remote-control manuals swung outward. At the same time, Bonnett's voice came over the intercom. "The control bank's free, Skipper. I can take it from here. Get that damned fool out of there. He may still have a chance." Bonnett was almost sobbing.

"I'm coming in after you," said Sparrow.

"You don't understand," shouted Garcia. "Stay out of here, Skipper!"

"I'm coming," repeated Sparrow. He freed the detergent hose from its reel clip.

Garcia's voice rose almost to a scream. "Skipper! I'm your spy! Don't be a fool!"

"You're my engineering officer," said Sparrow. He bent for the tunnel, slid into it, dragging hose and ABG suit behind him.

Garcia's voice came to them: "You can't—" He fell silent, choked, coughed, collapsed onto the reactor-room floor.

Around Ramsey in the engine room, lights brightened, the four motors resumed their normal humming. He could feel the *Ram*'s response through his feet as though it were a report from someone outside himself. He was unable to tear his gaze from the screen. The giant manual arm swung out over Garcia's prone figure, clasped him gently, lifted him into the tunnel, replaced the cover plates.

"I've got him," said Sparrow. A gush of detergent washed out the mouth of the tunnel.

He was afraid to look back at the snooper above the tunnel door. Jammed in the red. *We've had it, but good,* he thought.

Bonnett was still at the helm as Ramsey entered the control room. "Wouldn't let me help," he said. He motioned toward the door aft.

Ramsey continued after the line of wet footprints. *Naked of soul, naked of body,* he thought. *Now we're down to the simplest essentials.*

Ramsey jumped to the bulkhead console, started a pump removing the hot fluid.

"Johnny!" Sparrow's voice.

He spoke into his suit mike. "Here, Skipper."

Sparrow's voice lowered. "You don't have to help in this, Johnny. Get away from the tunnel mouth if you value your virility. Joe's hot. Very hot."

"I've already got two kids," said Ramsey. "Bring him out."

"Here he is."

Garcia's limp body was extruded from the tunnel mouth like an insect from its burrow. Ramsey eased him to the deck. Sparrow followed.

"I almost drowned him in detergent getting him into his suit. It's already too hot."

Ramsey bent over, unzipped the front of Garcia's suit. Sparrow helped him pull the limp figure from it. They hustled Garcia into the decontamination chamber. Sparrow removed his own suit, went in with Garcia. Ramsey took the suits, stuffed them into the tunnel mouth, stripped off his own and pressed it in after the others. He closed the door, wedged it with the Stillson wrench.

The door to the decon chamber popped open. Sparrow emerged nude, dragging Garcia after him in like condition. "We'll have to replace every drop of his blood," said Sparrow. "Get in there and shed your clothes, then come up to the rec room." He stooped, lifted Garcia over his shoulder and went up the ladder to the catwalk, muscles knotting on his legs and back with the strain of the load.

Ramsey paused to speak into his chest mike. "Les, Skipper is bringing Joe up. Better lend a hand." Then he ducked into the decon chamber, slapped the medium-jet control. The harsh streams, designed for a man in a protective suit, bit into his flesh with a stinging pressure. Ramsey shucked out of his clothes, kicked them into a corner, stopped the spray, went out, and followed Sparrow's wet footprints up the ladder.

In the rec room, Sparrow had Garcia stretched out on a cot, a plasma bottle hung above him, its tube leading into a vein. Sparrow was setting up a blood-exchange unit on the opposite side of the cot, adjusting the vein and artery taps, the flow meters, the height of the armrest.

Ramsey went to the live-blood storage, checked the automatic circulation and revitalization systems, found them operative.

"Blood ready," he said. He turned.

Sparrow said, "Right." He plugged the blood exchange into the live-blood circulating system, put a hand on the valve. "Monitor what we pump out of him."

Ramsey went to the head of the blood-exchange unit, glanced at the taps which Sparrow had adjusted to Garcia's arm. The engineering officer's breath was coming in slow, shallow rhythm, the movement of his chest discernible. The skin of his face and chest had a mottled blue cyanotic appearance.

Sparrow opened the exchange valve. Blood from Garcia's body began to flow into the unit's lead-lined storage system as the new blood was pumped into his body. Immediately, Ramsey's monitor snooper swung far right, stuck there.

"He's off the meter, Skipper."

Sparrow nodded. "Shall I use it all?"

"What do you mean?"

"There won't be any blood left for us."

Ramsey's memory flashed back to a vision of the

tunnel snooper jammed in the red. "We'll get by with plasma," he said.

"My thought. I'm glad you agree." He came around the cot, unhooked the plasma tube from Garcia's left arm. "If we need it, that is. And I'm more apt to than you are. I was in that tunnel."

"Let's save a couple of changes for you," said Ramsey.

"You never can—"

"I'll be all right."

Ramsey fell silent, watching the monitor dial. It stayed against the right-hand pin.

"I got his shots into him and took my own before you came up," said Sparrow. "We'd better check you now."

"Go ahead," said Ramsey. He held out his left arm, kept his gaze on the monitor dial. "Three changes through him by now for sure and he's still off the meter. Skipper, I've never heard of—"

"This is the de-carb," said Sparrow. "It'll hurt." He grasped Ramsey's arm, injected the serum precipitate into the muscle. "Don't worry about Joe. He's in God's hands, now."

"Aren't we all," said Ramsey.

"Skipper!" It was Bonnett's voice over the intercom.

Sparrow stepped to a wall mike, flipped the switch. "Go ahead."

"I've just checked out the pile. All secure."

"Set course for Charleston," said Sparrow. "Force speed."

"Aye. How's Joe?"

"It's too soon to know."

"Tell me if—"

"We will." Sparrow closed the switch.

Garcia stirred on the cot; his lips moved and he twisted his head from side to side. Suddenly, he spoke, his voice surprisingly strong. "I've gotta do it, Bea! They'll get at me through our kids, don't you understand?"

He seemed to be listening.

"I can't tell anybody! They'd shoot me!"

"Easy, Joe," said Sparrow.

Garcia's eyes flickered open, closed, opened. He stared blankly at Sparrow. "Where's Bea! Did they hurt her?"

"She'll be all right," said Sparrow.

Garcia shuddered. "If we could've just gone somewheres and changed our name. That's all." He closed his eyes.

"Do you know where you are?" asked Sparrow.

Garcia nodded. "Nightmare."

"He's on the meter," said Ramsey. "But so far into the probable fatal that—"

"Be quiet," said Sparrow. He checked the change-count dial in the blood system. "Eight down."

"And sixteen to go," said Ramsey.

Sparrow reduced the rate of flow.

"You should've left me in there," said Garcia.

"Don't talk foolish," said Sparrow.

"I was trained Buenos Aires spy school," said Garcia. "Twenty years ago. Then I came up here an' met Bea. So I quit. Easy. They'd taught me how to hide in plain sight."

"He shouldn't be talking," said Ramsey. "Blood pressure's up."

"Gotta talk," said Garcia. "They found me six months ago, said 'Come through, or else!' Our kids. Y' understand?"

"Sure, Joe," said Sparrow. "Now, please be quiet. Save your strength."

"First time in my life I ever belonged anywhere—really belonged—was with your crew," said Garcia. "With Bea, sure. But that's different."

"You have to conserve your strength," said Sparrow.

"Why? So Johnny Security can take me back to stand trial?"

"I'm not Security, Joe."

"He's a BuPsych," said Sparrow. "They put him on to ride herd on me."

Ramsey's mouth dropped open.

"I spotted that the day we first went down overlimit," said Sparrow. "It was the way he treated Les."

"Security, too," said Garcia.

"Only by adoption," said Ramsey. "And I can't—"

"If you spill this," said Sparrow, "I'll—"

"I was about to say that I can't hear so well," said Ramsey. He grinned, then frowned and looked down at Garcia. "Did you have anything to do with the death of that Security inspector?"

"Nothing, so help me God," said Garcia.

"How about the sabotage?"

"That was my old friends just being doubly sure." He shook his head. "I was just supposed to tip off the location of the well when we reached it. Instead, I set it off while we were still in our own waters. Thought they'd just force us up, capture us."

"How'd you do it?" asked Sparrow.

"By stepping up the sono-pulse system, keyed to weak tube plate."

"When did you decide not to tip them to the well?"

"I never decided *to* do it."

Sparrow seemed to relax.

"I told Bea to take our kids and go to Security as soon as we were out of pursuit range with the *Ram*." He fell silent.

"Try to rest," said Sparrow.

Garcia sniffed. "What's the needle say now, Johnny?"

Ramsey looked at Sparrow, who nodded assent.

"P-F," said Ramsey.

"Probable fatal," translated Garcia.

"The needle has come down some," said Ramsey.

"Do you want to chance an overdose of de-phos and de-calse?" asked Sparrow.

Garcia looked up at him. "Carry on the jolly battle a little longer, eh?" He smiled. "If you say so, Skipper. But keep me under morph, will you?" His grin became tight, like a death's head. "Convulsions are so messy!"

Sparrow took a deep breath, hesitated.

"It's his only chance," said Ramsey. "If you can call that a chance."

"All right," said Sparrow. He stepped to the pharmacy rack, readied the shots, returned.

"The morphine," reminded Garcia.

Sparrow held up an ampule.

"Thanks for everything, Skipper," said Garcia. "One favor: Will you look after Bea and the kids?"

Sparrow nodded curtly, bent, and administered the injections—one, two, three.

They watched the morphine take effect.

"Eight more blood changes left in the machine," said Ramsey.

"Give him maximum flow rate," said Sparrow.

Ramsey adjusted the valve.

"Now, Johnny, I want the whole story from you," said Sparrow. He spoke without taking his gaze from Garcia.

"Evidently, you already know it," said Ramsey.

"Not in detail. That's what I want now."

Ramsey thought: *The cloak-and-dagger role is a farce. Sparrow's had me spotted for some time—and that's probably Garcia's doing. I've been flying blind and didn't know it. Or did I?* He thought back over his vague feelings of misgiving.

Sparrow said, "Well?"

Stalling for time to think, Ramsey said, "How much detail?"

"Start from the beginning," said Sparrow.

Ramsey mentally crossed his fingers, thought: *This is the crisis. If Sparrow's really psycho, he'll blow. But I have to chance it. I don't know how much he's discovered. I can't pull any punches.*

"You can start right now," said Sparrow. "That's an order."

Ramsey took a deep breath, began with the message from Dr. Oberhausen and the conference with Admiral Belland in Sec. I.

"This telemetering equipment," said Sparrow. "What does it tell you about me?"

"That you're like a part of this submarine. You react

like one of its instruments instead of like a human being."

"I'm a machine?"

"If you want."

"Are you sure of your little black box?"

"The body's own juices don't lie."

"I suppose they don't. But interpretations can be mis-
taken. For instance, I don't think you've correctly eval-
uated the adjustment we have to make to exist down
here in the deeps."

"How do you mean?"

"Do you recall the day you broke down in the
shack?"

Ramsey remembered his fear, his inability to move,
the reassuring influence of Sparrow. He nodded.

"What would you call that experience?"

"A temporary psychotic break."

"Temporary?"

Ramsey stared at Sparrow. "What's that supposed to
mean?"

"Would you say that all of your actions aboard the
*Ram* have been completely sane?"

Ramsey colored, feeling the hot flush of blood in his
face. "What kind of a machine are you now, Skipper?"

"A computing machine," said Sparrow. "Now listen
to me and listen carefully. Here in the subtugs, we have
adapted to about as great a mental pressure as human
beings can take and still remain operative. We have
*adapted*. Some to a greater degree than others. Some
one way and some another. But whatever the method of
adaptation, there's this fact about it which remains always the same: viewed in the light of people who exist
under lesser pressures, our adaptation is not sane."

"How do you know?"

"I've had to know," said Sparrow. "As you've observed, my particular adaptation has been machine-
like. Considered in the light of human normality, you
psych people have a name for that adaptation."

"Schizoid."

"So I've compartmentalized my life," said Sparrow.

"I have a part of me—call it a circuit if you want—which keeps me going down here. It believes in the hereafter because it has to—"

Ramsey caught the third-person reference to self; he tensed.

"Who's to deny me the right to be whatever I have to be down here?" asked Sparrow. He rubbed the side of his jaw with his long-fingered hand. "I had to know what it was I was doing. So I studied me. I analyzed me. I computed me against every background I could think of. I was completely ruthless with me." He fell silent.

Cautiously, Ramsey said, "And?"

"I'm nuts," said Sparrow. "But I'm nuts in a way which fits me perfectly to my world. That makes my world nuts and me normal. Not sane. Normal. Adapted."

"You're saying the world's schizoid, fragmented."

"Hasn't it always been?" asked Sparrow. "Where are there completely unbroken lines of communication? Show me complete social integration." He shook his long head from side to side in a slow negation. "It's the pressure, Johnny."

Ramsey made a minute adjustment on the flow meter controlling the exchange of blood in Garcia's body. He looked down at the drugged engineering officer. Face relaxed, peaceful. Pressures gone for the moment.

"We look to a Utopian existence as sanity," said Sparrow. "No pressures against survival. That's why we get a dreamy nostalgia about us when we think of the old South Seas. Minimum threat to survival." Again he shook his head. "Whatever the pressure and whatever the adaptation, that adaptation is definable by your science as non-sane. I sometimes think that's the proper interpretation of the Biblical phrase: 'A child shall lead them.' Children generally don't have survival pressures. *Ergo*: They're more sane than adults."

"They have their pressures," said Ramsey.

"Of a different character," said Sparrow. He bent, felt Garcia's pulse. "How many changes left?"

"Two."

"What's the radiation reading?"

Ramsey's head jerked as he turned to stare fully at the dial. "Fifty-fifty."

"He'll live," said Sparrow. His voice carried a tone of absolute decision, an irrevocable judgment.

Ramsey fought down an unaccountable irritation. "How can you be so damned sure?"

"You were startled when you focused on the meter," said Sparrow.

"It's a miracle he's come this far." In spite of himself, Ramsey's voice betrayed his irritation.

"That's right, a miracle," said Sparrow. "Listen to me, Johnny. In spite of all your science and your medicine, there's something you people often refuse to admit."

"Which is?" Now his voice was openly hostile.

"There's such a thing as being on God's side. Being right with the world. That's really the thing behind miracles. It's quite simple. You get in . . . well, phase. That's the mechanical way of saying it. You ride the wave instead of bucking it." Sparrow's voice carried a tone of calm detachment.

Ramsey pressed his lips together to keep from speaking his thoughts. And over it all, his own psychological training was feeding data to a train of thought: *Religious fanaticism. Fragmentation. Impenetrable belief in own righteousness. The evidence for a diagnosis of paranoiac type is very strong.*

"Your particular adaptation is dictation by your psychological training," said Sparrow. "You have a function: to keep operating. Call it normal. You have to believe I'm insane and that your diagnosis of insanity type is accurate. That way, you're on top; you're in control. It's your way to survival. You can guide me and direct me like the proper animal that I am, and I'll take you back where the pressures are reduced."

"This is nonsense," barked Ramsey. "Psychological nonsense! You don't know what you're talking about!"

"If your diagnosis is correct, what's the probable course of my life?" asked Sparrow.

Before he could stop himself, Ramsey said, "You'll go completely psychotic! Completely—" He broke off.

Sparrow laughed. He shook his head. "No, Johnny. I'll go back where the pressures are less. And I'll take a deep breath. And I'll play a little poker at Garden Glen. And I'll get drunk a time or two because it's expected of me. I'll have another honeymoon with my wife. She'll be very nice to me. Very contrite because of all the times she's cuckolded me while I've been away. That's her adaptation. It doesn't really hurt me. Why should it?"

Ramsey stared at him.

"And, of course, I'll do some more wondering: What's this all about? What are we human animals? What's the meaning behind all this? If there is a meaning. But my roots are solid, Johnny. I've seen miracles." He nodded toward Garcia. "I've known the outcome of events before even the events. That gives me a—"

The warning buzzer sounded on the blood-exchange unit. Ramsey slapped the transfer switch. Sparrow moved around the cot, disengaged the artery and vein taps.

"Sixty-forty," said Ramsey.

"We'll be at Charleston in twenty-two hours," said Sparrow. He looked at Ramsey. "What do you intend to tell Admiral Belland's boys about Joe?"

"I don't remember anything about Joe worth telling Belland," said Ramsey.

A slow smile formed on Sparrow's lips. "That's normal," he said. "Not sane, but normal."

Ramsey sniffed. *Why am I irritated?* he asked himself. And his psychological training gave him the unavoidable answer: *Because I'm not facing something about myself. There's something I don't want to see.*

"Let's talk about Heppner," said Sparrow.

Ramsey suppressed an urge to shout: *For Christ's sake! What for?*

"He got to wondering about sanity," continued Sparrow. "And one day the truth dawned on him that I'm not particularly sane. Then he got to wondering:

What is sanity? He talked about some of his thoughts. And he found he couldn't define sanity. Not for sure. Which meant to him that he himself was off balance." Sparrow closed his eyes.

"So?" whispered Ramsey.

"So he applied for a transfer out of the subtugs. He gave me the application to submit when we landed. That last trip."

Ramsey said, "He cast himself adrift."

Sparrow nodded. "And he'd already admitted to himself that he had no anchor, no point of reference from which to navigate."

Ramsey felt a curious internal stimulation, as though he were on the brink of a great revelation.

"And that," said Sparrow, "is why I have to train another new electronics officer. You have to go back to BuPsych where you have your roots. That's an ocean in which you can navigate."

Ramsey could contain the question no longer. "What's your definition of sanity, Skipper?"

"The ability to swim," said Sparrow.

Ramsey felt a cold shock, as though he had been immersed suddenly in freezing water. He had to force himself to continue breathing normally. As though from a great distance, he heard Sparrow's voice:

"That means the sane person has to understand *currents,* has to know what's required in different waters."

Ramsey heard a heavy thundering, counterpoint to Sparrow's matter-of-fact tones.

"Insanity is something like drowning," said Sparrow. "You go under; you flounder without direction; you— Johnny! What's wrong?"

He heard the words, but they lacked meaning. The room was a spinning centrifuge with himself at the rim . . . faster . . . faster . . . faster . . . He caught at the blood-exchange unit, missed, crashed to the floor. A detached part of him sensed hands on his face, a finger lifting an eyelid.

Sparrow's voice squeaked insanely down an inverted funnel: "Shock!"

Thud! Thud! Thud! Thud!

footsteps

slamming of cabinet door

clinking of glass

He floated in a gelatin hammock, bound in upon himself. A miniature stage opened before his eyes. Sparrow, Garcia, and Bonnett stood arm in arm, doll figures staring across Lilliputian footlights.

Puppets.

In a dull monotone, the miniature Sparrow said, "I am a Commander, Submarine, Portable, Mark I."

The miniature Garcia said, "I am an Engineering Officer, Submarine, Portable, Mark I."

The miniature Bonnett said, "I am a First Officer, Submarine, Portable, Mark I."

Ramsey tried to speak, but his lips would not respond.

On the doll stage, Sparrow said, "I am not sane; he is not sane; you are not sane; we are not sane; they are not sane."

Garcia said, "I regret to report the failure of a component: myself." He dissolved, leaving Sparrow and Bonnett separated by a space.

Bonnett said, "That Ramsey is a catalyst."

Sparrow said, "I cannot help you; he cannot help you; we cannot help you; they cannot help you; you cannot help yourself."

Garcia's voice came from the empty space, "I regret that I cannot thank you in person."

Bonnett said, "My generation doesn't believe in vampires."

Again Ramsey tried to speak, but no sound came.

In unison, Sparrow and Bonnett began to recite: "Be quiet . . . be quiet . . . be quiet . . . be quiet . . . be quiet . . . be quiet . . ."

fainter

fainter

fainter

Garcia's voice was a faint echo, slightly off beat.
deep enfolding darkness
an amniotic darkness

Ramsey felt movement, a humming: the motors.
Bonnett's voice: "I think he's coming around."

Sparrow: "Can you hear me, Johnny?"

He didn't want to answer. That would take energy.
It would give substance to the world. His years of
psychological training abruptly said to him: *You are
in a tight foetal position.*

Sparrow: "Let's try to straighten him out. That may
help."

Bonnett: "Break it to him gently, Skipper."

Hands touched his legs, his arms, pulling him from
the curled ball. He wanted to resist, but his muscles
felt like weak putty.

*Break what gently?*

Sparrow's voice was imperative: "Johnny!"

Ramsey wet his dry lips with a reluctant tongue.
*Break what gently?* His voice came out faintly: "Yeah."

"Open your eyes, Johnny."

He obeyed, looked straight up into a crosshatch of
pipes and conduits. Control room. He sensed Sparrow
beside him, turned. The skipper looked down at him,
a worried frown tensing the long face. Beyond him,
Bonnett stood at the controls, back to them.

"Wha's—wha's——" He tried to clear his throat.

Sparrow said, "We brought you in here where we
could keep an eye on you. We're almost at Charleston."

Ramsey sensed the life pulse of subtug around him,
sank into it momentarily. *Break what gently?* He said,
"What happened?"

"You reacted to something," said Sparrow. "Maybe
the decalcification shot. It may have had something to
do with our over-pressure dives, increased anhydrase.
How do you feel?"

"Lousy. How's Joe?"

Sparrow seemed to retreat within himself. He took
a deep breath. "Joe ran out of red cells. Nothing we
could do."

*And there went your miracle,* thought Ramsey. He said, "I'm sorry, Skipper."

Sparrow passed a hand over his eyes. "Perhaps it was for the best." He shrugged. "He was too—"

"I have something on the ranging scope," said Bonnett. He keyed the IFF circuits, tested them. "It's a Monitor. One of ours. Coming fast."

Sparrow whirled, went to the communications board, tested the relays from the shack. "Are we close enough for voice?"

Bonnett studied his instruments. "Yes."

Sparrow turned a rheostat, closed the microphone key. "This is Able John. Repeat. This is Able John. We have a full slug. One crewman down with radiation sickness. Request clearance for Charleston. Over."

A voice came from the wall speaker with the eerie wavering of pulse modulation. "Hello, Able John. You're a bit hot. Stand by for snooping. Over."

Bonnett depressed the drive bar and their speed slackened.

From his position on the cot, Ramsey could see the ranging scope, blip lines growing deeper and deeper as the Monitor approached.

Again the eerie voice wavered from the speaker. "Monitor to Able John. You'll pass, Able John. Proceed at entrance depth. We will flank you. Over."

Bonnett pulled up the drive bar. The *Ram* surged ahead.

"Give us the bow eyes," said Sparrow.

The big screen above the search board came to life. Green water and occasional help.

Sparrow turned toward Ramsey. "We'll have you in good hands soon, Johnny. Before you know it."

Ramsey felt a strange dragging at his senses. He tried to imagine the Charleston tunnel entrance—a black hole in the wall of an underwater canyon. His mind sheered away. *Why was that?* he asked himself. Then: *Break what gently?* Part of him seemed to be standing off, making clinical notes. *You don't want to*

*go back. Why? A bit ago you were in a rolled-up ball.*
*Remember? Very interesting.*

He sensed an answer, said, "Skipper."

"Yes, Johnny?"

"I went catatonic, didn't I? Catatonic shock?"

Sparrow's voice became brisk. "Just shock."

The tone told Ramsey what he wanted to know.
The clinical part of his mind said, *Catatonic. Well, well.*
He was suddenly very aware of the cot beneath him,
pressure of his own weight against his back. In the
same instant, pieces of his puzzle started clicking into
place. He took a deep breath.

"Just take it easy," said Sparrow.

Bonnett glanced back, a look of wariness about his
eyes.

"I'm all right," said Ramsey. And he was surprised
at the full extent of truth in that statement. Strength
was pouring into him. "I went into a full retreat," he
said. "But now I know why."

Sparrow stepped to the side of the cot, put the
back of his hand against Ramsey's forehead. "You
should try to relax."

Ramsey repressed an urge to laugh. "Joe told me,
Skipper, but I didn't believe him."

Sparrow's reply was little more than a whisper:
"What did Joe tell you?"

"That you've had this situation pegged and under
control all along." He nodded. "That marine tunnel's
a birth canal. Going through it is like being born.
This sub is a perambulating womb looking for a place
to spew us out."

Sparrow said, "Maybe you hadn't better talk now."

"I want to talk. We're born into another set of real-
ities. There's one kind of insanity down here; another
up there. Just look at the old *Ram* here. An enveloped
world with its own special ecology. Damp atmosphere,
ever present menace from the outside, a constant
rhythm in motion—"

"Like a heartbeat," said Sparrow quietly.

Ramsey smiled. "We're afloat in amniotic fluid."

"How's that?"

"Salt water. It's chemically almost identical with the fluid surrounding an unborn baby. The unconscious knows. And here we are headed for birth."

"You make a more detailed comparison than I ever have," said Sparrow. "What's our umbilical cord?"

"Experience. The kind of experience that ties you to your boat, makes you a part of it. Petite perception. You're the perfect symbiote. We become siblings, brothers, with all the emotional ties and rivalry that—"

"First checkpoint," said Bonnett flatly. "Now on heading for the Charleston mole. Do you want to take over, Skipper?"

"Take her in, Les," said Sparrow. "You've earned the right."

Bonnett reached up, adjusted the range-response dial. His shoulders seemed to take on a new, more positive set. Ramsey realized abruptly that Bonnett had come of age on this voyage, that he was ready to cut his own cord. The thought gave Ramsey a tug of possessive fondness for Bonnett, an emotion touched by nostalgia at the thought of separation.

*Truly like brothers,* he thought.

Sparrow looked down at Ramsey. "Why don't you transfer out of BuPsych and into the subtugs?" asked Sparrow.

"Yeah," echoed Bonnett. "We need good men."

Sadness tightened Ramsey's chest. "That's the finest compliment I've ever received," he said. "But I can't. I was sent out here to solve a problem: Why were submariners breaking down? You gave me the answer. Now, I'll have to take a hand in applying that answer." He swallowed a lump in his throat. "Dr. Oberhausen of BuPsych has promised me my own department dealing with problems of submariners."

Sparrow said, "That's wonderful, Johnny! A big-time shore job."

"We're going to hate losing you," said Bonnett. "Will you still talk to the likes of us when you're an important brass type?"

"Never fear," said Ramsey.

"What is this solution?" asked Sparrow.

"The breakdowns are a rejection of birth by men who have unconsciously retreated into the world of prebirth. What child would seek birth if he knew that pain and fear—a constant menace—awaited him on the other side?"

"There's menace down here," said Sparrow.

"But our little world under the sea fools and confuses the unconscious," said Ramsey.

Bonnett spoke up, faint note of sarcasm in his voice. "That makes sense even to me . . . I think." He kept one hand on the wheel, stepped aside to adjust the tow controls.

"We have to make the complete cycle desirable," said Ramsey. "I'm going to recommend a whole new procedure: the best quarters for submariners. A big jump in pay for each mission."

"That's for me!" said Bonnett.

"There are going to be some changes made," said Ramsey.

"Johnny, do me a favor," said Sparrow.

"Name it."

Sparrow looked away, swallowed. "It sounds like you're going to be a VIP and—" He hesitated. "Will you do what you can to cushion things for Joe's wife?"

"Anything I can do," said Ramsey. "I promise." He took a deep breath. "Who's going to get the dirty job of telling her?"

"I will," said Sparrow. "I'll break it to her as gently as I can."

A sudden chill swept over Ramsey's body. *Break it gently!* He cleared his throat. "Skipper, that reminds me. I heard Les say something about breaking a bit of news to me. What?"

Sparrow wet his lips with his tongue, looked across at Bonnett working with the controls.

"Break what gently?" repeated Ramsey.

"Joe's death."

"But—"

"Each time we tried to bring you out of shock, you—"

"Each time?"

"We tried four or five times. Each time you raved for Joe to come back. We guessed it was delirium, but—"

Silence fell between them.

"The unconscious senses many things," said Ramsey. He felt a deep emptiness and suddenly recalled his nightmare. Garcia's voice: *"I regret that I cannot thank you in person."*

*For what?*

Ramsey said, "We had a lot in common. Joe understood me. He saw right through my act . . . said so. I guess I resented it. Joe was better at my game than I was."

"He admired you," said Sparrow.

Ramsey's eyes burned and smarted.

"He was awake at the end," said Sparrow. "Worried about you. He said he'd given you a raw deal by feeling our suspicions. Joe thought you had the makings of a top submariner."

Ramsey turned away.

"Will you do what you can for his wife?" asked Sparrow.

Ramsey nodded, unable to speak.

"We're approaching the mole," said Bonnett, his voice oddly casual. "Bottom-marker number two coming up." He indicated the screen above him.

Through a green haze of water, two high-piercement lights keyed to their IFF circuits winked at them.

"Are we set for the automatic pickup?" asked Sparrow.

"All set," said Bonnett.

"We've brought home the bacon," said Ramsey.

Bonnett's voice took on an unconscious mimicry of Garcia's bantering accent: "We're a bunch of bloody heroes!"

It was peaceful in Dr. Oberhausen's Charleston office. The wizened BuPsych chief sat behind a desk like all other BuPsych office desks, leaning back with his hands steepled beneath his goatee. His bat-eye radar box, disconnected from its shoulder harness, rested on the patterned wood of the desk top. Dr. Oberhausen's sightless ball-bearing eyes seemed to be staring at Ramsey, who sat across the desk from him.

Ramsey rubbed a hand over his head, feeling the stubble of returning hair. "That's pretty much the story," he said. "Most of it was in my notes. You've had those, even though the medics wouldn't let you talk to me."

Dr. Oberhausen nodded silently.

Ramsey leaned back in his chair. It creaked and Ramsey suddenly realized that Dr. Oberhausen purposely surrounded himself with creaking chairs—reassuring signals for a blind man.

"A close thing with you, Johnny. Radiation sickness is a peculiar thing." He passed a hand across his own radiation-blinded eyes. "It is fortunate that BuPsych agents are virtually indestructible."

"Does this check with my notes and the telemeter tapes?" asked Ramsey.

Dr. Oberhausen nodded. "Yes, it checks. Sparrow became almost literally a part of his boat, sensitive to everything about it—including his crew. An odd mating of the right mentality and the right experiences has made him a master psychologist. I'm going to see about taking him into the department."

"What about my recommendation for preventing those psychotic breaks?"

Dr. Oberhausen pursed his lips, tugged at his goatee. "The old Napoleonic fancy-uniform therapy: fanfare coming and going." He nodded. "Security will kick and scream that it will prevent secrecy of departures, but they've already made one concession."

"What?"

"They've announced officially that we're pirating oil from the EPs."

"That was a senseless secret anyway."

"They were reluctant."

"We'd be better off without Security," muttered Ramsey. "We should be working to get rid of it. Security stifles communication. It's creating social schizophrenia."

Dr. Oberhausen gave a negative shake of his head. "No, Johnny, we shouldn't get rid of Security. That's an old fallacy. Use Captain Sparrow's analogy: In an insane society, a crazy man is normal. Security has the kind of insanity that's normal for wartime. Normal and needed."

"But *after* the war, Obe! You know they're going to keep right on!"

"They'll try, Johnny. But by that time we'll have Security under the control of BuPsych. We'll be able to nullify them quite effectively."

Ramsey stared at him, then chuckled. "So that's why you've been moving in on Belland."

"Not just Belland, Johnny."

"You scare me sometimes, Obe."

Dr. Oberhausen's goatee twitched. "Good. That means my pose of omnipotence is effective even with those who know better." He smiled.

Ramsey grinned, stirred in his chair. "If that's all, Obe, I'd like to get away. They wouldn't let Janet and the kids anywhere near me while I was in the hospital, and now that—"

"I waited, too, Johnny. BuMed's little dictatorship halted even the great BuPsych. There's an area of autonomy in radiation medicine that—" He shook his head slowly.

"Well?" asked Ramsey.

"The impatience of youth," said Dr. Oberhausen. "There are just a few more points to be cleared up. Why do you believe we never saw the need for this fancy-uniform therapy?"

"Partly Security," said Ramsey. "But it really wasn't obvious. Wrong symptoms. Napoleon was looking to build up enlistments and stop his gunners from going over the hill. We've never had that trouble. In fact, our submariners seemed eager to return to duty. That's the paradox: they found threat in both spheres—ashore and at sea. When they were ashore they seemed to forget about the menace of the sea because the subconscious masked it. The boat spelled enveloping safety, a return to the womb. But when the men came ashore, that was birth: exposure. The sky's a hideous thing to men who want to hide from it."

Dr. Oberhausen cleared his throat. His voice took on a crisp, business-like tone. "Now, I'd like to go back to your notes for just a moment. You say BuPsych should emphasize religious training. Explain your reasoning."

Ramsey leaned forward and the telltale chair creaked. "Because it's sanity, Obe. That's the—"

"It smacks of a panacea, Johnny. A nostrum."

"No, Obe. A church provides a common bond for people, a clear line of communication." He shook his head. "Unless BuPsych can uncover telepathy or absolute proof of the hereafter, it can't substitute for religion. The sooner we face that, the sooner we'll be able to offer—"

Dr. Oberhausen slapped his hand on the desk top. "Religion is not scientific! It's faith!" He said *faith* as he might have said *dirty*.

*He's needling me,* thought Ramsey. He said, "Okay, Obe. All I'm saying is this: We don't have a substitute for religion. But we're offering our so-called science as a substitute. That's all I'm—"

"So-called?"

"How many distinct schools of psychology can you name?"

Dr. Oberhausen smiled thinly. "At least as many as there are distinct religions."

"We're following the pattern even there," said Ramsey.

The BuPsych chief chuckled. "Did I interrupt a chain of thought?"

Ramsey paused. "Only that I've never met a psychoanalyst who didn't—at least subconsciously—offer his system as a substitute for religion. Present company included. We set ourselves up as little gods—all-knowing, all-healing. People resent that and rightly. We have polite labels for our failures. We agree among ourselves that anything bearing one of those labels is, of course, incurable."

Dr. Oberhausen's voice held a sense of remoteness. "That's quite an indictment, Johnny. Do I take it that you've been *converted* by our good Captain Sparrow?"

Ramsey leaned back, laughed. "Hell, no! I'm just going to stop posing as a messiah."

Dr. Oberhausen took a deep breath. "That's encouraging."

"And I guess I'll go on poking around inside people's minds. If that describes whatever it is we do." He smiled. "I'll keep on being a psychologist."

"What do you expect to find?"

Ramsey was silent a moment, then: "A good scientist doesn't *expect* to find anything, Obe. He reports what he sees."

Dr. Oberhausen clasped his hands. "If you find God, please let me know."

"I'll do that." Ramsey forced briskness into his voice. "As long as we're clearing up loose ends, what about me? When do I get out of this damned uniform and into my nice new department of BuPsych?"

Dr. Oberhausen pushed his chair back, resting his hands on the edge of the desk. He tipped his head down, appeared to be staring at the bat-eye box. "First, you'll have to play out your hero role. The President's going to pin medals on all of you. That's Belland's doing. By the way, the admiral has given Mrs. Garcia a job in his department, his polite way of keeping her under surveillance. But it works out for the best of all concerned."

"In this best of all possible worlds," said Ramsey. He sensed hesitancy in Dr. Oberhausen's manner. "But when *do* I get out of the service?"

Dr. Oberhausen lifted his chin. "I may not be able to get you out immediately, Johnny."

Ramsey felt pressure building up inside him. "Why?"

"Well, you're a hero. They'll want to exploit that." The BuPsych chief cleared his throat. "Some things are difficult even for BuPsych. Look, I couldn't even get past BuMed and in to see you while—"

"You promised me a—"

"And I'll keep my promise, Johnny. In time." He leaned back. "Meanwhile, there's a commodore on the board of classification and promotion. He's a presidential errand boy and he needs an—an aide-de-camp."

"Oh no!" Ramsey stared at Dr. Oberhausen.

The little doctor shrugged. "Well, Johnny, he found out that you're the clever Long John Ramsey who improvised a vampire gauge from a hypodermic and two glass tubes and saved the *Dolphin* during that training-mission breakdown. He wants—"

Ramsey groaned.

"You'll be jumped to lieutenant," said Dr. Oberhausen.

"Thanks," said Ramsey bitterly. He curled his lips, copied Dr. Oberhausen's voice: "Sure, Johnny. You'll have your own department."

"You're young," said Dr. Oberhausen. "There's time."

"He'll have me polishing his shoes."

"Oh no. He's quite impressed by your talents. Says you're too good for BuPsych. Bringing home that oil has done nothing to reduce his admiration." Again the BuPsych chief cleared his throat. "And while you're with the commodore, there are some things about this department that I'd like you to—"

"So that's it!" barked Ramsey. "Another of your damned spy jobs! You want me to ferret out the dope on the commodore so you can move in on him. I'll bet you set this job up yourself."

"I'm sure you see the necessity," said Dr. Oberhausen. "That way lies sanity."

"I'm not so sure," said Ramsey.

"I like your Captain Sparrow's analogy about sanity and swimming," said Dr. Oberhausen. "But I would add to it, the swimmer must be prepared at all times to grasp a paddle."

Ramsey smiled even as he realized that Dr. Oberhausen was amusing him to ease the tension between them. "Okay, Obe. One more. But I'm telling you now: that's all."

"Fair enough, Johnny. Now, if you'll just—"

A door slammed in the outer hall behind Ramsey. He heard a flurry of sounds. A woman's voice shouted: "You can't stop me from going in there!"

*Janet!*

His pulse quickened.

The woman's voice mounted almost to a scream: "I know he's in there with that damned Dr. Oberhausen! And by Heaven I'm going in!"

The office door behind Ramsey burst open. He turned. It was a secretary. "Please excuse me," she said. "There's—"

"Let her come in," said Dr. Oberhausen.

Ramsey stood up, feeling suddenly giddy. Janet came rushing through the door and into his arms. A familiar perfume. The contours of a familiar face pressing against his cheek, a familiar body against his own.

"Johnny! Oh, Johnny!"

He heard Dr. Oberhausen get up, saw him walk past him toward the office door, fastening the bat-eye box to his shoulder as he went.

"Johnny, I missed you so."

"I missed you, too," he said.

"I never knew it would be so dangerous. Why, they told me—"

"It wasn't bad, Janet. Really."

"But you were so long in the hospital!"

Dr. Oberhausen paused at the door, a figure in new perspective, grown suddenly smaller, giving off a sense of loneliness. Ramsey wanted to call out something but didn't know what. He said, "Obe."

The BuPsych chief turned.

"We'll see you soon," said Ramsey.

The doctor smiled, nodded, went out, closing the door behind him.

And then Ramsey had to explain to Janet why he wanted to include "that awful old Obe" in their reunion plans.